P9-EML-397

Cade wondered if he was dreaming

He had to be. No way was Brynn creeping into his bedroom, wearing nothing but a soft, sheer nightgown.

But there she stood, her beautiful face barely visible in the moonlight.

"You want me to keep you *occupied*, Cade?" Her sexy whisper shot shivers down his spine.

Before he could gather his wits enough to reply, she sank a knee into the mattress and knelt beside him. Her eyes, oddly shining, seemed to look straight through him. "Don't think for a minute that I can't 'keep you occupied.'"

He sat up, stunned beyond words. After all this time, was Brynn trying to seduce him?

"You don't think I'm up to it?" Her words teased him as he thought of all the ways she could occupy him.

"Let's give it a go, Romeo." And with a suddenness that startled him, she yanked her nightgown over her head.

It was all the invitation he needed....

Dear Reader,

Life is complicated enough without having your subconscious mind play tricks on you…such as sending you dreams so vivid and lifelike you can't help but rise out of bed to participate. I'm talking about sleepwalking. It's been a curse to me for as long as I can remember. Many times I've woken up in places other than my bed with only jumbled, nonsensical memories of how I'd gotten there.

These occasional nighttime adventures inspired me to write *Sex and the Sleepwalker*. Imagine the complications that could arise when the owner of a bed-and-breakfast inn wanders the halls in her sleep…and wakes up in bed with a sexy male guest.

I hope you enjoy Brynn's misadventures—and her resulting relationship with a macho U.S. marshal, Cade Hunter. Happy reading, dear readers. And always follow your dreams…but only when you're awake.

Feel free to e-mail me at donnasterling@mindspring.com. And don't forget to check out www.tryblaze.com.

Sincerely,

Donna Sterling

Books by Donna Sterling

HARLEQUIN TEMPTATION   HARLEQUIN SUPERROMANCE
726—SAY "AHHH…"   1017—WIFE BY DECEPTION
738—TEMPERATURE'S RISING
754—THE DADDY DECISION
777—HOT-BLOODED HERO
803—INTIMATE STRANGER

Don't miss any of our special offers. Write to us at the following address for information on our newest releases.

Harlequin Reader Service
U.S.: 3010 Walden Ave., P.O. Box 1325, Buffalo, NY 14269
Canadian: P.O. Box 609, Fort Erie, Ont. L2A 5X3

SEX AND THE SLEEPWALKER

Donna Sterling

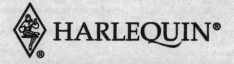

HARLEQUIN®

TORONTO • NEW YORK • LONDON
AMSTERDAM • PARIS • SYDNEY • HAMBURG
STOCKHOLM • ATHENS • TOKYO • MILAN • MADRID
PRAGUE • WARSAW • BUDAPEST • AUCKLAND

If you purchased this book without a cover you should be aware
that this book is stolen property. It was reported as "unsold and
destroyed" to the publisher, and neither the author nor the
publisher has received any payment for this "stripped book."

To my parents, my husband and my conference
roommates—for all the times your sleep was disrupted
by my sleepwalking adventures. Feel free to "seize the day."
I've got the nights covered.

ISBN 0-373-79101-1

SEX AND THE SLEEPWALKER

Copyright © 2003 by Donna Fejes.

All rights reserved. Except for use in any review, the reproduction or
utilization of this work in whole or in part in any form by any electronic,
mechanical or other means, now known or hereafter invented, including
xerography, photocopying and recording, or in any information storage
or retrieval system, is forbidden without the written permission of the
publisher, Harlequin Enterprises Limited, 225 Duncan Mill Road,
Don Mills, Ontario, Canada M3B 3K9.

All characters in this book have no existence outside the imagination of
the author and have no relation whatsoever to anyone bearing the same
name or names. They are not even distantly inspired by any individual
known or unknown to the author, and all incidents are pure invention.

This edition published by arrangement with Harlequin Books S.A.

® and TM are trademarks of the publisher. Trademarks indicated with
® are registered in the United States Patent and Trademark Office, the
Canadian Trade Marks Office and in other countries.

Visit us at www.eHarlequin.com

Printed in U.S.A.

1

SHE SPOTTED HIM the moment she stepped onstage.

There he sat in the front row of the crowded auditorium, his muscular arms crossed, his long legs comfortably extended, his mouth slanted in that slight but infuriating smirk she remembered so well from their college days. Cade Hunter. Of all the rotten luck, why did *Cade Hunter* have to show up at the most important award ceremony of her life?

"It's my pleasure to present this award to the incredible, incomparable, one-and-only Ms. Brynn Sutherland," the president of the United States had just announced, a woman who bore a striking resemblance to Brynn's softball coach in seventh grade, "for running the best bed-and-breakfast in the history of the free world!"

The auditorium had exploded with applause and the audience had risen to their feet. It was Brynn's shining moment—success beyond her wildest imagining. But as she tried to cross the stage to accept the huge gold trophy—which looked exactly like an Oscar—she found herself moving in slow motion, as if she were walking through dense, soupy muck. And it was all *his* fault. He was the only one not clapping, the only one not standing and smiling in admiration.

She tried not to scowl at him. She was supposed to

be smiling and approaching the podium to accept her award, not fuming over Cade Hunter's insolent attitude.

Before she managed to tear her gaze away from his rugged but oddly appealing face, she saw his lips move. And though she couldn't hear his voice, she knew what he said. "Prude."

Prude! Oh, he knew how to push her buttons! This was an important occasion for her. A business function. A public affirmation of her talent as an innkeeper—not to mention great promo for the Three Sisters Bed & Breakfast Inn. Yet Cade Hunter had taken it upon himself to show up, uninvited, just to rehash old arguments.

Balling her hands into fists, Brynn pivoted away from him and resumed her slow motion trek toward the podium. The president, she noticed, had morphed into Candice Bergen, and the trophy now looked like a mermaid from a tuna can label. Brynn didn't mind that too much, though.

She was still too ticked over Cade Hunter's gall. *Prude,* he'd called her. Didn't he see that she'd changed? Couldn't he tell she was no longer the virginal teenager he'd known, but a sultry urban adventuress with more notches on her bedpost than the gals on *Sex and the City?*

"Prick tease," he taunted.

That stopped her dead in her tracks, not three feet from the podium. How dare he? Nine years ago, he might have had grounds to call her such a thing—though he never had, to her knowledge. No, he'd never called her anything worse than a prude, which had been bad enough. But now he seemed determined to publicly humiliate her.

And he was succeeding. For some inexplicable reason, another man in the audience repeated the accusation. "Prick tease." Then someone else said it.

Soon the entire audience took up a chant: "Prick tease. Prick tease. Prick tease."

"That's not fair," Brynn yelled over the commotion. "I had good reasons not to go all the way with him. I was only eighteen. I wasn't ready!"

The audience didn't listen. Their chanting had grown thunderous. With that cocky gleam in his honey-gold eyes, Cade Hunter uttered, "She's probably frigid, anyway."

"Frigid! Me?" *That* was more than any self-respecting urban adventuress could take. Shaking with outrage, Brynn stalked past Candice Bergen to the side of the stage and descended a flight of stairs, glaring all the while at the despicable Cade Hunter. "You think I'm frigid, Cade? And a prude? A 'prick tease'? Well, let's just see about that, why don't we?" With every step she took, she jerked open her silk blouse a bit more, popping off the mother-of-pearl buttons like microwave popcorn. "Come on, big boy." She yanked the blouse off her shoulders and reached for the zipper of her designer slacks. "You want a piece of me? Let's give it a go, Romeo...."

She never saw it coming. Out of nowhere, a long, hard protrusion sprang up and hit her in the jaw, knocking her into a wall. Metal clanged around her. Something damp and limp folded over her face. The lights went out, plunging her into darkness, and pain shot through her body.

It took a moment—a long, agonizing moment of stunned bewilderment—before her eyes adjusted to the dark, her senses fully returned and she recognized where she was.

In the broom closet. More specifically, on the cold tile floor of the broom closet, with a broom handle lying across her throat, a mop hanging in her face, her bare breasts jutting free of her torn pajama top and one bare foot wedged painfully in a metal bucket.

And though she hadn't seen him in nine years and hoped to never see him again, it was all Cade Hunter's fault.

STRESS. Simple stress. That's what had caused her nighttime wandering, Brynn had deduced by the next morning. Football season was beginning—her busiest time of year, with alumni flocking back to cheer on the Georgia Bulldogs. Fun, but hectic for local inns, especially for the Three Sisters Bed & Breakfast Inn, a former sorority house that she and two of her sorority sisters had bought and refurbished. Turning a decent profit during football season could make the difference between success and failure. And unlike the previous three years, they were not booked to capacity for the first game. The state of the economy had clearly taken its toll. Brynn had good reason to be stressed.

And it wasn't much of a mystery why Cade Hunter starred in the dream, either. Trish Howell Hightower, her gorgeous blond business partner, had mentioned running into him yesterday at a local café. He was in town on business, it seemed. The thought of having Cade Hunter anywhere nearby was enough to give

Brynn nightmares. Nine years ago, he'd broken her heart and, as the saying went, "stomped that sucker flat."

She'd gotten over it, of course. She didn't care in the least about Cade Hunter anymore. But unless he'd changed greatly, he was a menace to any vulnerable woman who caught his eye. Brynn hated to think of the emotional carnage he could wreak upon their small town. Or, God forbid, on Trish. Newly divorced and on the rebound, she'd be ripe for the picking.

"What's wrong, Brynn? Don't tell me you're siding with Trish on the barbecue sauce issue!" Lexi Dupree's anxious question brought Brynn back to the present. They were sitting in wicker rockers on the columned front porch of the antebellum mansion, taking full advantage of the mild August morning, lounging with virgin Bloody Marys—it was too early for mint juleps—and discussing the food they would serve during the tailgating parties this weekend.

"Barbecue sauce?" Brynn repeated, struggling to comprehend what Lexi had been saying.

"I thought you loved my barbecue sauce. Guests rave about it. Just because some gourmet guru gave Trish a new recipe doesn't mean we have to stop using mine."

"Oh…right. I agree. We won't make any changes without a taste test."

"A taste test!" Lexi crossed her pale, rounded arms and frowned. "I thought *I* was in charge of the food…and I like the sauce we've been using. Why should I change it for Trish? She already messed around with the breakfast buffet, the evening dessert and my weekend schedule. She's supposed to be a silent partner, remember? *Silent.*"

"Yes, but she did put up most of the money. She owns fifty-one percent. We can't ignore her suggestions."

"She put up most of the cash, but you and I invested pretty heavily, too—with the agreement that you'd manage the inn and I'd take care of the food and activities. Trish shouldn't be interfering."

Brynn sensed that Lexi's annoyance with Trish was rising to a dangerous level. And she understood why. Trish had a tendency to dominate. They probably should have known when she offered to help finance their venture that she wouldn't be able to stay hands-off forever. Now that she'd gotten involved in the day-to-day running of the inn, it was only a matter of time before she drove them both whacko. Lexi seemed near the breaking point already, and Trish had only moved in two weeks ago. Brynn hated conflict between her friends. Or anywhere, for that matter.

"I'll talk to her," she promised, not looking forward to the task. It wasn't the first time she'd be negotiating peace between her business partners. Although the three of them had been friends since their sorority-house days, business concerns had put a strain on their sisterhood. "But, Lex, try to be patient with Trish. She *does* have good ideas, and she knows what's popular in society circles. If we plan to cater to sorority alumni, we need to know that. Besides, she's going through a hard time, trying to adjust to the single lifestyle and map out a new route for her life."

"Yeah, well, I'd be happy to tell her which route to take," Lexi mumbled, though the sulky expression in her large dark eyes was softened somewhat. With her hair bleached platinum and cropped in spiky wisps around her cute, plump face, she looked like a baby doll whose tresses had been shorn by some exuberant little girl. The multitude of silver hoops and studs lining her ears, the guitar tattooed on her shoulder and the skimpy half-T she wore showed her for the hip, sexy musician she really was—a persona that had fully emerged only in the last couple of years.

Trish, a classical purist in both music and fashion, disapproved of Lexi's tattoo and platinum bleach job. If Lex had tried either of those innovations during their sorority days, she would have caught hell; Trish had been the queen bee at the sorority house, too.

Brynn, on the other hand, thought the changes in Lexi were refreshing. The image fit Lexi's character perfectly. In a way, Brynn envied her for her metamorphosis. Back in college, she and Lexi had been the quiet brunettes in a sorority full of vivacious blondes and redheads. Brynn had always suspected that she and Lex had been recruited for their grade point averages.

"Hey," Lexi said in a tone of realization, "with her fifty-one percent ownership, Trish can fire me, can't she?"

"I suppose, but she'd never do that. She's a pain in the butt at times, but Trish loves you, Lex. We started this business together, and we'll make a success of it *together*."

Looking troubled, Lexi shrugged and turned her attention to the menus she had planned for their weekend guests.

Just as the discussion was coming to a close, a

sporty red Porsche jetted into the circular drive and squealed to a halt at the bottom of the garden steps. Trish popped out.

"'Morning, y'all," she called, ascending the stairs in a short tennis dress, her blond hair cut in a classic chin-length bob, swaying. Tall and slender with wide blue eyes, a Mediterranean-acquired tan and the easy poise of those born to great wealth, Trish looked exactly like the coed she'd once been. "Lexi, have you mixed up a batch of that barbecue sauce yet? Can't wait for you to try it. It's all the rage in Manhattan. I *begged* the chef of Club Noir for the recipe."

Despite the lighthearted tone of Trish's cultured Southern voice, Lexi visibly bristled, and Brynn hurriedly answered for her. "We've been too busy with our planning session for Lexi to do much of anything in the kitchen yet. Why don't you grab a virgin Mary from the pitcher in the fridge and come join us?"

"Can't. Have to shower, then hurry downtown for a lunch date at eleven." The look in Trish's eyes made it clear that she wasn't exactly thrilled by the date. She hadn't had much luck with dating over the past year. "But I'll be back by two to man the front desk."

"I don't have you scheduled for desk duty," Brynn said. She knew Trish was focusing a lot on the business to avoid thinking about her personal life.

"Thought I'd give you a break. Let you prepare for the weekend rush." She shifted toward the door, then paused. "By the way, Brynnie…was there some kind of problem last night?"

"Problem?"

"At breakfast, Mrs. Hornsby mentioned she heard a ruckus coming from your suite. Yelling, thudding and clanging, she said. I didn't hear a thing, but then my room is at the other end of the inn. Was there something going on?''

Both Trish and Lexi gazed at her in curiosity, and Brynn felt her color rise. ''Must have been my television.'' Guilt pricked her for having disturbed a guest, and even more so for lying about it. But she didn't want anyone to know about her sleepwalking episode. Especially not Trish. God knows what she'd make of it. Brynn herself considered it not far from a psychotic breakdown.

Trish raised her fair brows. ''*You* were watching television at three in the morning? You're usually conked out by eleven.''

''I fell asleep with it on.''

''Oh. I'm glad there wasn't a problem. But, um, maybe you should try to keep the volume down, hmm?'' With a parting smile, Trish continued on her way into the inn.

Brynn drew in a breath and tried not to react negatively to the sweetly spoken rebuke. Trish had every right to expect the manager of her inn to refrain from waking the guests at three in the morning.

''So, what *really* happened?''

Brynn slanted Lexi a glance. ''You think I'm lying?''

''Like a rug. I'd recognize that guilty blush anywhere. Something went on last night.''

''Nothing. It was nothing. Really.''

Lexi's eagle-eyed gaze lighted on Brynn's swollen, purplish toes, visible in her strappy sandal. ''Then what happened to your foot? I don't remember seeing that bruise yesterday.''

"I stubbed my toes, that's all." She *had* to think of a way to change the subject. "While I was rushing to answer the phone. It was my brother. They haven't caught that abductor yet—you know, the case John has been investigating—and he called to warn me again about taking in suspicious strangers. Now how, I ask you, can we not take in strangers when we run a bed-and-breakfast? Having a cop in the family is enough to make anyone paranoid."

"Don't try to change the subject. Who was yelling and banging things around last night, and how did you get hurt? Tell the truth." When Brynn didn't answer, Lexi leaned closer and whispered with concern, "Did Antoine lose his temper about something?"

"Antoine!" If Brynn hadn't been so surprised, she would've laughed. "Of course not. I've never seen Antoine lose his temper. He's a sweetheart. Besides, he's too urbane, too polished, to resort to violence."

"Urbane and polished don't have anything to do with a man's violent tendencies. And there's something you're not telling me." Studying her with an intensity that increased Brynn's tension, Lexi's eyes suddenly widened. "Were you and Antoine doing something…you know…kinky? Some kind of love play that got out of hand? I've heard that French lovers can be highly creative."

Brynn laughed out loud at that. "Not even close." Lexi would be so disappointed if she knew the truth about Antoine and her.

She wasn't about to let that cat out of the bag. Lexi had been thrilled when Brynn started dating handsome, charming, artistic Antoine. Lexi had been certain Brynn had finally found a red-hot lover. Until then, she'd been involved in a series of long-term relationships with scholarly types more inclined toward philosophical stimulation than physical. Brynn guessed she just felt secure with that kind of guy. Secure, but sexually bored and frustrated. Lexi had recognized the problem and persuaded her to "go for the gusto." Trish helped by introducing her to Antoine, her cousin who had recently moved to Georgia from France. He'd taken a flattering interest in Brynn, and they'd been dating ever since.

It wasn't Antoine's fault that the boredom hadn't left her. *She* was the problem. She found herself thinking too much during intimate times. Analyzing every move.

Not that she'd always been that way. Far from it. There'd been a time in her life when a man's touch had set her ablaze. But she refused to think about that man. It was bad enough she'd dreamed about him.

Maybe she'd just grown too cerebral to experience sexual bliss. After five weeks of dating her, Antoine had probably realized as much. Hence all those recent business trips.

Had she really thought of herself as an urban adventuress in her dream last night, with more notches on her bedpost than the gals on *Sex and the City?* She nearly snorted at the thought. In real life, her notches were few and far between.

But *not* nonexistent. She'd had pleasurable affairs. She was far from frigid, as Cade Hunter had claimed last night. Dream or no dream, that accusation still smarted.

"If Antoine laid a hand on you in anger," Lexi said, "I'll stomp his butt. I don't hold with violence."

Brynn resisted the urge to point out the irony in those two statements, or to laugh at the image of petite Lexi stomping a big guy like Antoine. "He didn't do anything, I swear. He wasn't even here last night. He left town after dinner for another business trip."

Seeing the doubt on Lexi's face, Brynn realized she had to come clean about what had really happened, or Antoine would be labeled a woman-beater. But how she hated to confess! Her sleepwalking was sure to make Lexi and Trish worry, considering Brynn's role as resident manager of the inn. Roaming about in a zombielike state couldn't be good for business.

"If you must know, I caused the ruckus myself last night," Brynn admitted. "I was dreaming."

Lexi frowned, perplexed. "What does dreaming have to do with—" She broke off as understanding dawned. "Oh, no. You haven't started sleepwalking again, have you?"

Brynn assumed she was remembering the night in the sorority house when Lexi had woken to find her wandering around their bedroom, carrying on about Daytona Beach and a Pontiac Firebird. Thank goodness her roommate hadn't paid much attention to what she'd been saying. The near miss of having her deepest, darkest secret exposed had shaken Brynn so much that she'd spent months taking herbs, sleeping aids, meditation therapy and biofeedback sessions to stop her from walking or blabbing in her sleep. Brynn believed it had been pure determination that had eventually broken the habit.

"Last night was the first time I've walked in my sleep since college," Brynn said, hoping to reassure Lexi with that fact. "I guess the onset of football season was just too much for me to take, um, lying down.''

"So what did you do?"

"Rammed into a wall. Woke up in a closet.'' She didn't mention that it had been the basement broom closet. Lexi didn't need to know she'd actually left her bedroom suite.

"That's pitiful." Lexi shook her spiky platinum head in grim reflection. "I'll bet I know why this happened. You're keeping too much bottled up inside. You're still sexually repressed."

Brynn stared at her in astonishment. How had she arrived at that conclusion? For all Lexi knew, her sex life was hotter than ever with Antoine.

"Oh, don't look so surprised. I know you, Brynn Sutherland. If you were getting any decent action, you'd be giddy with relief, after all those years of pressure building up. Believe me, I have personal experience with this phenomenon.'' She slumped back in her chair and sighed. "I had such high hopes for you and Antoine."

Brynn rested her head against the back of the rocker. "It's not his fault. It's mine."

"You just haven't found the right guy."

Hating to get her started again on a campaign to find her a red-hot lover, Brynn steered the conversation back to its original track. "I doubt that my sex life has anything to do with the sleepwalking, anyway. It's stress related."

"You've been stressed more than this plenty of times, but I haven't heard about your sleepwalking until now. What was your dream about?"

The question caught Brynn off guard. "Nothing.

Nobody. That is, nobody I know.'' She felt unreasonably shaken by the inquiry. ''I mean, I might have known them, but…uh…'' Impromptu lying had never been her strong suit.

That intent look came over Lexi's face again, and Brynn nearly groaned. Her friend would hound her until she confessed. With Lexi's truth-seeking, mind-probing talents, it was a wonder Brynn was able to keep any secrets from her at all.

She did, though. The important one. The one about Daytona Beach and the Firebird.

''I don't see how this is pertinent,'' Brynn said, caving under the pressure, ''but the only person I recognized in the dream other than Candice Bergen was Cade Hunter.''

''Cade Hunter.'' Lexi contemplated the information, then broke into a small, self-congratulatory smile. ''So I was right. The sleepwalking does have to do with your sex life.''

''It does not! It's just that Trish mentioned running into him yesterday.''

''Cade Hunter was the last guy you really went crazy over.''

''I didn't go crazy over him.''

''You know you did. Half the girls in our sorority house did, and he wasn't even a frat boy. That man was one well-built, good-looking hunk of masculinity.''

''Not good-looking, really. Appealing, you could say.''

''You could say a whole lot more than that! He's a *manly* man. And more to the point, he's an old flame of yours, which means that time has probably glorified him in your mind.''

''*Glorified* him? Cade? You've got to be kidding.''

''Everyone knows that old flames burn hotter in a woman's memory than they ever did in real life.''

Brynn considered the statement and wondered if it was true. As much as she despised him for his heartless behavior, she couldn't deny that her memories of Cade Hunter sparked more sensuous heat in her than any of her later relationships. He and she hadn't made love per se, but their make-out sessions had always stirred an intense longing. Had the passage of time exaggerated that longing, until no flesh-and-blood man could ever compete? It was a startling thought.

''A woman in your unfulfilled state, dreaming about an old flame as hot as Cade Hunter...'' Lexi shook her head, pondering the situation. ''No wonder you got so worked up.''

''I wasn't 'worked up' over Cade! At least, not in a sexual way. I was angry because he was insulting me.''

''Insulting you how?''

Telltale warmth crept into her face again. She didn't want to say he'd been calling her a ''prick tease.'' That would lead Lexi to analyze the underlying reason she'd dreamed such things...and Brynn didn't want to talk about how she and Cade had broken off their relationship all those years ago. *Make love to me, Brynn, or we're through.*

She still had a hard time even thinking about his ultimatum, let alone discussing it. She'd been falling in love with him—deeply, desperately—while Cade had clearly wanted her only for sex. Hurt, angry and humiliated, she'd broken up with him. He'd lost no time finding someone else. A sorority sister of hers, no less, who soon turned up pregnant.

That had been years ago. Brynn now viewed the entire episode as a lesson learned. She'd fully recuperated from the devastation, of course, and was much wiser to the ways of unscrupulous heartbreakers like Cade Hunter.

But she didn't want to talk about it, now or ever.

"I don't remember exactly how he was insulting me," she said, avoiding Lexi's probing gaze.

"Uh-huh." Clearly she knew Brynn was withholding information. Fortunately, Lexi didn't press the issue.

Brynn couldn't have been more relieved. Because even though she *had* been angry with Cade in the dream, she'd also ripped open her pajama top in the throes of an erotic challenge. Maybe her sexual stagnation was affecting her more than she'd thought.

"Take my advice, girlfriend," Lexi said. "Go find a man you're really hot for and let loose with that pent-up energy. Otherwise, who knows what'll become of you?"

Words of wisdom, no doubt. But Brynn wasn't someone who could easily "let loose." Except, of course, in her dreams.

"WE'VE GOT OUR 'IN'," Cade Hunter murmured into his cell phone as he drove through the old, tree-shaded neighborhood surrounding the Three Sisters Bed & Breakfast Inn. He'd found it necessary to refamiliarize himself with the lay of the land. It had been too many years since he'd lived nearby to remember all the details. "I followed Trish to a café yesterday. Made contact. She invited me to stay at the inn. I'm on my way."

His associate murmured his approval, and Cade disconnected the call. If this encounter with Trish hadn't produced an invitation, he'd had another ruse ready to justify his visit. This would be better, though. Trish had invited him, an old college chum, and he'd accepted. No suspicions would be raised about his motive for being there.

And that was important.

Pocketing the cell phone, Cade turned his open-topped sports-utility vehicle toward the inn. Trish had mentioned she'd be manning the registration desk this afternoon while Lexi and Brynn worked on preparations for the weekend's activities. He couldn't have asked for a luckier break.

Because if Brynn were working the front desk, he had no doubt she'd whip out the No Vacancy sign and swear the inn was full. She'd always been good at turning him away.

But he was here to do an important job, and he wouldn't let Miss Brynn Sexy-As-Sin Hold-But-Don't-Have Sutherland stop him. Nor would he let himself obsess over her again. She'd probably changed quite a bit over the years, anyway. With any luck, he would hardly recognize her.

Not that he was worried about seeing her again. The last nine years had taught him a lot. Made him stronger and smarter, especially when it came to women. Friends called him jaded. He preferred to think of himself as enlightened.

Turning his SUV into the shady, asphalt driveway

of the antebellum mansion that had once been Brynn's sorority house, Cade forced his grip to loosen from the wheel and the muscles of his body to unclench.

She'd demanded "self-control" from him, all those years ago. Since then, he had mastered the art. No matter what she did or said, how she looked—or smelled, smiled, sounded—there was no way in hell he would let her get to him.

2

OKAY, SO SHE WASN'T an urban adventuress, or gloriously liberated like Lexi, or "in the know" about cosmopolitan social trends, like Trish. And if either of them knew about her personal history, chances were they never would have allowed her into their social circle in the first place, which, in a way, made Brynn feel like a fraud.

But there was one area in which she felt entirely comfortable, and that was welcoming guests. She loved meeting new people, greeting those she'd entertained before, and hearing about their lives, travels and interests. Every new arrival filled her with anticipation, as if she were embarking on a new adventure. And every person who became a friend made her feel that much richer. She considered the most important part of her job to be making her guests feel comfortable. At home. Sincerely welcome.

With this in mind, Brynn allowed Trish to work the registration desk while she herself played hostess to the new arrivals in the parlor, offering them high tea—or happy hour, as some preferred to call it, although the guests had to provide their own "happy" libations to go with the soft drinks, tea and coffee served there.

As Brynn and Lexi set trays of pastries, cheese and veggies on the antique sideboard for their Thursday afternoon guests, a thunderous roar came from the entryway.

"GO *DAWGS!* Sic 'em! *Rrrf, rrrf, rrrf…*"

In any other part of the country, the sound of men barking, growling and howling might have raised an alarm. But in Athens, Georgia, home of the University of Georgia Bulldogs, the commotion merely drew smiles from a few of the guests in the parlor. Brynn and Lexi went a little further and answered the barking with howls of their own.

"Hey, guys, I do believe we've found some Easy DZs," remarked Smitty, the biggest and loudest of the four beer-bellied, middle-aged newcomers. The group had quit barking to pause at the wide, arched doorway of the parlor and leer playfully at Brynn and Lexi.

"I beg your pardon?" Brynn asked in mock affront at the age-old slur to her sorority. These guys were some of her favorite regulars who stayed at the inn every year for the football season opener. "Did you say Easy DZs? That's Easy Delta Zetas to you."

"Leave it to those Kappa Alpha boys to get it wrong," Lexi added, which prompted the men to break into a bawdy song about their beloved fraternity.

"Go put your paw prints on a registration form at the desk, you crazy dawgs, you," Brynn called out over their singing while she poured coffee for three young, pretty recent graduates. As former beauty queens—Miss Athens, Miss Clarke County and Miss Georgia—the girls were slated to participate in opening-day celebrations on campus. They seemed to be saving their smiles for the occasion; they looked bored at the moment and annoyed by the commotion.

Brynn moved away to fill cups for the more congenial guests. She would have to find a way to draw these young women into the fun-loving spirit of the weekend.

Before she could make an effort to change the girls' spoilsport attitudes, her radio beeper went off, and Trish asked if she'd take a look at a faulty air conditioner. Brynn hurried upstairs to handle the problem. August in Georgia definitely required air-conditioning.

Forty minutes later, after nearly dismantling the wall unit, Brynn called a repairman. It was at times like these that she truly appreciated Trish's help. At least she knew the front desk was being run properly while problems kept her elsewhere. She hated missing high tea, though, especially when her Kappa Alpha guys would be trooping in there—with a twelve-pack of beer, probably—and unwittingly annoying the beauty queens. Hopefully Lexi would keep things amiable, regardless of what tactics the guys might use to get the attention of the three young ladies.

Hoping for the best, but fearing the worst, Brynn finally made her way downstairs. If things hadn't gone well between the Kappa Alphas and the beauty queens, high tea may have ended prematurely, which wouldn't bode well for the weekend. A congenial atmosphere was vital during football season, when people wanted the freedom to make fools of themselves and have others appreciate them for it. Brynn had to do her utmost to promote a fun-loving spirit among her guests.

Armed with that resolve, she marched toward the parlor, passing Trish, who was deeply involved in a phone conversation at the reception desk. A glance toward the kitchen showed Lexi retreating with an armful of empty snack trays.

Assuming that the tea had ended early, Brynn was surprised as she drew closer to the parlor to hear lively voices and peals of laughter, both masculine and feminine. Mystified, she paused at the parlor entrance and gaped. The guests were clustered around a table—the Kappa Alpha men, the beauty queens, a married couple who were both retired professors, and big, gruff old Mrs. Hornsby, all watching some central action.

Only when Brynn crept closer did she realize that an arm-wrestling match was taking place. Smitty, the Kappa Alphas' earlier spokesman, was involved in the match, his beefy face red with exertion, his brawny arm raised and quivering under the strain, his hand clasped in a death grip with a darker, leaner hand.

Brynn then caught sight of the other contestant's face. And the breath left her body. God help her…it was Cade Hunter!

Why was he here? Had he come to see *her?* She couldn't imagine why he would. They hadn't parted on friendly terms. And if he'd come for a social visit, why was he involving himself with her guests?

The beauty queens looked pleased at his presence; they were clustered around him in seductive poses, their gazes glued to his lean, strong-jawed face. The men, all caught up in the macho contest, cheered their fellow Kappa Alpha on, and even the older guests watched with interest. Cade's attention was trained solely on his opponent.

Brynn couldn't help but take the opportunity to study the man who had broken her heart nine years ago—the last man she'd been ''crazy'' about. His shoulders looked broader now, his chest and arms more powerful, but that might have been because of the muscles flexing with exertion. His jet-black hair was as thick and wavy as ever, but cropped shorter than it had been then. Subtle strands of silver now gleamed near his temples. Surprising, considering he was only thirty. His skin, a dark, natural bronze, looked more weathered, giving his already rugged face a craggier look than she remembered. But his eyes, the amber color of sunlit honey, glinted with the same look of wry amusement and quiet intelligence that had first attracted her to him.

He had no business being here! This get-together was for guests only, not the general public. She had to set him straight on that matter.

Unless, of course, he was a friend of the Kappa Alphas, just dropping in for a visit. She couldn't chase off a friend of her guests. But her Kappa Alpha men were at least ten years older than Cade; he wouldn't have attended UGA at the same time they had. And Cade hadn't been in a fraternity. He'd belonged to a different kind of brotherhood—the criminal-justice majors, who hung out together at the gym, pumping iron, or at the firing range, honing their aim in hopes of entering the police academy or FBI. Her brother had been one of his crowd. Brynn's sorority sisters had referred to them as "cop wannabes." Because they weren't in a fraternity, they were generally considered beneath the notice of the Delta Zetas. At the same time, most red-blooded women couldn't help but admire the rock-hard physiques and protective attitudes of those criminal-justice boys.

Cade had never lacked for female admirers.

Which brought up another possibility—that he'd come to visit one of the beauty queens. But they were recent graduates, and Cade hadn't been in Athens for nine years, as far as Brynn knew.

Before she had time to reflect on other possibilities, Cade pinned his opponent's arm to the table. Cheers erupted from the beauty queens, who congratulated him as if he'd made the winning touchdown at a championship game. His defeated opponent flushed, laughed and mumbled something about tennis elbow.

"My turn to take him on," another Kappa Alpha announced, nudging his frat brother out of the chair. "And this time, use your right arm, buddy. I'll put you down, anyway."

Brynn realized that Cade had been using his non-dominant arm, probably as a handicap against the age difference. Interesting. In arm-wrestling, he actually had scruples.

But he had no business being at *her* high tea.

It was time to assert her authority. "Excuse me." She shouldered her way through the Kappa Alphas, who were hunkering around the table for the next match, while the girls fluttered and cooed around Cade, expressing their faith in his endurance. "I hate to interrupt the action, but…"

Cade's attention swung to her then. Her breath halted. Her stomach dropped. She'd forgotten how powerful his gaze could be. She felt as if he'd physically grabbed her and lifted her high into the air. She actually experienced the heady rush of vertigo.

Coming to her senses, she shook it off, and reminded herself who he was and what he'd done. It had been years since she'd confronted him in anything but her fantasies. Oh, how she'd torn into him then! And how she longed to do that now. She couldn't, of course. She had to think of her guests, and the harmonious spirit she intended to promote.

Restraining herself, she said in an admirably civilized tone, "I'm afraid this function is for registered guests of the inn only."

Cade confused the issue immediately by smiling at her as if he were mildly pleased to see her. Only mildly, mind you. But that was enough to distract her, to kick her pulse into high gear. "Hello, there. You remember me, don't you? From UGA. Cade Hunter." He extended a hand to her—a smooth, practiced move that she automatically responded to. His grip was firm, warm and dry—and the fit of his palm against hers was utterly perfect. Immediately intimate. Frighteningly familiar. "You're...Brenda, right?"

Brenda. Brenda!

Brynn pulled her hand back from his and stared at him. He'd forgotten her name. All these years, she'd been harboring fantasies of whittling him down to size with her sharp wit and icy demeanor, while he hadn't given her a thought.

"Brynn," corrected Mrs. Hornsby in her gruff, cantankerous voice from somewhere behind her. "Her name's Brynn."

"Brynn," Cade repeated. "That's right. Sorry. I'm terrible with names. How've you been?"

Delusional, it seemed. She'd been sure he would never forget her. How *dared* he forget her? "This gathering is for registered guests only, Mr...Hunt, did you say?"

"Hunter." His smile didn't waver as he reached

into the pocket of his tight jeans, pulled out a room key and held it up for her inspection. "And I *am* a registered guest."

Stunned for the second time in mere moments, Brynn stared at his room key in horror. Registered! He'd registered as a guest? He would be staying here, under her roof? And in the Dogwood Room, according to his key. Two doors down from her suite. No!

"For the *whole weekend?*" She forgot to even try hiding her dismay.

"Not the weekend." Before she could breathe a sigh of relief that he'd only be here for the night, he added, "I'll be staying a couple of weeks. Maybe three, depending on my schedule."

Brynn couldn't have been more appalled.

"Let's go, big guy," urged the Alpha Kappa sitting across the table from him, sliding his raised arm toward Cade in challenge.

Through a nightmarish haze, Brynn watched Cade plant his elbow next to the challenger's, grip his hand and engage in another battle, while the other guests moved closer and cheered them on. The air virtually hummed with testosterone.

Brynn backed away from the action, struggling to come to grips with the reality of the situation. How had this happened? How could Cade Hunter be a registered guest at her inn—for two or three weeks, yet?

It had to have been Trish. The moment Brynn had turned her back, Trish had allowed riffraff of the worst kind to register at their inn. Not that Trish could have known how Brynn felt about this particular specimen of riffraff. Brynn had had her pride back in college and hadn't carried on about her feelings, bad or otherwise, for Cade Hunter. They were merely two people who had once dated, fought and gone their separate ways, as far as any of her friends would remember.

And not even that, as far as Cade remembered. *Brenda,* he'd called her. Why should that sting as much as it did?

The remainder of high tea passed in something of a blur for Brynn. Lexi, whose shift had ended after she'd set out the snacks, had left for the day, hurrying to get ready for a hot date with her guitarist boyfriend, and Trish remained occupied at the registration desk. Cade continued to win arm-wrestling contests until the last match, when a Kappa Alpha finally beat him.

He then challenged the winner to a double-or-nothing competition that involved balancing stacks of beer-bottle caps on their noses. Every one of the Kappa Alphas joined in, and the beauty queens found the men's antics delightfully amusing.

"Double or nothing, did you say?" Brynn cried, unable to refrain from pouncing on this transgression. She arched her brows at Cade and said in her most quelling voice, "I hope you're not *gambling* in my establishment."

Immediately the merry chatter and comical action ceased. Smiles wilted. Bottle caps fell off of noses. All eyes turned her way. All faces took on varying degrees of surprise, dismay and contrition.

So much for promoting a happy, tolerant environment.

Cade settled back in his chair and regarded her with the expectant air of a bystander watching a spectacle. Brynn wished she could retract her hasty rebuke, but didn't know how.

Quietly, apologetically, Smitty broke the silence. "Aww, Brynn, we're not playing for money. Only for beers. You know, like we always do."

Only then did she realize the full extent of her mistake. Of course they always wagered for beers, usually regarding football. She'd never complained about their betting before.

Forcing a smile despite the heat blazing in her face, she said, "I…I meant to say…surely you're not gambling in my establishment…um, without letting me in on the action."

Smiles returned to her guests' faces. Smitty hurried to accept her bet, and bottle caps were promptly realigned on the Kappa Alphas' noses.

Tongue clearly tucked in his cheek, Cade met her gaze. His tawny eyes brimmed with silent laughter. She swore he knew perfectly well what had driven her to that outburst. *He* had. But how could he realize that unless he remembered their past relationship? The suspicion that he was playing some kind of secret game with her flooded Brynn with an oddly energizing heat.

They'd played many secret games together, once upon a time….

The heat took on a sensual burn, and she pivoted away from him, feeling shaken. This would never do! How could she bear to have Cade Hunter here for two or three weeks?

Teatime lasted forever. Though she tried to focus her attention on the refreshments and the needs of her other guests, she found herself preoccupied with her awareness of Cade, an awareness she'd rather die than show. By the time the guests went their separate ways for the evening, her face ached from forcing a smile.

On their way out, the Kappa Alphas and the beauty queens told Cade they hoped to see him around the inn that weekend. As usual, he'd been a big hit.

It was enough to turn Brynn's stomach.

Most disturbing of all, though, was when Trish ran into Cade on his way out of the parlor. For the first time since her divorce from her cheating ex, a sparkle leaped in her bright blue eyes. With flushed animation, she talked to him, flirted with him and insisted that he have dinner with her to "catch up"—although they'd never been close friends.

"Brynn, you'll come too, won't you?" she asked as an afterthought, probably because they were the only three people left in the entryway.

Brynn actually considered going, just to prevent Trish from being alone with the big bad wolf. The thought of Cade and Trish as a couple, even for the briefest time, was too horrible to tolerate. But if they were intent on pursuing a relationship, she couldn't imagine anything worse than being with them as a third wheel. "No, you go ahead. I've had a busy day."

"So have I," Cade said, surprising her. "And I have a lot of work to catch up on," he added, surprising her even more. Brynn wondered what kind of work he did. "Think I'll turn in early, too," he said.

The crestfallen look on Trish's face made Brynn want to shake her.

"But let me take a rain check on those dinner plans, huh, Trish?" Cade's smile was as rich, warm and powerful as cognac.

Trish visibly brightened and assured him he could. Brynn gritted her teeth. Of all the guys her friend could have gotten interested in, why Cade? She'd be going from one lowlife to another.

"If you two are turning in early," Trish said, "I'm going over to the campus to help decorate for the festivities tomorrow." With a wink at Cade, she made her exit.

Which left Brynn very much alone with him. Her tension shifted into higher gear as they stood watching the door close behind Trish. Brynn braced herself for whatever he might say or do.

But with nothing more than a courteous nod, he turned and strode to the stairway.

Again he'd surprised her. And not in a good way. She felt curiously deflated. Robbed, even. He apparently thought he could slink off to his room without a face-to-face confrontation with her.

She allowed him that delusion as she followed him silently up the stairs to the second floor. All the way to his door, actually. It wasn't until he pushed his key into the lock that Brynn halted beside him.

He glanced at her in surprise.

She scowled. "You might not remember much about me, *Cal*," she said in a furious undertone, deliberately getting his name wrong, "but I remember plenty about you. Trish is my friend. She's been through a tough time lately, and she doesn't need a wolf like you ready to pounce on her. Stay away from her."

One corner of his mouth tipped up, and he leaned a broad shoulder against the doorjamb. "So, you're worried about your friend, are you?" His gaze played over her face with gathering intensity. "Then maybe you'd better keep me occupied."

A dark thrill shot into her stomach. A spear of sensual heat, the kind she hadn't felt for years. Nine years. The realization alarmed her. "Don't play your mind games here. *With anyone.* Or I promise you, I will be your worst nightmare."

With that passionate threat, she whipped around, stalked to her room and shut the door behind her, her knees deplorably weak, her blood humming in her ears. She had no idea how she would ever carry out that threat, but she meant it. Something about Cade Hunter never failed to incite her to passion, one way or another.

Maybe you'd better keep me occupied. Why should that hoarsely uttered suggestion have given her such a thrill? He had to know she wanted nothing to do with him. He was only taunting her. Laughing at her, no doubt.

How she wished that just once she could turn the tables on him. Slay him with a single gaze. Wipe that cockiness off his face. Bring him to his knees.

But that highly satisfying image soon elicited memories. Vivid, hot, sensually arousing memories. Not appropriate for this situation. The last thing she wanted was any kind of sexual relationship with him.

Of course she didn't. He infuriated her, that was all. She only hoped she could calm down enough to sleep.

HE WAS HAVING TROUBLE sleeping. He wasn't sure why.

It wasn't because of his work. He had all the precautions in place, and things were proceeding as planned. It wasn't because of jet lag, either. He'd been in Georgia for two days, long enough for him to adjust from Colorado time. There was no good reason for him to lie here staring at the ceiling.

Hell, Hunter, this undercover work has got you lying to yourself. He knew damn well why he couldn't sleep: because of Brynn. He'd been so determined to take their reunion in stride, to treat her with the same casual lightness he treated everyone else. Yet here he was, reliving every moment he'd spent in her presence.

He'd been a little stunned when he'd seen her today.

Nine years ago, she'd been a soft-spoken, dark-haired beauty with natural warmth and kindness shining from her hazel eyes and heart-shaped face. He'd first seen her at a UGA football game, and he hadn't been able to look away. She'd been there with his buddy John from crim law class—a good friend, although they hadn't known each other long. Cade had felt a sinking in his chest, a heaviness in his gut, because he'd known, after one long look at Brynn, that he would do everything in his power to take her away from John. There was just something about her that struck him as so damn beautiful. So damn *unique*. He traded seats with the guy behind them, and was more than a little relieved when John introduced Brynn as his sister. Then he heard her voice. Talked with her. Laughed with her. And the certainty grew. She had to be his.

That had been nine years ago, when he was twenty-one. He'd done a lot of hard, fast living since then, had more than his share of beautiful women. When he'd checked into the inn today, he'd expected to see her with new eyes. *Jaded* eyes, as his friends might say. He'd also expected her to have changed in some fairly major ways.

But then he'd looked up from his arm-wrestling match and felt a sudden clutch in his gut. A sinking in his chest. A heaviness in his stomach. Because she was so damn beautiful. That same unique, angelic beauty still radiated from her. Still took his breath away.

And that had surprised the hell out of him. In his experience, life had a way of hardening people. Changing them from the inside out. After all he'd seen and heard in the course of his work, he doubted that the kid he'd once been even existed in his body anymore.

But Brynn hadn't seemed to have changed in any major way. Her long dark hair was styled differently— in some fancy braid—and her slender figure had filled out into rounder curves. She now wore an air of authority with surprising ease. But the sweetness still glowed from her face and eyes, even when she was trying her damnedest to drive him away.

Maybe that was why he hadn't been able to resist testing her, prodding her, to see how she'd react. "Maybe you'd better keep me occupied," he'd told her.

And that, he realized, was the real reason he couldn't sleep. He was angry with himself. He'd started out so well, pretending not even to remember her name. His time here would pass much easier if he could avoid any meaningful personal contact with her. He'd almost made it to his room with his mask firmly in place. But then he'd taken the bait and allowed her to lure him out of his "impersonal" mode.

He'd gazed into her eyes, up close and personal, and breathed in her scent. And lost a little bit of his mind.

The old heated awareness had flooded her face, and so had that look of alarm. Which meant nothing had changed. She was still running from him. He still couldn't have her.

That was another reason he couldn't sleep. He was angry with her—because she still jumped to the wrong conclusions about him. Assumed the very worst about his character. "Trish doesn't need a wolf like you ready to pounce on her," she'd said.

Wasn't that the story of his life, though? Hadn't all the people he'd loved believed the very worst about his actions, his motives? His mother had given up custody of him when he was seven because he'd been "a handful"—and he hadn't even known he'd been misbehaving. To this day, his father and stepmother considered him bad news, and their son and daughter naturally excluded him from family gatherings.

Cade should have learned by now. When it came to the important people in his life, he didn't have whatever it took to be trusted, or even given the benefit of the doubt. He'd thought he'd learned to live with that.

In a way, he was glad his annoyance with Brynn had rescued him this evening. Otherwise, he might have started wanting her again. And that would be pure hell. He'd spent weeks, months, maybe years, reliving the long, hot hours they'd spent kissing, necking, petting. She hadn't let him make love to her. Not all the way. But he'd known how to make her hot, and how to make her come. And he'd relished the power, the heat…and had wanted, *needed*, so much more.

It had become a constant craving. The scent of her, the feel, the taste—all made him believe that she had been made for him. He'd wanted to drive himself deep into her body. To fill her entirely. To possess her completely.

It hadn't happened.

Make love to me, Brynn, or we're through. They'd been words of desperation. Stupid, foolish, asinine. His ultimatum had only alienated her. He'd then compounded the mistake by trying to make her jealous.

But he wouldn't think about any of that now. Those desperate, churning emotions were long dead and buried, and he was damn glad of it. He never wanted to want her again.

Punching the old-fashioned down pillow into shape, he glanced at the bedside clock: 2:00 a.m. He laid his head back down and shut his eyes, determined to sleep. He had a serious job to do here, and needed his rest.

No sooner had he begun to drift off, though, than he heard a faint jingling, like the rattle of keys. And a click. Then another noise. Half-asleep as he was, he vaguely recognized it as the squeak of a door opening. But, of course, he must be dreaming.

Or maybe not. His eyes flew open just in time to see a figure gliding toward him in the dark. His instincts kicked in, and he reached for the gun beside the bed, his mind instantly alert, his body poised for attack.

But then his eyes adjusted to the dark, and the shadowy figure materialized into a woman. A woman with long, free-flowing dark hair, wearing a soft, sheer nightgown.

Brynn.

3

HE WONDERED IF HE WAS dreaming. He had to be. No way in hell was Brynn Sutherland creeping into his bedroom in the middle of the night. But there she stood, right beside his bed, her beautiful, wide-eyed face faintly visible in the moonlight seeping between the drawn curtains.

"You want me to keep you *occupied,* Cade?" The fierce whisper sprang at him, like a cat, from the darkness.

Before he could gather his wits enough to reply, she sank a knee into the mattress, levered herself up and knelt beside him on the bed, her long hair billowing in sleep-mussed tangles around her. Her eyes, oddly shining, seemed to look straight through him. "Don't think for a minute that I can't 'keep you occupied.'"

He sat up in bed, stunned beyond words.

"Oh, you don't think I'm up to it?" she cried. "You think I'm a prude, a tease? You think I'm a dud in bed?"

"No! God, no."

"I'm anything but a dud, or…or frigid."

"Frigid? I never said—"

"Let's give it a go, Romeo." And with a suddenness that startled him, she yanked her gown over her head, struggled briefly to free her arms, then flung the garment aside. The effort threw her off balance. She swayed.

He grabbed her, pulled her to him. And his breath left him in a whoosh of sudden sensation. Her bare, jutting breasts, firm and full and impossibly soft, pressed against his chest, and a lavish abundance of cool, fragrant hair spilled over him. And her scent…ahh, her scent. He'd almost forgotten.

"Brynn," he breathed, holding her tightly to him. She felt incredibly good. Incredibly *right.*

He fell back against the pillows with her, feeling as if he'd fallen into a fantasy. A purr hummed in her throat—a long, low moan of approval—and her breath steamed against his shoulder. His temperature spiked. His body hardened in arousal.

Sweeping his hand down her back, he relished the softness and warmth of her skin. It had been so long since he'd touched her. She wore panties, he discovered. But only panties. And she was here, in his arms, in his bed. Brynn.

She shifted against him, their bodies connecting fully from breast to hip, and she murmured something he didn't quite catch. He rolled onto his side and pressed her down onto the bed, twining his leg with hers. He wanted to kiss her. Connect with her. Delve into her sweetness and heat. See if the magic could possibly be as potent as he remembered.

Her eyes were closed, her lips parted. He swept his mouth across them, wanting her. *Wanting* her.

"Mmm," she moaned. And smiled. And turned her head.

Turned her head? The surprise of that made him draw back. Never had she failed to respond to his kiss.

It was her one true weakness. His doorway to heaven. If his lips touched hers, he'd always been assured of long, lush kisses, each one hotter and wilder than the last. He believed that was the reason she'd never let him too near, after they'd broken up. Because she couldn't resist his kisses. Yet she'd turned her head just now. Something was wrong. Very wrong.

"Brynn?"

As he watched, she lapsed into deep, rhythmic breathing, as if she were asleep. Which was impossible. No one went from anger to passion to sleep in a matter of minutes.

Thoroughly confused, he rose up on an elbow, reached for the bedside lamp and switched it on. He saw her clearly then. Lots of creamy skin with a natural honey glow. Dark, lustrous hair spread over the pillows. Sinfully beautiful, she was. And nearly naked beneath him. And, unquestionably, asleep.

But...but how? Why? It made no sense.

A vague memory stirred. A bothersome suspicion.

The light, or maybe the shifting of his weight on the bed, disturbed her, and she frowned. Blinked. Opened her eyes. For a moment, she stared blankly, toward nothing in particular. Perplexity entered her gaze. And then she turned her head and focused on him.

Her eyes widened and she shot up into a sitting position, gaping at him as if he were a two-headed space alien. "Cade! What are you doing here?" It was as much an accusation as a question.

As if *he'd* done something questionable. "What am *I* doing here? That takes some nerve."

She glanced around the room, and gradually her expression turned from perplexed surprise to distressed understanding. "Oh no," she whispered, clearly mortified. "I'm in *your* room."

He didn't bother to confirm that conclusion. He just watched her through narrowed eyes. Maybe she understood what had happened, but he didn't. Or maybe he didn't want to understand.

"I...I guess I was...sleepwalking."

"Sleepwalking." He said it as if the idea was ludicrous, although the suspicion had flitted through his mind. He remembered hearing something about her sleepwalking in the sorority house. But, damn it, he didn't want to accept that as the explanation. She'd come to him, *wanted* him. There was no mistaking that. He forced a nonchalant shrug and leaned back against the pillows. "Whatever you say, darlin'."

"It's true," she insisted vehemently. "I *was* sleepwalking."

He nodded and smiled.

She glared at him, then glanced down at her naked breasts, so high and round and pretty, with their proud coral tips and lilting bounce. With a little cry, she grabbed for the rumpled sheet and yanked it up to cover herself. The accusation returned to her gaze. "What did we do?"

Now *that* irked him. Did she really think it would be possible, if they'd made love or anything close to it, for her to *sleep through it?* He managed not to grit his teeth. "You're telling me you don't know? That you were unaware of what you were doing when you came to my room, unlocked my door, climbed into my bed and got naked?"

"I'm not naked!"

Heat sluiced through him in a surprising rush, just from thinking about her sitting there in nothing but those little panties and a bedsheet. He wanted his hands on her. And his mouth.

Along with the heat came unreasonable resentment. She'd been in his arms, ready and willing. He would not disregard that. "Oh, you're not naked?" His gaze traveled pointedly to the sheet she clasped to her slim form. "Then show me what you're wearing."

Her fists tightened on the sheet. "I'm sure you know."

"And why is that?" He tilted his face close to hers, the anger and the desire flaring in him. "Because you crawled into my bed wearing only those little panties and rubbed your body against mine, promising to keep me *occupied.*"

She looked stricken. "Oh, God."

"Then you said something like, 'Let's go, Romeo.'"

"No!"

"You want me to believe you don't remember any of that?"

His chiding pushed her too far, it seemed, and the spunk and sass returned to her face. Leaning back against the pillows, she crossed her long, shapely arms and lifted her delightfully cleft chin. "I don't care what you believe. The truth is I was walking and talking in my sleep. It meant nothing."

"At the very least it means you were dreaming about me. Dreaming about having sex with me." The thought pleased him. Immensely. He raised a brow. "How often does that happen?"

"Don't flatter yourself. You could have been anybody. I had no idea who you were."

"You said my name. You called me Cade. How many Cades do you know? And how many are registered to this room?"

"If I was dreaming about you, which I don't remember at all, it had to be the first time. I haven't given you a thought in years."

He might have believed her if rosy color hadn't climbed her cheekbones and she hadn't averted her eyes. She was, without a doubt, lying. She'd dreamed about him before. Pleasure warmed him like fine whiskey. He wondered how often she'd dreamed of him, and if those dreams always involved sex. He hoped so.

But then another question occurred to him. "My God, Brynn...how often do you walk in your sleep? How many guests have you surprised like this?"

Her mouth opened and hung ajar for two or three heartbeats. "I've never done this before," she cried, aghast. "I haven't walked in my sleep since college. Well, except for once, when I ended up in the broom closet. Alone. Wearing pajamas."

He believed her, and couldn't have been more relieved—or more pleased that thoughts of him and him alone had stirred her to rise from her bed at night.

Then again... "If you don't remember your actions after you wake up, how can you be sure? Maybe this happens more than you realize."

"It doesn't. I would know."

He rubbed his chin and regarded her doubtfully. "I'm not too sure about that. You seemed pretty popular with those frat guys I met in the parlor. And if I understood correctly, they *do* come back year after year.''

Surprisingly, she didn't hit him, storm out of the room or cut him to shreds with a razor-sharp comeback. Instead, she caught her lower lip between her teeth to suppress a smile. ''Are you accusing me of being…promiscuous?''

He stared at her, not because of what she'd said, but because her emerging smile caught him off guard. A dimple now danced beside her mouth and cute little she-devils played in her eyes. It had been damn near a decade since she'd sparkled at him like that. ''I didn't accuse you of anything,'' he murmured, feeling shell-shocked.

''But you implied it. You implied that I climb into my guests' beds on a regular basis.'' With a toss of her thick, tangled hair, she held up her hands, like a perp surrendering to police. ''You caught me. I can't deny it. I never know which bed I'll wake up in.'' She looked so pleased at the notion that Cade almost laughed. Almost. But the sheet had drifted lower across her breasts, ending just above her hardened nipples, and he was helplessly aroused. ''I see more action than those girls on *Sex and the City,*'' she boasted. ''I'm one hot mama.''

Cade rested his bare shoulders against the headboard and studied her, aroused, amused, mystified and intrigued. ''That's odd, then…considering what you said when you climbed into my bed.''

A watchful stillness came over her. ''What?''

He didn't answer right away, enjoying the sudden intensity of her gaze. He still couldn't believe she was actually sitting here beside him in bed, talking about sex, wearing next to nothing, while he wore only his briefs. The possibilities were endless. And he couldn't help dwelling on them.

"Cade, what did I say?"

"Well, at one point, you mentioned something about your being a dud in bed."

The chagrin that filled her eyes said more than words ever could. He'd clearly hit a raw nerve.

So, of course, he prodded a little more. "I believe you also said something about being frigid."

Her color flared. "What I say in a dream means nothing." She nearly choked on the words. "Just a lot of garbled nonsense." She looked wounded and terribly vulnerable.

Why? *Of course* it was nonsense. He had no doubt about that. But, incredibly, it seemed that she did have doubts. "Don't tell me someone's got you believing you're no good in bed!"

"Of course not. It's none of your business, anyway."

He strongly felt that it was. "Are you involved with someone now?"

"Yes, and he's a wonderful man. An excellent lover."

"Who makes you think you're frigid."

"No!"

Cade ignored her denial, amazed that she could believe herself sexually inadequate in any way. She, the epitome of desirability. The standard by which he measured all others. A standard no one else had met.

He was also suddenly, violently, jealous of anyone who had had her. Anyone who had known her intimately. It took Cade a moment to find his voice and form coherent words. "You're not frigid, Brynn, or a dud in bed. Nothing could be further from the truth."

That wary stillness came over her again, and she concentrated her attention on him like a ray of noon-day sun through a magnifying glass. "And how would you know that?"

He released a surge of breath and realized he was angry. She was wounded. Unfairly wounded. And he wanted to punish whomever was responsible. And tend to her wounds...

Sliding an arm around her, he cradled her against his chest and brushed a tendril of hair from her face. "I've never known a woman more responsive than you," he said, meaning every word. "One who made me hot with just a kiss. No one, Brynn. Ever."

Her breath caught, her neediness apparent. "Really?"

"Honest to God. I can't tell you how many times over the last nine years I've gotten hard just thinking about you, and the things we used to do. With only our hands..." He trailed his fingers down her arm to her slender wrist and rubbed his thumb over the center of her palm. His gaze then drifted to her lips. "And our mouths." Desire coursed through him, hot and strong, making his voice gruff. "Don't you remember?"

"Yes, I remember," she admitted with a trembly exhalation.

"Things couldn't have changed that much. At least, not between you and me."

Her eyes darkened in that old familiar way, and the need to kiss her propelled him closer, until he breathed in the honied warmth of her mouth. But before his lips touched hers, she pulled back, pressing deeper into the pillow. "If you remember me so clearly, Cade, how is it that you didn't quite recall my name?"

He pressed his lips together to keep from cursing—not at her, but at himself. He should have known that that silly, impulsive ploy would cost him. He'd just *had* to call her Brenda. "I was trying to slow you down a little. You were ready to throw me out on the street. As if we were enemies or something."

"I hate to break this to you, Cade, but we're not exactly friends. We didn't part on a friendly note."

He couldn't deny that. The last few times he'd seen her on campus, she'd looked straight through him. "You're right. We didn't part on friendly terms. And it was my fault. I never should have given you that ultimatum." *Make love to me, Brynn, or we're through.* He winced at the memory. "I'm sorry for that. It was stupid and cruel, and I've wished a thousand times that I'd never said it."

"Forget it." Her voice and eyes remained cool, though. "No harm done."

No harm done.

An odd urgency gripped him. He couldn't allow her to hide behind coolness again—not after she'd smiled at him and very nearly kissed him. "I've never forgotten you, Brynn," he vowed. "Not for a single day. And, believe me, I've tried."

Surprise entered her eyes, and she searched his face as if trying to gauge his sincerity. The very fact that it mattered to her gave him hope.

He had to convince her. Had to convey his feelings. Had to close the distance between them and keep her here, in his bed. Make her want him again. Make her need him…deep inside this time.

Splaying his fingers along the delicate curve of her face, he kissed her.

It began as a gentle nudge of his mouth. A signal of intent. A silky, sweet "Hello, may I come in?" With a sigh—not of reluctance, but of pleasure—she opened to him. The kiss progressed slowly at first, into a simple inhalation of mingled breath, a savoring of scent and texture. A blossoming of erotic warmth. A sensuous sliding of smooth, tender flesh in a sumptuous, mutual tasting.

Ahh, but that wasn't nearly enough. Not for him or for her. In a simultaneous rush, they surged closer, delved deeper. The heat intensified with startling suddenness, like a flame touched to tinder.

Cade reveled in the blaze, in the freedom to hold, squeeze, feel and indulge. She reveled in it, too, he knew, her pleasure evident in the quickening of her breath and the tiny hums and moans vibrating her throat. He'd forgotten how eloquent her kisses were.

And he'd forgotten the way she moved whenever he kissed her—the provocative arching of her back. The instinctive ebb and flow of her hips. The crush and rub of her breasts against him, as if she were driven to get close, closer, closest….

No, he *hadn't* forgotten. Any of it. Every detail was indelibly etched somewhere in his being. He'd deliberately turned away from those memories. But she was back in his arms now, his body conforming to hers, moving with hers, moving *against* hers, with a growing need to dominate, penetrate. Merge. The subtle movement of her pelvis stroked him to unbearable hardness.

He slid his hands down the bare, lush curves of her body, captured her bottom and rocked his arousal against her, straining at the barrier of their underwear. And each new joining of their mouths incited an even more voluptuous kiss.

The fire leaping inside him was one he hadn't felt for nine years, and he fed it now with serious intent. Hooking his thumbs into the sides of her little satin panties, he tugged them down to midthigh. He'd have to get a condom from his wallet, he knew, but not quite yet. He couldn't bear to pause just yet....

"Cade." She broke the kiss, flushed and panting. "We've got to stop."

Stop? He couldn't have understood her. Or maybe she'd meant that it was time to get a condom.

"Soon," he murmured, loath to release her even for a moment. He kissed her again and led her back to those enticing undulations, spreading her thighs as far as the panties would allow. The satin garment had to go. And so did his briefs.

"Now," she whispered faintly against his mouth as he tugged at the waistband of his briefs. "We have to stop now."

He kissed her again into silence, not allowing himself to worry too much. This wasn't like their make-out sessions in college. She wouldn't leave him high and dry. They were adults, and she wanted him. She'd come to his bed, stripped off her gown and was kissing him even now with a feverish need, a very sexual need.

A tortured groan escaped her, and she caught his

hands in her own. "Cade, I...I have to think about this."

Think about this, she'd said. Not *get a condom.* Surprise made Cade pull back to read her face. "Think about what?"

"This. Us." Her expression was troubled as she squirmed from beneath him and sat up. "Having sex."

"Don't think so much." He levered himself up on one arm and hijacked her mouth in another kiss—a little more urgent than the ones they'd been sharing. A little more impatient.

She matched his impatience with a roughness of her own, an exhilarating thrust and parry that roused him all the more.

But then she broke away, panting as if she'd been wrestling rather than kissing. "I know you're right. I *do* think too much. And you're right about our kisses, too." She paused to catch her breath, her eyes luminous, her color high, her hair tousled and sexy. "Just kissing you makes me hotter than...than...oh, never mind."

She initiated the kiss this time.

Fire leaped within him, and his next kiss pressed her back against the pillows. She groaned, wrapped an arm around his neck and arched against him. He rubbed a greedy hand over her breast until the tender peak stood high and tight and scraped across his palm.

She gasped, writhed and ran her silky knee up his thigh...up, up, up, to the tip of his erection, sending shards of heat through his groin.

With a sharp hiss of breath, he plunged his hand in a downward path toward the dark curls glistening between her thighs.

She caught his hand again, though, just shy of his destination, and held it. "This is wrong. I can't let myself do this." She pulled away from him and scooted to the side of the bed.

Dazed and shaken, Cade watched in disbelief as she rose and pulled up her panties. "I'm sorry, Cade."

Sorry. Which meant she was doing it again! Just as she had in college—leaving him all hot and bothered and half-crazed. "Brynn," he said, his voice inhumanly gruff, "what the hell are you doing?"

"I'm going back to my room." She found her rumpled nightgown on the floor, slipped the filmy fabric over her head and smoothed it down her maddening body.

"Why?"

"Because I can't jump into bed with you without even thinking about it."

He sprang from the bed, crossed the room in two long strides and trapped her against the dresser, anchoring his arms on either side of her. "In case you don't remember, you *did* jump into bed with me without even thinking about it. You also stripped off your clothes, kissed me into a goddamn fever—"

"I know, I know!" She glanced at the erection straining beneath his briefs, and looked away with a guilty wince. "I'm sorry about that, but—"

"What are you afraid of, Brynn?"

"I'm not afraid."

"Then what is it?" A thought hit him, and he asked with a curious tightness in his jaw, "Are you in love with someone else?" The tightness spread to his chest. "The guy who makes you think you're frigid?"

"No!" She frowned at him, and relief rushed

through his veins. "I'm not in love with anyone. And don't talk about Antoine that way."

"Antoine? He's French?"

She nodded, and Cade scowled. There was something about Frenchmen that drove women a little crazy. "If you're not in love with this Antoine, then what's stopping you from having sex with me? If you think you don't want to, you're lying to yourself."

"Oh, I know I *want* to." Her voice had gone all throaty and her gaze warmed. "There's always been sexual chemistry between us. I've never denied that."

Cade pressed closer, longing for the taste of her mouth, the feel of her body moving beneath his.

Her gaze grew apologetic, though, and he had to hold back a curse. "But...well..." She searched for words that clearly evaded her.

"But what, damn it?"

"You're...*Cade Hunter.*"

He stared at her, nonplussed. What the hell did she mean by that? Before he was able to decipher the statement in any rational way, she ducked under his arm and fled across the room, her sheer gown billowing out behind her.

"That's no answer," he called, bewildered, riled and more sexually frustrated than he'd thought humanly possible.

She didn't reply, stopping only to scoop up the keys she'd dropped when she first entered the room.

He fisted his hands to keep from grabbing her and carrying her back to bed. "If you walk out that door, Brynn," he warned, his voice harsh and uncompromising, "don't—"

He stopped, precariously on the verge of saying,

Don't come back to my room unless you're ready to make love.

As if she heard what he'd left unsaid, she froze on the way to the door and turned a forbidding frown on him. "Don't…what?"

"Don't…forget that you…said you were going to think about it—about…finishing what we started." He forced the impromptu words through a throat severely constricted by pent-up pressure. "So, do that. Think about it."

She regarded him in clear surprise, then slowly nodded. "I will." Bowing her head, she hurried out of his room.

Cade released an explosive breath, feeling as if he'd stopped just short of driving blindly off a cliff. He'd come close to giving her the same ultimatum he'd been cursing himself over for nine long years.

At least he'd learned from his mistake.

And that just might have earned him what he now wanted more than anything—one more chance with her.

4

THE FIRST THING BRYNN DID the next morning was to order from a local health-food store a special combination of herbs she'd taken back in college to help stop her sleepwalking. She wasn't sure if the herbs had worked, but she *had* eventually stopped the disturbing habit, so it seemed worth taking the concoction again.

She also dug through the crate of papers, letters and mementos she'd kept from her college days until she found the meditation cassettes that might have helped, as well. Again, she wasn't sure that they had, but they certainly hadn't hurt.

She then called the nearest security company and ordered a computerized lock for her bedroom door that required fairly complex steps to open. Steps she couldn't possibly follow in her sleep. Hoping the new lock would keep her in her own bedroom at night, she paid an exorbitant fee to have it installed that day.

At least she would have control of her whereabouts at night. Any amount of money was worth ensuring *that*.

A workman arrived that morning. As Brynn watched him install the lock, she thought about last night's debacle. She couldn't believe she'd gone to Cade's room, stripped off her gown and climbed into bed with him. As humiliating as that loss of self-control had been, she'd learned something she'd wanted to know. Time had not glorified her memories of Cade. He still kindled an awesome heat in her that no one else ever had.

Should she explore that heat and see how far it could take her toward the bliss she remembered from long ago? Or should she forget about the utterly thrilling moments she'd spent in his bed, and keep him at a distance?

It had taken her years to get over the emotional damage he'd done to her, to forget her feelings for him, to convince herself she was better off without him. Now was not the time to backslide. And after being kissed into a sensual heat that still simmered in her blood, she was afraid she could easily do so.

She wished she didn't have to see Cade until she had decided what to do. Her duties, however, called for her to put in an appearance at the Friday lunch buffet.

She didn't stay long. Uncertain about her plans regarding him and feeling guilty for interrupting his sleep, then leaving him unsatisfied, she barely risked a glance at him while she chatted with the other guests. She escaped to her private suite as soon as possible with a sandwich and cup of cappuccino.

That was why she missed his startling revelation about himself, which sent Trish and Lexi scurrying to her sitting room immediately after lunch for an emergency meeting.

"A travel journalist?" Brynn frowned at her business partners as if they'd been lacing their coffee with too much Irish Cream again. "Cade told you he's a journalist?"

"An author of four travel books." Trish tossed a business card into Brynn's lap, on top of a stack of paperwork. Brynn set her work aside, curled her legs beside her on the armchair and read Cade's card, while Lexi sank down onto the sofa and watched her face for a reaction.

Brynn's incredulity grew. "I had no idea. Cade majored in criminal justice in college." She glanced at her friends in wonder. "Who knew that he'd end up a writer?"

"And a photographer," Lexi said. "He showed me the photos he took of the lakes and rivers around here, and they're all gorgeous. He's doing a series of books about his travels through the Southeast."

Brynn could barely believe it. The Cade she'd known had shown very little interest in writing. "He never mentioned this to me," she murmured, feeling as if she didn't know him at all. "He always wanted to be a cop."

"Guess he came to his senses," Trish theorized, her eyes brimming with excitement. Brynn hadn't seen her this interested in anything since their sorority days. "You do realize what this means, don't you, Brynn?"

"What?"

"If he's impressed enough with our inn, he'll put us in his book."

"He includes all his favorite spots and experiences." Lexi sounded as excited at the prospect as Trish did. "Restaurants, beaches, parks, gardens... *historic inns.*"

"I've already given him a printout of our inn's history from the 1870s," Trish said. "And, of course, he knows that Georgia has the oldest state-chartered university in America.''

"He's been taking pictures of the house," Lexi said. "He even had us pose with our guests at breakfast on the sunporch. I made sure he had a menu of my specialties, too, in case he wants to include it in his new book."

Trish dropped down onto the couch beside Lexi, and they beamed at each other in rare camaraderie. Brynn wasn't sure why she felt a twinge of foreboding at their excitement.

"Anyway, Brynn," said Trish, "we felt we'd better talk to you about this so you can change your attitude."

"My attitude?"

"Toward Cade. We think it's important that you make him feel at home here. Welcomed. Pampered."

Brynn stared at her, aghast. Trish had no idea what she was asking.

"He's really not a bad guy, Brynnie. I know your relationship with him ended badly, and any time you want to talk about that, hon, you know I'm here for you." Trish paused, looking both sympathetic and avidly curious. She clearly couldn't remember the details from nine years ago, and Brynn was glad. When she didn't avail herself of the opportunity to rehash her humiliation and heartbreak, Trish sighed in disappointment and went on. "He's a paying customer now, and he writes travel books. We have to treat him cordially."

Brynn wondered if climbing into bed with him last night could be considered cordial. And if he'd add it to his list of favorite experiences. Highly doubtful. She forced back a hysterical giggle. "I thought I *was* treating him cordially."

Trish and Lexi exchanged glances. "Mrs. Hornsby told me that you nearly threw him out of the inn yesterday at tea," Trish said.

"At the time I didn't know he was a registered guest."

"And I saw for myself the way you were glaring at him in the foyer before I left for the evening. And today at lunch you greeted everyone except him. It was *painfully* obvious you were dissing him. I'm sure he was humiliated."

Although he had sent her a searching stare, he hadn't looked humiliated at all to Brynn. He'd looked as if he might pull her aside and demand to know if she intended to sleep with him. She'd gathered that from one quick, sidelong glance that had left her uncomfortably warm and shaken. "If I didn't greet him, it was just an oversight."

"Oh, come on, Brynn. It's *us* you're talking to," Lexi chided, propping her sandaled feet with their toe rings and chain anklets on the ottoman of Brynn's armchair.

It wasn't like Lexi to side with Trish against her, and Brynn felt betrayed. After all the conflicts she'd resolved between these two, how dare they gang up on her?

Trish went on to remind Brynn that they were trying to generate a buzz about the Three Sisters, and how devastating a bad report in a travel book could be. Lexi sat there nodding at every word Trish said.

Trish then rose from the far end of the sofa with regal poise, her flawless face adopting its executiveat-work look. "I'm sure you wouldn't want to alienate a customer. So try a little harder to make Cade feel welcome, hmm? I'd be so unhappy if he were to check out early or leave with a bad taste in his mouth." Glancing at her delicate gold Rolex watch and murmuring something about an appointment at the spa, she left Brynn's office.

"Traitor," Brynn said with a glare as soon as she and Lexi were alone.

"We're only thinking of the business, *Brynnie,*" she said, using Trish's pet name for her with mischief in her dark eyes. "And Trish might be thinking of the fringe benefits of having a hunk like Cade sleeping beneath her roof—which is something maybe *you* should think about."

Brynn wasn't ready to talk about Cade yet. Even with Lexi. She answered with a disinterested smile and shifted her attention to her cup of cappuccino.

"You're passing up a monumental opportunity here, Brynn."

"For what?"

"To broaden your sexual horizons. Just the thought of Cade worked you up enough to make you sleepwalk into a closet. And you *have* been looking for a red-hot lover."

"No, *you've* been looking for a red-hot lover for me. I'm perfectly satisfied as I am."

"That's not what you said the other day. Have you even talked to Cade alone?"

"Some."

"Well, that's a start. I myself found him perfectly charming. I didn't know him very well in school, but this morning he helped me set up tables and chairs in the yard for tonight's party.''

Brynn had noticed from the upstairs window that Cade had spent a considerable amount of time with Lexi this morning, and that he'd obviously charmed her. They'd had a high old time laughing, talking and teasing each other. ''Well, we'll have to put a star next to his name for helping,'' she responded lightly, ''and give him an extra cookie at playtime.''

Lexi nudged Brynn's knee with her foot in protest of the sarcasm. ''I really appreciated his help. He didn't have to do it, you know. But now that I think about it, he probably did have an ulterior motive.''

Brynn hoped her friend wasn't about to tell her that Cade had come on to her. For some reason, the thought bothered her way too much.

''I think he still has a thing for you.''

Her heart contracted, but she merely raised her brows in a silent invitation for her friend to elaborate.

''He kept bringing the conversation back to you. He seemed especially interested in the men in your life. I'm thinking he's sizing up the competition,'' Lexi said.

''Or trying to find more ammunition to annoy me with. Did you tell him anything about Antoine?''

''Not really. I don't know Antoine very well. He seems to always drop by after my shift is over. But what I saw of him I liked, and I told Cade as much. Six-foot-something, hunky build. Tawny hair streaked blond from the sun. Continental charm. Sexy accent. Old family money. What's not to like?''

Brynn nodded absently. Cade was learning far too much about her private business. *You're not in love with the guy who makes you think you're frigid, are you?* She had to learn to sleep with her mouth firmly shut!

"Then again," Lexi continued, "Cade isn't exactly dog food. If a guy like him showed interest in me, I'd give serious thought to seeing if he's changed since his wild youth. I know he hurt you, Brynn, but we've all done some stupid things in our past that we regret."

She couldn't argue there. Her own regret kept her up some nights.

But she couldn't take much more of Lexi's endorsement of Cade. Brynn was already too preoccupied with thoughts of him, and felt as if a battle were being fought inside her head, with both sides taking a beating. "It's not just a matter of him hurting me. There was also that thing with Rhiannon."

"Rhiannon Jeffries, our sorority sister?"

Brynn bit her lip, immediately regretting the slip. She hadn't meant to share her suspicion with anyone. It was, after all, just a suspicion.

"She's the one he started dating after he broke up with you, isn't she?"

"I broke up with *him*," Brynn said, hoping to distract Lexi from that train of thought. "Don't you remember? I—"

"Rhiannon left school in the middle of that semester because she was pregnant," Lexi interrupted, too immersed in her musing to be distracted.

Brynn's lips tightened. This was much too painful a subject to talk about.

"Do you think Cade was the father?" Lexi asked, her eyes growing round.

"I'm really not sure," Brynn admitted in an attempt to be fair, "so I shouldn't have said anything."

"Didn't Rhiannon say that the father of her baby refused to take responsibility?"

Brynn focused on the far wall, hating to discuss the subject. It still brought a lump to her throat and a pain to her heart. Which, if she was smart, should solve the dilemma of whether or not to sleep with Cade. If unproved suspicions from nine years ago had the power to hurt her, she definitely should not sleep with him.

Lexi absorbed the implications in silence, flopped back against the couch and shook her head. "We can't make assumptions like that. It's unfair to Cade. I don't believe he'd act that way if he'd fathered a child."

"You barely know him."

"He just didn't strike me as the type."

"I didn't think so, either," Brynn said. "But then, I never thought he'd give me an ultimatum like he did."

"What ultimatum?"

Brynn shut her eyes, swearing to have her mouth sewn shut. If Lexi didn't remember—which wasn't surprising, considering nine years had gone by— Brynn certainly didn't want to remind her. "It was nothing. Something silly back in college."

"Oh, yeah. I remember now. 'Have sex with me or we're through,' right?"

Annoyed that she'd remembered—and even more so that Lexi didn't seem particularly outraged on her friend's behalf—Brynn forced an almost imperceptible nod.

"Don't tell me that's still bugging you. That ultimatum is the college boy's time-honored weapon of last resort. As a reformed 'good girl,' I should know. I heard it a few times myself.''

''You never mentioned it.''

''Why should I?''

Brynn wished she could dismiss it as casually as Lexi had. But she couldn't. She'd really believed that Cade had felt something special for her. He'd hurt her deeply with that ultimatum—and even more so by taking up immediately with Rhiannon. He'd then gone on to carve many more notches in his bedpost, leaving other girls pining for him, or so Brynn had heard.

''Look at this through adult eyes, Brynn. He's grown up since college, and even if he's not your ultimate dream man, he's a good candidate for a sexual adventure or two. The most important question is, does he still get the old furnace blazing?''

Brynn let out a laugh, shifted her eyes away from Lexi's and, without conscious thought, fanned her face with her hand.

When she again glanced at her friend, Lexi was peering at her with an arrested expression of discovery. ''You're holding out on me. You *have* spent some up-close-and-personal time with him, haven't you?''

''A little.'' The admission made Brynn uncomfortable. She didn't want to worry Lexi with the sleepwalking problem. And if Trish heard about what had happened, she'd probably haul Brynn off to a sleep clinic and refuse to let her work as resident manager until she'd been cured. Brynn knew from experience that sleepwalking wasn't easy to cure.

Realizing that Lexi was still waiting for an explanation of the time she'd recently spent with Cade, she said, ''Nothing serious happened between us.''

"You mean, nothing sexual?"

"That's exactly what I mean."

"Oh, Brynn, why didn't you give the guy a try? Just days ago you were saying how Antoine doesn't do it for you. The breakup will have to be handled diplomatically, considering he's Trish's cousin, but why not let Antoine know it's over and see how great sex could be with a lover like Cade?"

Brynn shrugged as if the matter wasn't very important to her. As if she hadn't been asking herself those very questions all night and day. But she'd always answered with another question: would she be able to remain emotionally detached if she made love to Cade?

He had a way of making her feel things too deeply, such as the anger and sense of betrayal that had stayed with her for way too long. If she ever did something as stupid as falling in love with him again, he'd surely shatter her heart. He wasn't a one-woman type of guy, and he wasn't interested in anything more than sex.

Maybe that was why she'd been devastated—because his kisses had made her believe he was. What was worse, *they still did.*

No, she couldn't get intimately involved with Cade unless she could see him as merely an enjoyable passtime. A carnival ride. A sexual adventure.

Why couldn't she accept that and get on with it, like any good urban adventuress would?

HE WAITED UNTIL ALL THREE innkeepers were busy elsewhere—Trish away from the inn, Lexi in the kitchen and Brynn in the backyard telling her guests about the colorful history of Athens. Even Mrs.

Hornsby, the sharp-eyed old busybody, listened, entranced, beneath the big old magnolias, pines and dogwoods.

The upstairs floor of the inn was entirely his.

Cade lost no time making the most of the opportunity. With a tool he carried with him everywhere, he opened the locked doors and quickly searched each room for anything telling. Unfortunately, he found very little.

He then bugged the phones in Trish's and Brynn's rooms. He would have bugged Lexi's phone, too, but she lived in a house of her own. Brynn's cell phone, unfortunately, was nowhere to be found. She probably carried it with her. He'd have to find a way to bug it later. A wealth of information could be learned from phone calls.

Most importantly, he installed a motion sensor on Brynn's bedroom door. With the sophisticated new lock she'd had installed, she would never notice the tiny motion sensor. No one would be leaving this room—or entering it—without his knowing.

He then returned to his own room, booted up his laptop and uploaded the digital photos he'd taken of the inn's staff and guests. A click of the mouse sent the images whizzing through cyberspace.

BRYNN STAYED BUSY for most of that Friday afternoon, preparing for the evening party, catering to guests who hadn't gone off for the day and trying the entire time not to notice what Cade was doing or whom he was doing it with. He hung around the inn with his camera and a notebook—presumably to work on his book—while he held court with the other guests, all seemingly enthralled by his work as a travel writer.

Brynn managed to avoid him until late that afternoon, when she found herself virtually alone with him in the television room. Although Mrs. Hornsby sat in a rocker near the window, the bulky, grim-faced woman was snoring over a mystery novel that lay abandoned in her lap when Cade strolled in. Brynn, who'd been dusting furniture and adjusting the cushions on the sofas, couldn't very well stop her work and run out, although she was tempted to do just that.

Cade dropped down into an armchair and greeted her with a smile that any woman would have found impossible to ignore.

Hoping that Mrs. Hornsby's presence would prevent him from initiating intimate conversation, Brynn took refuge in the relatively impersonal subject of his career. While plumping the sofa cushions, she said in an offhand way, "So, I heard that you're a travel journalist."

"I suppose you did."

When he said nothing more, she glanced at him in mild surprise. She'd expected him to elaborate at least a little. Instead, he lounged silently in the chair, his elbow on the armrest, his chin in his hand, and watched her. The silence made her uncomfortable.

"You never seemed interested in writing, as far as I remember," she said. "Or in traveling, for that matter."

"People change." Another moment of disarming silence went by before he added, "At least, *some* people do."

Uneasiness knotted her insides. She knew he was

referring to her behavior last night, when she'd left him as sexually frustrated as she had in college. Conscious of Mrs. Hornsby sitting within easy earshot, Brynn ignored the implication, yanked the dust cloth from the pocket of the pinstriped apron she wore over her jeans, and turned her effort to polishing an end table. "I thought for sure you'd work in some kind of law enforcement capacity."

"Where's the future in that?"

She halted her polishing and stared at him. The 180-degree change in direction suddenly struck her as incomprehensible. He'd always been intensely interested in police detective work, FBI profiling techniques and the noble cause of putting dangerous criminals behind bars.

In fact, there'd been times when his passion on the subject had bothered her. She'd had gut-wrenching qualms about how he might react, how his feelings for her might change, if he learned too much about her younger days—specifically, the ones she'd spent at a certain Florida beach community. Of course, that worry had applied to virtually everyone in her life.

Although she hadn't particularly liked Cade's passion for hunting down criminals, she'd understood it. His maternal grandfather had been a cop. Cade hadn't known him very well, but he'd taken to heart stories of his valor. The old man had obviously passed on to his young grandson an enthusiasm for confronting the bad guys. Brynn would have staked her life that Cade would specialize in some area of law enforcement.

And though it was none of her business, and, in many ways, she had to admit he was wise to choose the safe, potentially lucrative job of travel writing, she was ridiculously disappointed that he hadn't pursued his dream.

"Do I sense disapproval?" he asked incredulously. "Of my *writing career?*"

"Not disapproval. Who could disapprove of a writer's career when he's already published several books?"

"But you're not especially impressed."

"It's impressive enough." She turned back to her dusting.

"But...?"

"But..." Oh, *why* couldn't she keep her opinions to herself? "...it just seems that you sold out."

"Sold out." He narrowed his eyes as if to decipher unintelligible words.

"You majored in criminal justice," she reminded him.

"Are you telling me you think I should have been a cop?"

"Or a fed. A judge. A prosecutor. I think those lines of work would have suited you." She rubbed harder at the smooth, glossy finish of the oak table, watching him surreptitiously in her peripheral vision.

He leaned forward in the chair, rested his forearms across his knees and studied her profile. "You've never struck me as the cop-groupie type."

"The cop-groupie type!" She clutched the dust cloth in her fist and turned to him, ready to give him a quick, hard, verbal right hook. But she reconsidered. He'd called her a prude once, and just moments ago insinuated that she hadn't changed. "A cop groupie, huh?" She rested the fist with the dust cloth against her hip and tilted her head in contemplation. "A fascinating idea, really—to shamelessly pursue macho men in uniform for tawdry sexual kicks."

His mouth flexed and laugh lines creased beside his amber-brown eyes. "Okay, so you're not a cop groupie. But you're the first nongroupie of the female persuasion I've ever known who'd actually encourage a guy to be a cop."

"I wouldn't encourage just *any* guy to be a cop."

"Then why me?"

"You were always fascinated by police work, and…and by being one of the good guys." That, she realized, had been the driving force behind his zeal. She wasn't even sure how she knew. "You were *passionate* about it. It was part of you. And I'm sorry to hear you've left that part behind."

Surprise entered his eyes, then turned into something deeper. As if she'd somehow touched him. "I was passionate about other things, too."

Her heart took a leap, and she felt the sensual warmth rise in her again. Yes, she remembered very clearly. He had indeed been passionate.

She wrenched her gaze away from his mesmerizing one and resumed polishing the end table. He was simply too good at luring her into an erotic state of mind.

She couldn't have been more relieved when, moments later, the Kappa Alpha guys trooped in to watch the Braves game on the big-screen television. Mrs. Hornsby quit her snoring to watch the game, too.

Brynn kept herself busy by serving drinks and snacks, thereby avoiding further conversation with Cade. At least she had made up her mind on the question of whether or not to sleep with him. She wouldn't. If a conversation about his job had the power to stir her emotions, how could she ever survive sexual involvement?

Then again, how could she ignore the potent sexual attraction she felt for him when she felt it for no one else?

Okay, so maybe her mind wasn't entirely made up.

Her attention was torn from her inner debate when the baseball game was interrupted by a special newscast. A headline banner ran across the television screen: Serial Abductor: "The Pied Piper."

The anchorwoman announced, "Just in from police—three separate incidences of women disappearing from their homes in Georgia this summer have now been linked to a single abductor. Police recently received in the mail photographs of all three women, along with a note that read, 'Dancing to my tune now.' The note was signed, 'The Pied Piper.' So far, no ransom has been demanded. Police believe the abductor befriended each victim prior to her disappearance. More on this story at eleven."

Brynn recognized the case her brother was investigating—the abductor he'd warned her about, although he hadn't mentioned the sensational details about the photos and note. He'd merely warned her to beware of strangers because some creep abductor had been targeting women "just like her," whatever that meant. John had also told her that they didn't know if the women were still alive. Brynn shuddered at the implication. The thought that her brother dealt with such dangerous psychos in the course of his work hit her harder than ever before.

Had she been crazy, telling Cade he should have been a cop? He was much better off as a writer! She should have praised his change in career plans, not criticized it.

Most of the men gathered around the television had paid little attention to the broadcast, other than to grumble about the interruption to the ball game. Cade, however, had seemed to focus intently on the newscast. And though someone who didn't know him probably wouldn't have noticed, Brynn suspected he'd been disturbed by it. Not just concerned over the news, as she was, but *angered* by it.

An odd reaction.

But then he laughed at something a Kappa Alpha was saying, and returned his attention to the Braves game. Brynn assumed she'd misjudged his fleeting reaction.

5

THE BIDDING STOPPED at one hundred twenty thousand, and the painting of a wilted corsage was sold to some social butterfly who would hang it on her wall so her fluff-brained friends could ooh and ahh over it as if the damn thing had real merit.

Anger percolated through his veins and throbbed in his temples with such fierceness that he had to shoulder his way through the crowd and leave the gallery. A hundred twenty big ones—while his own vastly superior work went for mere hundreds, if he was lucky.

He strode out the door and down a bustling Atlanta street at a furious pace, longing to wreak violence on something or someone, to give in to the all-consuming rage. And for the umpteenth time, he swore he understood the mindset of Jack the Ripper. He'd read the theory that the killer had been a suffering Impressionist painter. Too bad his notoriety as the Ripper hadn't brought attention to his art. Of course, they would have hanged him. Which might have caused his work to fetch even higher prices.

The black humor in that irony helped to calm him. He didn't consider himself a violent man, and he couldn't let the injustice of the art world get to him like this.

He had to keep in mind that soon his work would

command top dollar at galleries around the world. And his name would be known not only by art patrons, but by everyone who read newspapers or watched the news. Because he had devised a way to cash in on notoriety without having to die for it.

Approaching an exclusive shopping district, he slowed his pace to a stroll in order to peer into the faces of the women he passed. Each drew him in her own way. Each possessed a unique beauty that he could easily translate into art. And he knew he could persuade any of them to sit for him. Ironically enough, he had discovered his aptitude for art while using it as a ruse to get close to wealthy women. Long before that, he'd made his living by charming the fairer sex into parting with money they didn't particularly need, anyway. In return, he gave them the thrill of his attention.

Women always loved him. He made sure of it.

But, at the moment, he had no need to woo any more women for profit, or to hunt for exceptionally striking models. He'd already chosen the ones that would take him where he wanted to go. He'd spent years deciding on these particular ones, and, so far, his thorough research and preparation had been paying off. Things were moving along according to plan.

As he crossed a side street with a chatty mob of mostly female shoppers, he passed by a patrol car. Casually he averted his face from the cop behind the wheel and merged deeper into the concealing crowd. Not that he worried about being collared. He'd been very careful in his latest ventures and didn't believe the cops had any idea what he looked like.

It was just an old reflex, to hide from the law. The

one time a mark of his had turned on him and pressed charges, he'd spent hard time behind bars. He didn't let the memories of the disrespectful treatment he'd suffered at the hands of Atlanta cops upset him anymore. Because now he had the upper hand. Now, they were dancing to *his* tune.

His spirits lifted at the thought, and self-satisfaction added a bounce to his step. The plan he'd concocted to elevate his status in the art world was serving more than one purpose. The delicious irony of it all delighted him.

He was, quite simply, a master at his game, and the world would someday marvel at his ingenuity.

And clamor to buy a painting by the artist formerly known as the Pied Piper.

THE WEATHER ON FRIDAY evening was perfect for a cookout, without the oppressive humidity or heat so common to late-August days in Georgia. More like an evening at his mountain home in Colorado, Cade decided, leaning against a column on the inn's front porch as he watched the crowd.

Brynn and Lexi had decorated the yard with red and black streamers around trees, balloons on the porch columns, Go Dawgs! signs and a Skin Those Wildcats! banner that spanned the entire roofline. A glance down the street in either direction showed that almost every yard was decorated, with students and alumni milling around, drinks in hand. Laughter and music blared from the sorority and fraternity houses lining the street.

Tables draped in red surrounded by black folding chairs were set up in the front yard of the inn, with a

long, central table bearing food, buffet-style, for registered guests. Lexi, with a little G for "Georgia"
painted on her face, flipped hamburgers and chicken
breasts on a nearby grill. Coolers were stocked with
icy beer and soft drinks. Classic rock music played
from high-quality stereo speakers.

The weekend-long tailgating party had begun.

Two of the beauty queens danced provocatively
with Kappa Alpha guys in a grassy clearing between
tables, no doubt killing time before joining parties on
campus or at frat houses. Other guests watched,
clapped and whistled.

Brynn, dressed in a red University of Georgia
T-shirt and tiny black shorts that hugged her slender
hips and nicely rounded bottom in a seriously distracting way, was encouraging the retired professors to
dance, making sure no one was left out of the action.

Cade tried not to glare at Smitty, the likable yet
annoying frat-boy-turned-insurance-salesman who was
admiring Brynn's trim backside a little too much for
his liking. As long as the guy kept his hands to himself, Cade supposed he'd have to let him live.

Whether she realized it or not, all of the men
watched her on the sly. She'd attracted a lot of male
attention back in college, too. She hadn't seemed to
notice then, either. She'd been aware of *his* interest,
though. Openly aware. Undeniably aware.

Now she avoided him with that same intensity.

God help the poor sucker who tried to get her alone.

*Calm down, Hunter. You can't stop her from choos-
ing another man to spend time with…even intimate
time, if it comes to that.* But the thought that it might
had kept him on edge all evening. He wasn't sure what

he'd do if she took on male company for the night. Unless, of course, she chose *him.*

He no longer held out much hope for that. She'd been avoiding him since their talk that afternoon.

Maybe she shied away from him out of loyalty to her boyfriend, Antoine, Trish's cousin with the "continental charm." Cade wondered when he'd show up. That thought, too, made him unreasonably tense. Cade didn't think he could take it if Brynn showed signs of being in love with the guy. Or even of being in lust with him.

Cade mentally scoffed at himself. So much for his vow never to let Brynn Sutherland under his skin again.

But how could he resist a woman who got upset that he hadn't followed his dreams? He didn't know anyone else who'd ever given a thought to what his dreams were or whether he'd achieved them. She'd also recognized the force that had driven him since he was a kid: to be one of the "good guys." He hadn't consciously recognized that motivation in himself until she'd said it. It stunned him to realize anyone knew him that well, let alone someone he hadn't seen in years.

When she'd broken off their conversation today and gone back to ignoring him, he'd been as disappointed as he had last night, when she'd run from his bed.

This afternoon's television broadcast hadn't helped his mood any, either. He hadn't expected the news of the abductor's note and "Pied Piper" moniker to become public so soon. Media attention was, without a doubt, what the perp craved. Publicity could encourage him to strike again, and sooner rather than later.

At least some of the details hadn't been publicized yet. Like the fact that every woman he'd taken was a loved one of an Atlanta cop. Two were wives, the other a daughter. That juicy little tidbit would be leaked to the media soon enough, Cade guessed. And Brynn, knowing that her brother was not only an Atlanta cop, but the lead detective on the Piper's case, would realize how much danger she was in. Which would only complicate Cade's job all the more.

Annoyed by the media coverage—and the fact that Smitty had finally persuaded Brynn to dance with him—Cade decided to get on with another part of his job: to find out as much as he could from and about the people in her immediate environment.

Since he'd already talked with Lexi that morning and many of the guests throughout the day, he decided to spend some time with the one he'd spoken to the least. The one who could tell him the most about Brynn's boyfriend. Trish.

THE PARTY WAS CLEARLY a huge success. Everyone seemed to be having a fabulous time eating, drinking, dancing or flirting. Brynn couldn't wait until it ended.

Her less-than-sunny mood had nothing whatsoever to do with the fact that Trish, dressed in only a black bikini, high heels and a sheer little wrap around her slim hips, was practically welded to Cade's side. They'd sat at a table talking, just the two of them, for what seemed like hours. Now she stood arm in arm with him as he talked to other guests, flashing not-so-subtle invitations to him with her big ol' baby blues.

Brynn couldn't take another minute of it.

"Um, Trish, honey," she called, "I need your help

with something for a few moments. Would you mind?''

The look Trish shot her made it clear that she did indeed mind. Brynn smiled and crooked her finger. Reluctantly, Trish whispered something to Cade, then followed her up the porch steps and into the house.

When they reached the library, Brynn pulled Trish into the spacious, stately room and shut the door. ''Trish, please listen to me. I'm telling you for your own good—don't get involved with Cade Hunter.''

Trish frowned at her. ''Why not?''

''Because you're vulnerable right now. You're on the rebound after your divorce. Why get into another relationship that's bound to end badly?''

''What makes you think it'll end badly? Cade is nothing like my cheating, son-of-a-bitch ex.''

''Oh, you don't think so?'' This was just too much to take! ''Then let me tell you about how my relationship with him ended back in college. Cade demanded that I have sex with him, and when I wouldn't, he got it from someone else.''

There. She'd said it. It had hurt, yes—like a bandage being torn from a wound—but at least Trish had been warned.

''You wouldn't have sex with him?''

Brynn blinked. Her friend clearly hadn't gotten the point. And the incredulity in Trish's expression reminded her of why she hadn't discussed the matter in any great detail with Trish or her other sorority sisters. Her virginity had been something of an oddity.

''I was only eighteen, Trish! And I—I...'' Knowing her friend would never understand, Brynn threw her hands up in exasperation. ''What difference does it make why I didn't have sex with him? When I said no, he turned to someone else.''

''Well, what did you expect him to do?''

Brynn's exasperation grew. Trish just didn't get it. ''He turned to *one of our sorority sisters.*''

At last, shock and disapproval registered on Trish's face. Since her husband had slept with one of her friends from the yacht club, she was particularly sensitive to the issue of a man betraying a woman with one of her friends. ''That bastard!''

Much better. Brynn nodded, mollified.

''Who was it?'' Trish asked.

She bit her lip and shook her head, suddenly unsure if it had been wise to tell Trish about her heartbreak with Cade. She certainly wouldn't mention Rhiannon's name, as she had to Lexi that morning. It wouldn't be fair to spread unsubstantiated rumors about the possibility that Cade had fathered Rhiannon's baby. ''Who it was doesn't matter, Trish. The point is, *he broke my heart.* And it took years for me to get over it.''

''I'm so sorry, Brynnie.'' Compassion softened Trish's voice. She had spent hours telling Brynn about the anguish of discovering her husband's affair and her friend's betrayal. Brynn knew she now empathized completely. ''You don't still have feelings for him, do you?''

''No, of course not. I learned my lesson about Cade Hunter a long time ago.''

''Good.'' She hugged Brynn, then drew back with a lopsided smile. ''Then don't you worry about me, hon. I'm not in this for any long-term relationship. In fact, now that I know how he treated you, I believe

I'll punish him for all the wrong he's done and leave *him* with a broken heart. That would be poetic justice, wouldn't it?'' With a bittersweet grin, she squeezed Brynn's shoulders, turned away and left the library.

Brynn fought the urge to grab her by her pretty blond hair and yank her back in. Trish clearly had her mind set on seducing Cade. Brynn couldn't allow that to happen! Intent on running interference—although she had no clear idea how she'd do that—she made a move to rejoin the party.

But then a man stepped out of the shadowy hall, filling the library doorway. Brynn's heart turned over. *Cade.* She was too startled to speak.

His face was dark, serious. ''Was that true, Brynn? What you told Trish. Did I really…break your heart?''

''You were listening at the door,'' she accused, mortified.

''Your voice carried into the hall.'' He drew closer and repeated his question. ''Did I break your heart?''

She didn't want to admit that. Not to him. ''Of course you did.''

He stared at her, looking genuinely stunned. ''I didn't think you cared enough to get hurt. You broke up with me and didn't look back. You refused to talk to me or see me.''

''It doesn't matter anymore, anyway.'' She tried to move past him, but he caught her shoulders.

''It *does* matter.'' He searched her face with an intensity she hadn't seen in him since their early days, and she felt more naked now than she had last night. ''I didn't turn to any of your sorority sisters for sex.''

Her jaw went slack at the blatant lie. ''Are you forgetting about Rhiannon Jeffries?''

"I never slept with Rhiannon. We were friends. Platonic friends. Her family belonged to the same country club as my father. And because I spent six months a year at my father's house, I—"

"Give it a break, Cade. We were all at a party together, remember? Two days after we broke up. Or maybe you didn't notice I was there. You were on the sofa all evening, making out with your so-called platonic friend."

"So you *were* paying attention." He actually had the nerve to sound annoyed with her, as if she'd somehow deceived him. "You didn't act like you noticed or cared."

"Did you expect me to wail and gnash my teeth?"

He thinned his lips and took a deep breath. When he looked at her again, he made a clear attempt to start over. "Brynn, I admit I was wrong. I made a lot of bad choices. But, as unlikely as it sounds, sleeping with Rhiannon wasn't one of them. I never had sex with her. I brought her to that party just to make you jealous, hoping you'd come back to me. And Rhiannon went along with it to get to some other guy. Not the brightest of moves on our part...but we were both just so damn *desperate*."

Willingness to believe him welled up in her, but she fought it. Why should she believe him now when she hadn't back then? And why should she care now, one way or the other, whether he'd had sex with someone else?

He still made her feel things too deeply. That hadn't changed at all. Abruptly, she tried to break free from him.

He kept firm hold of her shoulders. "Brynn, I'm

sorry that I made you think I was involved with Rhiannon. And I'm sorry for giving you that ultimatum. I've never regretted anything more." Remorse showed in his eyes, the kind that bordered on heartsickness.

She was utterly tempted to forgive him and melt into his arms. Was she crazy to let down her defenses that much? This was the man who had ripped out her heart and stomped it flat!

"I forgive you." She forced a tight smile while her insides waged a battle. "We've both grown up, anyway. Moved on. Found happiness, et cetera, et cetera."

"Don't do that, Brynn." His hands tightened on her arms. "Don't shut me out. And don't be so sure I'm the only one to blame. You made me believe I was important to you while we were together. The way you held me, the way you kissed me. But then you kept pushing me away, and I realized I wasn't a part of your plans. You didn't want to get too attached. That's why you kept me at a distance. I just wanted to break down your barriers, Brynn, and close the distance between us."

"I was too young to get serious about anyone. We were both too young."

"I can see that now. But, at the time, all I saw was you. And I knew that your feelings for me went only so deep, and my time with you was limited." He released a harsh breath. And his voice turned wry, self-deprecating. "You'd think I'd have been used to that, but for some crazy reason—" He bit off the words and shook his head, as if to deny he'd said them. Or to shake off a painful thought.

The unfinished statement made sense to Brynn only

when she remembered what she'd pried out of him about his past. His wealthy, prominent father and exotic-dancer mother had waged an anticustody battle over him when he was seven. Neither side had wanted him. They were forced to share custody. He was shoved from one household to the other and back again. The significance of his childhood suddenly put his behavior toward her in a whole new light.

Your feelings for me went only so deep. My time with you was limited. You'd think I'd have been used to that….

She pressed a hand to her heart. Had *she* hurt *him?* No. This was just his way of turning things around. Shifting blame. Confusing her.

"We can't change what we did, Brynn, but we can decide what happens now." He ran his hands down to her elbows and pulled her against him. "You were right when you said we've both grown up and moved on. I'm not expecting you to change anything in your life for me, and I don't plan on hanging around too long. But I think there *is* something you want from me, just like I want it from you."

Heat fluttered in her stomach, and she looked away from him, knowing what he meant. Knowing he was right.

"Come to bed with me," he urged. "Tonight." With a soft, devastating note of humor in his voice, he added, "Awake this time."

Temptation rushed through her in a hot, dizzying surge. What would it hurt?

But she was having a harder time now than ever seeing him in his true light. She wasn't even sure any more what that was. She was pretty certain, though, that somewhere a bright, urgent warning should be flashing: Danger. Danger.

Unable to answer, or think clearly, or come to any kind of decision whatsoever, she mumbled a disjointed apology, pushed past him into the hallway and fled to the sanctuary of her private suite. Lexi could handle the rest of the party on her own. Social activities were, after all, Lexi's job. For once in her life, Brynn was heartily glad of that.

She was also thankful that she'd had the foresight to install that new computerized lock on the door to her suite. She could sleep secure in the knowledge that she wouldn't be climbing into Cade's bed without giving the prospect a lot of careful, rational thought.

The last thing she needed tonight was for her subconscious to play more tricks on her.

CADE STOOD BY THE LIBRARY door and watched her run away from him again. She believed he'd broken her heart! And it had taken her years to get over it, or so she'd told Trish. And she had no feelings left for him.

How the hell was he supposed to feel about all that? He couldn't help being a little gratified to know that she'd cared about him more than he'd thought. But he was angry, too. Furious with her. She'd seen his actions in the very worst light. On top of all that, he was disgusted with himself for hurting her. For losing her.

But he found it hard to accept that he'd been *that wrong* about her. For her to feel he'd broken her heart, she had to have loved him. Or at least, had to have thought she did.

Regret tore into him with sharp, punishing claws.

Had he failed to recognize the ultimate miracle when he'd found it? But no. He hadn't mistaken the situation. The barriers he'd sensed in her had been real.

And they were still there today, stronger than ever.

Yet he still wanted her with an urgency that baffled him.

THEY STORMED INTO her bedroom that night—a mob of angry, bickering women wearing nothing but black bikinis and spiked heels. Among them—and substantially more dressed—was the handsome, middle-aged anchorwoman who had delivered the newscast that afternoon. The crowd surrounded Brynn, yelling at her and at each other. She strained to understand what they were saying as she lay in bed, startled and bewildered.

The tallest, prettiest brunette, who looked like one of her beauty-queen guests, but of Amazonian proportions, addressed her directly. "Cade Hunter. I want him. Where is he? You said he'd be here."

"I did?"

"How could you want someone like him?" a buxom redhead shouted. "He's a son-of-a-bitch." To Brynn, she said, "I'm just glad you tipped us off to his true character."

Brynn frowned. "But I never—"

"I'm not worried about his character, as long as he's good in bed." An elegant blonde in white had shouldered her way through the contentious crowd that now filled Brynn's bedroom. Upon closer inspection, Brynn realized it was Trish. She was dressed as a bride, in the same pearl-seeded gown and veil she'd worn for her wedding to her ex. "Don't you worry,

Brynnie. I'll rip his heart out for you. Wouldn't that
be poetic justice?''

"No." Panic tweaked Brynn's stomach. Was Trish
going to *marry* Cade to punish him? "Trish, don't.''

"Why not? You don't want him for yourself, do
you?''

The Amazon beauty queen shoved Trish aside, her
impatience bordering on rage. "Where is he?''

"He's here," the newscaster stated in professional
tones of well-modulated urgency. "According to inside sources, Cade Hunter, the notorious heartthrob,
checked in on Thursday. Authorities believe he's on
the prowl for women to sleep with. More on this
breaking story at eleven.''

"He's here, all right," confirmed someone who
sounded like Mrs. Hornsby.

"It's my turn to have him," a woman cried in a
shrill voice, making Brynn cringe beneath her covers.

"I'll tear out his heart," snarled another.

Brynn suddenly understood what they would do.
They would take their pleasure with Cade, then punish
him for callously hurting her and Rhiannon, and refusing to acknowledge his own baby.

But *had* he callously hurt her, or had she somehow
misunderstood? And had he really fathered Rhiannon's baby, or had Brynn presumed too much? She
suddenly wasn't sure. Yet these wild, lustful women
were going to tear him apart.

"No, wait!" Brynn sprang to her knees on the bed.
"I might have been wrong about him.''

"Do you still have feelings for him?''

"Have you forgiven him?''

"Is he your lover?''

''If he's not your lover, then he'll be mine.''

Sweat beaded on Brynn's forehead and her tongue stuck to the roof of her mouth while the women turned into snarling, sharp-clawed cats, hissing and spitting at each other. Wildcats. And they were ready to tear Cade to pieces.

She had to warn him! Save him! It was all her fault, and she hadn't even been sure of his guilt!

Horrified by what she'd done, she leaped from the bed, nearly tripping over the covers that tangled around her legs. Her heart pounded and her head swam as she kicked free of them. She would need her keys to get to Cade before the intruders found him. Quickly she grabbed her key ring from the dresser. When she reached her door, though, she couldn't open it.

The new lock! She had to follow those complicated steps. Why, oh why, had she installed it? *Think, think.* How was she supposed to do it? Turn this, press that. Ah, yes, then the numbers. Thank God she remembered the code.

Wasting no time at all, she threw open the door and charged down the hall.

6

THE QUIET BUT INSISTENT beeping of the alarm on his watch roused Cade from the first deep sleep he'd had since he'd left Colorado. It took him a moment to clear his head and realize the alarm had been triggered by the movement sensor he'd planted on Brynn's door.

She had opened it. And his watch read 1:15 a.m. Was she sleepwalking again? Or had she changed her mind and decided to come to him? A surge of hope rose in him, then crashed head-on into another possibility. Was she opening her bedroom door to let someone in?

Fully alert now and tense beyond bearing, he sat up and listened. No, she'd left her room. Her footsteps thudded down the hall. Where was she going? Was she awake, or lost in some dream? She was headed in this direction. Would she stop at his door?

If not, he'd go after her. It was his duty to go after her. He couldn't let her wander around at night—even if she was awake.

He made a move to swing his legs over the side of the bed, but keys rattling in his lock stopped him. The knob turned. The door opened. Relief washed through him in hard, cleansing currents. She had come to him.

"Cade." She spoke in an urgent undertone as she shut the door behind her with both hands. "Oh,

Cade!'' She then launched herself toward the bed, wild-eyed, her dark hair streaming around her. ''They're coming for you.''

''Who?''

''The cats!''

He caught her as she landed on the bed. ''Cats?''

''They'll find you and tear you to shreds!'' She was talking nonsense. She had to be dreaming.

Damn. ''No, no. I'm good with cats,'' he assured her. Throwing the bedcovers aside, he drew her to him.

''I called them.'' She was trembling and cold. Terrified. ''I'm sorry, Cade. I'm so, so sorry.''

''Shh. It's okay.'' He smoothed his hands over her back, pressed her body against his and pulled the covers up to warm her. ''You're just dreaming.''

''I'm not dreaming,'' she insisted, surprising him. He hadn't thought a sleepwalker could carry on a discussion, let alone argue. ''They're here, they're really here, and they'll tear you to pieces.''

''And...you called them, huh?''

She pressed her velvety cheek against his bare shoulder. ''I shouldn't have told them about you.''

''What exactly did you tell them?''

She drew back and looked at him, her hazel eyes shining with regret, yet somehow not quite focusing on his. ''Is it true? Is any of it true, Cade?''

''Nah. None of it.'' He pulled her determinedly back into his embrace, wondering what she'd told the cats to make them want to tear him apart. And, more importantly, what made her regret it.

She pulled away, but only long enough to tug her nightgown up over her head and toss it aside. She then slid her arms around him, nestled her naked breasts against his chest and hugged him as if she'd never let him go.

His pulse drummed; his temperature soared. And the craving began. But he just held her. She murmured something incoherent. He felt as if he were eavesdropping through a keyhole, but he listened for anything else she might say.

"You're my sexual adventure," she murmured. And a few minutes later, with a restless turn of her head, "Just a carnival ride!"

He frowned. Was she still dreaming about him? Was she considering *him* in the light of a sexual adventure, a carnival ride?

Nothing wrong with that, he told himself. What man in his right mind wouldn't want to be considered a sexual adventure by a beautiful woman? Still, he found himself unaccountably tense as he listened for more clues to her thoughts. But her breathing soon grew deep, slow and rhythmic.

He would do nothing to wake her. She would sleep in his arms, by God. Just sleep. All night.

And in the morning, when she woke up, they'd have a long, serious talk. And maybe, just maybe, he'd take her on that carnival ride.

So her expensive new lock hadn't worked.

She knew that without even opening her eyes. She recognized Cade's night scent—a musky mix of soap, mint and man. She recognized the feel of his body curved against her back. Solid. Warm. Silken hair over toned muscle. She recognized the tensile strength in the arms holding her, the morning stubble on the chin resting against her ear and the callused hardness of the man-size palm cupping her breast.

Her bare breast.

Keeping her eyes shut despite the insistent morning light, she allowed herself to savor his physical nearness. How pleasing it was to lie with him. To wake up in his arms. She felt safe and coddled. Languorous, yet sensually charged. The merest tilting of her hips, the slightest arching of her body, the lowest purring in her throat, would pull him from his sleep. Bring tension to his muscles. Quickness to his breath. Purpose and drive to his hands.

Fighting the urge to undulate against his muscled thighs, Brynn forced herself to think beyond the moment, beyond her sensual compulsion to arouse him.

She didn't have to guess how she'd ended up in bed with Cade. He couldn't have gone to *her* bed. The door had been locked. She'd gone to his. She searched her memory, retrieving only vague, dreamlike images and emotions that made little sense. Most vivid was the feeling of impending doom. The need to hurry. Cade was in danger. She had to get to him.

Clearly, she'd succeeded.

Another fleeting memory returned: of tugging her gown over her head, whipping it aside…cuddling skin to skin…basking in the warmth, the safety, the sweet drowsy comfort. *Cade*. She'd known where she was, all right—exactly where she'd wanted to be. Damn that sleepwalking!

Damn, damn, damn. But since the damage to her pride was already done, and she felt this compulsive physical need with no other man, and the panic of her dream had reminded her that time with Cade was definitely limited...

She allowed her body to move. Just a little. The very slightest of motions. A subtle swish of her hips, like a whisper beneath the sheet. A brush of her buttocks across his pelvis, across his intimate heat. She turned her face and rested it against his jaw. Slid her hand along his hip. His sleek, bare hip.

He was naked. Although she'd known that, *felt* that, a moan gathered in her throat, a moan she couldn't quite contain.

She heard the rhythm of his breathing falter. Felt tension steal into his body. His hand tightened on her breast, and his muscles flexed in direct response to her seductive movements. She arched into him. Hardness burgeoned between his thighs, against the sensitive crevice of her backside, and he inhaled sharply.

"Brynn." The whisper heated her ear. "Are you awake?"

She smiled, ridiculously glad to know he cared. "Pinch me," she murmured, "just in case I'm dreaming."

He did exactly that—pinched her lightly, teasingly, on her bottom. He also sucked her earlobe into his mouth, sending tingles down her neck. He then traced the path of those tingles with a hot, wet swirl of his tongue.

She lost all restraint, allowing herself wanton moves, strokes and groans. He kneaded her breasts and worked his hand between her legs. Her pleasure grew hot and urgent while his erection pulsed to an awesome thickness between her legs.

She wanted him. Wanted him to go deep and hard.

Energized by a needful heat, she angled her hips to take him in. His fingertips stilled among the curls between her thighs, on the most sensitive part of her feminine mound, and pressed there—an even, steady pressure—while his arousal pushed up and in, probing for entry. The sharp, stunning sensation created by those two forces took her breath away.

A loud, sudden knock shook the door, rudely startling her. "Cade, are you in there?" The voice was Lexi's.

Brynn expelled a gasping breath and struggled to make sense of the intrusion. Cade crossed his dark, muscled arm between her breasts to hold her fast against him, like a hostage in a holdup. "Don't answer," he breathed into her ear. "We're not stopping, Brynn."

But Lexi rapped on the door again. "If you're in there, Cade, wake up. It's important."

They remained absolutely still and stared at the door, dismayed and disbelieving.

"Cade?" yelled Lexi. "I wouldn't bother you, but Brynn is missing."

Brynn squeezed her eyes shut and laid her head back against his shoulder. Cade let out a dry laugh that sounded like a curse.

"She didn't show up for work," Lexi explained through the wooden panel. "Her bedroom door was left open, and the covers were dragged off her bed. Things were knocked off her dresser. Her purse is still here, and so is her car, but—"

"I'm here, Lex."

The silence following Brynn's announcement was

rife with astonishment. "Oh," Lexi finally said, sounding dumbfounded. "Sorry to bother you, then."

Brynn glanced at the bedside clock. Eight thirty-five! Long past time to start work. "I'll be right down," she promised, consumed with guilt, yet incredibly frustrated at having to leave Cade's bed just now.

"Take your time. No need to rush," Lexi assured her. "I've got everything under control."

Nevertheless, at the sound of her receding footsteps, Brynn pulled out of her intimate pose with Cade and sat up to reach for her nightgown on the floor beside the bed. A masculine hand clamped around her arm, detaining her.

"Where you going? Lexi said not to rush."

The strength of Cade's hand on her arm, the impatience in his expression, the flush of arousal lingering beneath his tan, all revived the sensual heat that had been simmering in Brynn. "But I can't neglect my duties," she said, her voice throaty and hesitant. "We can talk later."

"Let's talk now." He pulled her down against the pillows. "As much as I love your company, and as welcome as you are in my bed—*anytime*—we've got to do something about your sleepwalking."

She caught her lip between her teeth. He had a point.

"It's dangerous, Brynn. Assuming that my bed is the only one you've visited so far, think about what might happen if you *did* go to someone else's."

"I won't go to anyone else's." She felt strangely sure of that.

He laid his hand alongside her face and searched

her gaze, as if trying to determine whether the statement was true. Warm emotion pulsed between them— the kind that always left her hungry for his kiss. "I'd like to believe it," he said with feeling, giving their conversation added meaning. "But you can't be sure what you'll do in your sleep. You might even leave the inn."

"No, I'd never do that."

"Dangerous people are out there. Didn't you hear the broadcast about the abductor snatching women from their homes? And he's just one of the scumbags lurking around. How safe do you think you'd be, wandering outside in your sleep?"

"I'm not disagreeing with you. I'd love to stop sleepwalking. Do you think it's fun, waking up somewhere other than where you went to bed?"

A teasing light entered his gaze. "You mean, like…here?" His voice had gone husky, and he ran the back of his fingers up her bare arm.

"Okay, maybe it *can* be fun," she allowed with a breathless laugh. Goose bumps followed the path of his fingers, making her hotly aware that the two of them were essentially naked beneath the covers…and lying flush against each other. Not the easiest way to carry on a rational conversation. Trying nonetheless, she said, "But you must know that if I'd been making logical decisions, I wouldn't be here with you."

He nodded, as if that fact didn't bother him in the least. "My point exactly." A tiny muscle moved in his jaw, though, at odds with his nonchalance.

"So what can I do? Chain myself to the bed?"

"There's an idea. I could help you make sure you're bound securely. I'd have to stay there with you, of course, in case of a fire. But I wouldn't mind. Especially if you'd wear a little leather. And high heels, maybe.''

Using the corner of the sheet, she whipped him across his brawny biceps.

He winced at every slash, though a wicked grin lit his eyes. "I surrender. Take me, punish me, oh mistress of the night."

"Careful, or you'll find yourself gagged."

"And handcuffed?"

"Without a doubt. Now, pay attention."

"Yes, *ma'am*."

They didn't smile at each other—in fact, they frowned as though still in character—but shared the enjoyment of the moment.

Then the tone subtly changed, with the sweep of his gaze across her mouth, and Brynn drew in a much-needed breath and forced her mind to the matter at hand. "Seriously, though," she managed to say.

"Seriously."

The sensuality in his stare was too distracting. "I bought the most expensive lock on the market," she said, determined to get them back on track, "and had it installed on my bedroom door. I thought it would prevent me from leaving the room." She lifted her hand in a helpless gesture. "I must have opened it in my sleep."

He contemplated that in silence for a moment. "So, what you're saying is, not even the most sophisticated lock on the market could stop you from coming to me."

She let out an exasperated huff. "Oh, *puh-leeze.*"

"Only stating the facts, ma'am. Just the facts."

Her lips shifted to the side in wry objection.

"Don't distract me," he murmured, brushing his thumb across her chin, "by doing things with your mouth."

Erotic warmth flushed through her. Holding on to her determination by a thread, she said, "Maybe I can get a dog. He could wake me up if I got out of bed. Oh, but if he barked, he'd disturb the guests."

"And how would you train him to know when you're dreaming? You argued with me in your sleep. I know damn well you'd order him to sit or stay, and you'd go on your merry way."

"I argued with you in my sleep?"

"You swore you weren't dreaming. I tried to tell you, but, as usual, you wouldn't listen. You were just too stubborn to acknowledge my superior wisdom."

"You're making that up."

"The argument, or my superior wisdom?"

"Both."

He shrugged. He clearly enjoyed having inside information to lord over her. "The point is, a dog would be bound to get confused, not knowing when to obey you or when to drag you back to bed. Could get pretty annoying if you had to leave your room at night for an emergency." He paused, then added in a sultry tone, "Like an urgent compulsion to come to my bed."

"Oh, you're impossible."

"Not at all. Actually, I'm easy. Give me a try."

"Be serious."

"You don't think I am?"

"This is all your fault, you know. If you would lock

your door with the security dead bolt like you're supposed to, I couldn't come in.''

"Now why the hell would I want to lock you out?"
He frowned at her as if she'd lost her mind.

"To help me stop sleepwalking."

"What makes you think you'd just go back to
bed?" He shook his head and tightened his arm
around her. "No, no. If you're walking in your sleep,
I want you to end up here. Right here. With me."

His protectiveness—or maybe it was possessive-
ness—spread warm, feminine gratification through
her. But then she realized he'd probably meant it for
purely sexual reasons. Which made her warmer in a
distinctly different way.

"Think about it, Brynn." He shifted onto his elbow
and rose above her to peer into her face. "There must
be a reason you're coming to my bed."

She cocked her head to one side and smiled into his
now-serious brown eyes. He really was irresistibly
gorgeous, with his morning stubble shadowing his
jaw, his ebony hair disheveled, his body taut and
strong against hers. "You think?"

"Know what I think?" His tone had gone soft and
throaty. "I think that deep down, beneath all the reasons you've found to keep me at a distance, you want
to make love to me."

She couldn't argue with that. She recognized the
truth when she heard it.

"And I believe," he softly continued, "that you
wanted to make love to me back in our college days,
too."

"Oh, I did," she agreed, relishing the heat growing

between them and the feel of his large, muscled body moving into a more provocative alignment with hers.

"I'm no psychologist, but I think the only way to stop your sleepwalking is to satisfy the unmet need that's causing it."

"Unmet need," she repeated, sliding her leg between his, certain now that she was, indeed, going to kiss him—

A knock rattled the door again, and Lexi called, "I'm so sorry, Brynn, but the pool man is here, wanting to be paid. And Professor Goldman said you ordered tickets for a concert this afternoon. And a sorority girl from next door dropped by and said she's got to talk to you about her date last night. I think she's the one whose mother died last year. I told her you were busy, but…"

"I'll be right down, Lex. Ten minutes, tops."

With a grateful murmur, Lexi left them again.

Sitting up with determination this time, Brynn cast a glance over her shoulder that was both apologetic and teasingly provocative. "We'll have to discuss my 'unmet need' later. And, uh, come up with a plan."

Cade sat back against the pillows and watched her rise from the bed. "It'll be my pleasure," he assured her.

As she left his room, she heard him softly whistling a tune she remembered from an old-fashioned carnival ride.

"I'M SORRY IT'S TAKEN so long to return your calls, *chérie*." Antoine's mellifluous, French-accented voice instigated a vague ache in Brynn's stomach. She hated breaking up with boyfriends. She hated disappointing them...or anyone, for that matter. But the time had definitely come to put an end to her relationship with Antoine. "My cell phone has not been reliable on the road," he was saying, "and my business has been keeping me much too busy."

"Antoine, I know this isn't the best time to discuss our relationship, but..." With her own cell phone to her ear, Brynn left the front desk of the inn, ducked into the small private office and shut the door. "Remember the discussion we had before you left?"

"Discussion? What discussion would that be?"

"Well, I said that maybe I'm not the right woman for you. You deserve someone who's more uninhibited, sexwise. You should be free to date other women, and I, too, should be free to—"

"Oh, *that* discussion. You see, I've put it completely out of my mind. You were speaking nonsense, Brynn. I am—how do you say?—crazy about you, and only you."

"I'm flattered, Antoine, but I've decided it's for the best if we, um, break up."

"Break up? I'm not sure what this phrase means, *chérie*. But you think I'm on the road too much, no? You are angry and bored, and lonely without me. I will make it up to you, *mon coeur*. I will be home soon. I will cancel all my—" A sound like static, or maybe scratching over the mouthpiece of the phone, interrupted his passionate declarations. "Brynn, are you there? Brynn, I adore you, and—" The harsh noise resumed, and the line went dead.

Brynn heaved a sigh of frustration and waited for him to call back. The phone did not ring. Either he was in an area that offered a poor connection for his cell phone, or he'd purposely ended the call.

But that last thought wasn't fair to Antoine. He'd never given her reason to think he was the scheming kind.

She'd simply have to wait for his next call to make him understand that their relationship was, in fact, over.

7

WHEN SHE FIRST LEFT his bed, Cade's plan was simple and direct. They'd have sex. As soon as possible. He could barely believe that after so many years of wanting Brynn, fantasizing about her, she was finally saying yes. That knowledge alone was an incredible turn-on.

But as he gave the situation more thought, he began to worry. From what she'd said in her sleep, she seemed to be looking for a "sexual adventure." And he'd assumed that their lovemaking, in and of itself, would more than qualify. From his perspective, nothing could be more thrilling than making love to Brynn, no matter where they were or how they did it. But what if she wanted something beyond good old-fashioned sex? Something more...adventurous?

He also had to keep in mind what she'd said the first time she'd come to his room in her sleep. She'd mentioned being frigid. A "dud in bed." And though she'd actually been insisting that she was neither of those things, he took it as a clear example of the lady protesting too much.

Not that he believed she was frigid or a dud in bed. He didn't. But what if her real "unmet need" was to be reassured? Once she had sex with him, she would be reassured. She'd then have no reason to make love to him again. With her psychological need fulfilled, he might become obsolete!

Okay, that chance was slim, since the sex was bound to be fantastic, but the chance did exist. And he wanted more than just one time with her. Nine years of bottled-up desire couldn't be discharged that easily, no matter how great the sex. It would take a whole week of being together, in his estimation. Maybe even two.

He clearly needed a better plan than just inviting her to his bed. Something adventurous. Something that would take longer than just one night.

He gave the matter constant thought and, over the course of that Saturday morning, a plan slowly evolved. An ingenious plan. One that would fulfill her needs along with his, and would require several days and nights of intimacy.

The wisdom of his new, improved plan was confirmed early that afternoon, just before the pregame festivities got into full swing. As he leaned against a column on the wide front porch of the inn, watching Brynn help the Kappa Alphas paint their faces red and black, his cell phone rang. Cade wandered into the yard to avoid being overheard.

"I'm running a check on the names and photos you sent." It was John Sutherland, detective with the Atlanta PD. Cade's college buddy. Brynn's brother.

"So am I," Cade said. "In case you miss something."

John grumbled at that—something about the "goddamn arrogant feds"— but it was only lighthearted, token resistance to sharing jurisdiction on the case. Ordinarily, he'd likely have fought any involvement of federal agents, Cade knew. In this instance, however, he had asked for Cade's help.

"I didn't get a photo of Antoine Moreau yet," Cade told him. "He's been away on a business trip, supposedly. Have you met him, by the way? Brynn's boyfriend."

"No. She hasn't said much about him, either."

Cade's suspicions about Antoine grew. Were they based on professional instinct, or personal jealousy? He had to admit, at least to himself, that he'd love to bust the guy just for his relationship with Brynn. "Trish told me he dropped by her mother's house a month ago—a nephew she hadn't seen in twenty years. Son of her late sister. Everyone bought it, without question. The timing bothers me."

"Yeah. It bothers me, too. Let's check him out." In an abrupt change of topic, John asked, "Have you seen the news?"

"Tell me the television coverage wasn't your idea."

"Hell, no, it wasn't. This precinct has more leaks than the *Titanic*. All we can do is hope that the publicity doesn't send the abductor underground. Then we'd have no way of finding his victims, or of knowing when or where he'll strike next. I don't think I could take that."

The suggestion of vulnerability wasn't like John. He'd never been one to show weakness of any kind. Cade understood why he did now, though. His sister could be targeted by this abductor, if the pattern held true. The fact that John was leading the investigation might make the challenge more attractive to the psycho—and make for dramatic press coverage. Right up the Piper's alley.

John, who'd been out of touch with Cade since college, had called him in to covertly check out the newcomers to Brynn's circle of acquaintances. And, of course, to protect her. John himself had his hands full, trying to protect his staff's families while working to apprehend the abductor.

Cade hadn't hesitated. He'd boarded a plane for Georgia before the authorization from his own supervisor had been final. And he'd been keeping his eye on Brynn ever since—with the help of an impromptu team of deputies in plain clothes who maintained a discreet perimeter around the inn.

Problem was, they had no idea whom they were guarding her against. They believed the Piper became personally involved with his victims in some way. There'd been no signs of struggle in any of the disappearances, and one woman—the wife of a patrolman—had left a phone message for him that she'd be home late because of a "business meeting." Which was odd, considering she worked as a waitress...and her co-workers had had no clue what she'd meant. The other two victims of the Piper had been described by their friends as "secretive" and "distracted" before their disappearance. The bastard clearly used some kind of psychological ploy to lure the women away from home. His choice of the nickname "Pied Piper" only added to that conclusion.

Cade intended to scrutinize every person who came into contact with Brynn, from now until the Piper was caught.

"One good thing came from the leak to the media, though, Bucko," John said.

Cade smiled at that. He'd forgotten John's habit of

calling his friends by whatever crazy nickname came to mind. Bud. Tiger. Jackeroo. They'd had some good times together, he and John, before his relationship with Brynn had strained their friendship. Amazing how life-threatening danger could put old conflicts into perspective. "What good came out of the media leak?" Cade asked.

"We got a tip from a hotel in Monticello, Florida. One of the maids swears she saw the latest victim the day after she'd been declared missing. She was seen leaving a hotel room with some guy."

Cade whistled, soft and low. He liked tips like that. "Did he use a credit card to check in, or flash any ID?"

"No. Paid cash. Wrote down an invalid license plate number. Signed in under 'J. Smith.'"

"Creative. Did we get a description of him, at least?"

"Not a great one, but the maid does remember that he was tall. Over six feet. Medium brown hair, she said. And he wore 'fancy' sunglasses."

Cade flashed back to the description Lexi had given him of Antoine Moreau. Over six feet tall. His hair "tawny." And he'd definitely sounded like the type to wear designer sunglasses. "It's more than we had to go on before," Cade murmured. "And we have a general direction to search in now, considering they were spotted in Florida. Did the suspect or victim leave anything behind in the hotel room?"

"No. And the room was cleaned after they left, then rented out several times since. Little chance of finding any useful fingerprints or fiber evidence. But this Piper bastard did leave us one more clue."

The anxious edge had returned to John's voice, Cade noticed. Bracing himself, he said, "Yeah?"

"Phone records show that he made a brief call from the hotel room."

"To whom?"

"The Three Sisters Bed & Breakfast Inn."

Anxiety formed a knot in Cade's chest. The abductor had called Brynn's inn. Which meant John's fear had been valid. She was one of the Piper's targets.

Had he been making a reservation at the inn, the first step in his plan to get close to her? Or had he already taken the preliminary steps, and was calling to touch base with his latest "girlfriend"?

Tense over that last possibility, Cade cast a glance at the gentle, beautiful, smiling woman who was now fitting a red-and-black dog collar around Smitty's neck. "I'd say it's time we tell her what's going on."

"I've been over this a thousand times in my mind," John said. "I'm so damned tempted to explain the situation, send her away somewhere safe—if there is such a place—and hunt this bastard down. But if we send Brynn away, he'll know we're on to him and just disappear...until he strikes again. His victims might never be found, and Brynn could end up living in fear the rest of her life, which might not be long if this nutcase is clever and ruthless enough. Right now, we know where he's headed. We can set a trap."

"With your sister as bait." Cade's stomach clenched.

"With my sister heavily guarded, and the U.S. Marshal Service's top man watching her every move."

Cade let the compliment slide by without acknowledgment. John was an astute cop. He knew that

Cade, with years of top-notch training, plus field experience guarding witnesses in the Federal Witness Protection Program, would give his life for anyone under his care, if need be. John also knew that Cade would give up whatever vacation he had coming or take a leave without pay, if necessary, to protect Brynn.

"Don't you see, Cade, that we can't even warn her?" John said. "If she knew that some psycho was planning to drop by and socialize, she'd close down the inn to protect her guests, and would warn all her friends about the danger. Even if we made her swear to keep the matter secret, there's no guarantee she would." He paused, then went on with a dry little laugh. "This might sound crazy, but when she gets stressed, she walks and talks in her sleep."

Cade made no comment. He wasn't about to admit that he knew. He wasn't sure how John would take the news that he'd been reaping the benefits from that particular vulnerability. Something told him Brynn's brother wouldn't be amused.

But John did have a valid point. Brynn could easily blow his cover in her sleep, or at least rouse suspicions.

"Even if she didn't talk in her sleep," John added, "everyone who knows her would be aware that something was seriously wrong. And the abductor would back off—until later, when our guard was down. We can't take that chance."

Unfortunately, Cade agreed. They couldn't take the chance. He couldn't even tell Brynn his real occupation. If the abductor got word that a U.S. marshal had suddenly come to stay with her, he'd smell a trap and run. There was only one logical course to take. While John used all his resources to track down the Pied Piper, Cade would have to expedite the investigation from the inside, as well as protect Brynn, all without letting her know his true purpose.

There was a silver lining behind the dark cloud, though. He now had every justification his conscience could possibly need to keep her with him, day and night, until the Piper was caught. And that could mean weeks.

The new plan he'd worked out to stop her from sleepwalking would fit in perfectly with that agenda. Now all he had to do was convince her to go along with it.

"HEY, WHAT D'YA CALL a Kentucky Wildcat in Sanford Stadium?" shouted a wiry, sunburned, shirtless student in a red-and-black Bulldog cap as he leaned out the window of a crowded SUV.

"The winner," a coed in blue yelled from the passenger seat of a convertible stuck in traffic behind the SUV.

"No. Dawg food!" The guys in the SUV cheered, barked and howled. Others called, "Here, kitty kitty kitty."

The gals in the convertible chanted pro-Wildcat slogans, drawing noisy support from passengers in other Kentucky-plated vehicles. The burly driver of a pickup truck with University of Kentucky flags shouted, "Hey, you dawgs! Tuck your tails between your legs. You probably don't have much else there."

Kentucky fans hooted, and the Bulldog fans switched from yelling "Kitty kitty kitty" to a word of the same meaning but with lewd connotations, much to the hilarity of pro-Georgia bystanders on both sides of the street.

Game day had arrived.

And game day in Athens, especially the season opener, meant all-day celebrations for both the home team's fans and the visitors. A ceaseless parade of traffic had been streaming onto campus and past the Three Sisters Bed & Breakfast Inn since early that morning. The choicest parking spots had been taken already by die-hard fans who had arrived on Friday and camped overnight. Vans, RVs, trucks and cars parked in nearby yards, lots and every open stretch of campus that wasn't posted as off-limits, as well as a few that were.

Students, alumni, faculty, staff and football fans of all ages set up for tailgating parties. Hopes were high for their team's new season. The Bulldog fans and the Wildcat supporters roasted each other with good-natured insults, boasts and challenges. Music—mostly Southern rock, bluegrass and rap—blared from every direction, along with sports commentary from portable televisions. Barbecue grills sizzled, and the afternoon air was fragrant with hickory smoke, beer, booze and the lush summer foliage of the wooded Georgia campus. Laughter, quips and shouts hummed all around like electricity over a high-voltage wire.

Brynn took in the excitement from the porch of the inn. Because the Three Sisters was tucked between sorority houses on "Greek Street," their lawn party merged with the activity in neighboring yards and with the lively parade of pedestrians on the sidewalks, creating one massive game-day celebration.

Brynn loved the holiday feel, and the sense of kinship among strangers. She loved the playful rivalry between schools and the grand traditions that held true across generations. Most of all, she loved the nostalgic feeling that transported her back to her earliest college days, when the excitement had been new.

That nostalgic feeling had never been as strong as it was today. Because Cade was here. Cade, who had been her first love. Her first college beau. Never mind that they had parted on such bad terms, or that she would never fully trust him again. Today was all about fun.

She'd thought about him the entire time she'd performed her daily duties. Anticipation had coursed beneath her skin like an underground river, utterly unstoppable.

And now that she'd finished her work for the day and changed into a sleeveless red midriff blouse and short black skirt—admittedly sexier clothes than she usually dressed in—she strolled down the steps and through the yard toward the street-side festivities, trying not to look as if she was searching for anyone in particular. She, who had always enjoyed socializing with guests and neighbors, found herself steering clear of conversations or anyone who might slow her down.

As she reached the main throng of people near the street and didn't see Cade, she began to worry that he'd gone somewhere else for the day.

Then a towering form stepped into her path, nearly causing her to collide with a broad male chest. "Looking for me?"

Breathing in the subtle scent of forest and man that she'd always associated with Cade, she blamed the surge of her heart on his sudden appearance. Certainly it wasn't her gladness to see him, or the fact that his black T-shirt stretched across his chest and showcased his dark, muscular arms to perfection, or that his jeans clung to his slim hips and athletic thighs in a blood-stirring way.

She forced her attention upward while she struggled to find her voice. "Whatever gave you that idea?"

"I wasn't looking for you, either." A wickedly irresistible smile curved his mouth and played in his light brown eyes.

"Then I'm glad we didn't find each other." She felt her pleasure beaming from her like rays of the sun.

His gaze meandered in clear enjoyment of her hair, which she'd left unbound to riffle in the hot summer breezes—the way he'd always liked her to wear it—then on to her tanned shoulders and crimson midriff blouse, which tied just above her navel. "Now that we've ignored each other in the rudest possible way," he murmured, stepping back to peruse her hip-hugging skirt and bare legs, "I guess we'll just have to be sociable, after all." His eyes returned to her face, and she saw that they'd heated to a dark, burnished gold.

Any retort she might have made was lost in an influx of heat and an almost painful pang of attraction.

"Cade! Hey, Cade! Over here!" The feminine shout disrupted their mutual trance, and they turned to see Trish waving and gesturing from a short distance away in the bustling crowd.

Without another word, Cade took hold of Brynn's elbow and steered her between clusters of people to where Trish stood with Lexi and a few of their women neighbors.

"Cade, I wanted to introduce you to some friends of ours. We were telling them about your books, and of course they're fascinated." Trish shifted to his free side with a proprietary air as she introduced him to the women.

His deep-voiced reply and potent virile presence drew their attention like flowers to sunlight. He said all that was courteous, charming every one of them, Brynn was sure, before he turned to Lexi. "I'm borrowing Brynn for a while. She's going to escort me around campus on game day to help put some local color in my writing."

"Great idea," Lexi replied.

"If Brynn has too much to do here, I'm free," Trish stated.

The other women, both younger and older, stout and trim, tall and petite, volunteered their services as tour guides, as well, each trying to outdo the other in comic attempts to explain her superior qualifications for the job and undying dedication to the literary arts.

Focusing on Cade rather than the lighthearted commotion he'd caused, Brynn lifted her brows, piqued that he'd spoken for her as if she were a child who needed permission to go out and play. "I don't remember you asking *me* if I'd go."

"Sure I did. Just like we *didn't* find each other."

She lifted her chin with a silent "Oh."

Lexi shifted a narrow-eyed glance from one to the other, as if suddenly concerned for their sanity.

Oblivious to their nonsense, Trish insisted, "I'd be happy to show you around, Cade. There are lots of places I can take you." She gave a beautifully dimpled smile and flashed her seductive blue eyes at him.

But his attention returned to Brynn and lingered there with the same playful yet sensual intensity he'd shown her earlier—as if they were entirely alone. She said to him, "I hope you're not assuming I agree to what you, um, didn't ask me?"

"No," he admitted. "That's why I've formulated a plan to force your hand, if need be."

"Force my hand?"

"Don't be stubborn, Brynn." Lexi gave her shoulder an emphatic nudge. "You're the perfect person to show Cade around. Who else knows as much about the place? You grew up here in Athens, for heaven's sake."

"I've spent quite a bit of time here myself, Lexi," Trish reminded her, sounding annoyed.

Only vaguely aware of the conflict brewing between her business partners, Brynn asked Cade, "How in the world would you force my hand?"

He replied by pointedly shifting his regard to Lexi, who was saying to Trish in a voice loud enough to draw a good deal of attention, "Don't leave us yet, Trish. Our guests have been enjoying your company *so* much." Those standing nearby, especially of the male persuasion, spoke up in hearty support. Lexi, her dark eyes gleaming with deviltry, and her spiky hairdo sprayed red-and-black, adding to the satanic look, continued her grandstanding. "I was hoping we could grill some ribs and wings with your new barbecue sauce, if you'd be willing to make a gallon or two. How 'bout it, Trish?"

The Kappa Alphas broke into a cheer of "Trish... Trish...Trish!"

The surrounding crowd picked up on it, until Trish,

the reigning authority on social graces, had little choice. "Okay, okay. I'll stay."

When the boisterous applause finally died down, Cade said to Trish, "Did I mention I'm devoting an entire chapter in my book to your inn and the Athens area?"

Recognizing a ploy when she heard one, Brynn rolled her eyes, but Trish brightened immediately, calling the idea "inspired." Lexi chimed in with vows to help in any way she could, and soon their voices unified in urging Brynn to spend as much time as Cade needed to get his "local color" just right.

Brynn pursed her lips and jabbed him in the ribs with her elbow, secretly thrilled that he'd forced her hand. Though, if truth be told, nothing less than a crisis would have stopped her from going with him.

Over the course of the night, she'd turned an important corner. Although she couldn't recall the exact details of her dream, she remembered the urgent, underlying message: that her time with Cade was limited. He would soon be gone, or snatched up by another woman, if Brynn didn't take action.

The time had come to do so. Even if he *was* an unscrupulous heartbreaker—which had yet to be proved without a doubt—he was definitely a good candidate for a sexual romp. *Tonight.* The prospect captivated her. Titillated her. She would expect nothing more from him than a good time.

With a small, droll smile, she capitulated. "If duty calls, one must answer."

"Yes, indeed, one must." His smile flashed brilliantly in his dark, rugged face.

And its effect on her left her with no doubt that she'd made the right decision.

8

WEAVING HIS LARGE, STRONG, tanned fingers through her fairer, slimmer ones, Cade led her across the lawn toward the street. Caught up in the pleasure of their palm-to-palm contact, Brynn barely noticed the people they passed as they crossed between slow-moving traffic to a sidewalk shaded by ancient oak trees. Merging into the flow of pedestrians, she and Cade trekked along with a jovial crowd of football fans until they came to a busy intersection.

Before she knew what he meant to do, Cade hooked an arm around her waist and swept her onto a bus that had whined to a wheezing stop beside them.

"What are we doing?" she asked, climbing the steps as the doors of the bus shut behind her with a blast of hot, street-scented air. She'd expected to walk through campus to downtown Athens. This bus was headed in a different direction.

"Making our getaway."

"From whom?"

"Everyone, I hope." He shot a glance out the window at the cheery mob on the sidewalk and beyond, as if he really was giving someone the slip. Looking satisfied, he paid the driver, then ushered Brynn through the crowded bus as it jerked into motion. The narrow aisle offered standing room only. Every passenger on board was dressed in red and black, it seemed, and all were talking or laughing loudly.

Cade spoke into her ear. "I want you to myself."

The words warmed her, thrilled her, but she asked breezily, "Sure you can handle it, Hercules?"

That surprised him into a laugh. She and John had teased him with that nickname in college because of his prowess in lifting weights, his resultant physique and the thick, wavy hair he'd worn longer than most criminal justice boys wore theirs. "I'm up for giving it a good hard try."

Aware of the double entendre in his husky reply, she laughed breathlessly. She hadn't flirted this way in years. Hadn't *felt* this way in years—light-headed, sexy and intoxicated by his nearness.

While the driver maneuvered the bus through stop-and-go traffic, Cade anchored one hand to the overhead rail and held her firmly against him. Swaying with every start, stop, bump and curve, she felt the vibrant rhythm of his heart against her breast through the thin cotton of their shirts. Inhaled the exotic woodsy scent of his skin and hair. Sensed the quickening of his blood and the hardening of his muscles as her hip lodged against his upper thigh.

"Our stop," he said, with a hot breath that sent tingles down her neck and shoulder.

Disoriented and way too warm, she gladly accepted his arm around her as the bus screeched to a halt and she descended the steps. They disembarked at Five Points, the popular intersection of Lumpkin Street and Milledge Avenue. "It's only right that we start our tour here," Cade said.

Brynn smiled in appreciation. Their first date had

been to the Sons of Italy Restaurant, whose outside deck was still teeming with students, probably from nearby fraternity and sorority houses.

"What'll it be?" Cade asked with a gesture that encompassed several storefronts. "Pizza and beer at Sons of Italy, or ice cream from Hodgson's?"

Hodgson's. She'd been addicted to the old-fashioned drugstore's heaping scoops of ice cream on hot summer days, while Cade had always gravitated more toward the beer. She was pleased that he remembered, after all these years.

"Since I'm older now, and more *adventurous*," she said, "let's go straight for the beer."

"Spoken like a true Delta Zeta."

She swatted his arm in mock punishment for the cheeky remark and then, with matching grins, they set out for Sons of Italy. As they crossed the street at the corner, Cade slanted her a curious glance. "Since when do you drink beer?"

"Since I came of age. When we were together, I was only eighteen. The real drinking age was twenty-one."

"Oh, yeah. I forgot what a wild outlaw you were."

The casual teasing, though spoken in an affectionate tone, made her uncomfortable. Touched a raw nerve. Reminded her of her secret shame—one of the few secrets she'd managed to keep well and truly buried. But she wouldn't let the Daytona Beach incident intrude now.

"Maybe not an outlaw," she replied, turning her attention toward clearing up at least one issue that had bugged her over the years, "but not a prude, either." Rounding on him with renewed outrage, she insisted,

"You have to admit that, Cade Hunter. I was not a prude."

He smiled, clearly delighted with her, even as she jabbed her finger reproachfully into his chest. Somehow the warmth in his smile healed the hurt she'd once felt at the charge. "I never called you a prude," he said.

She glared at him in rebuke, and he laughed. "If I did, I must have been sulking." He slid an arm around her and tugged her closer. "Must have been one of the many times I wanted more than you would give."

It wasn't an apology, but she accepted it as such and shied away from digging any deeper into that topic. She wanted no mention of the ultimatum that had torn them apart. She was having too much fun with him to ruin the mood.

Silently they strolled through the quaint commercial neighborhood that had once been their old stomping grounds.

And Cade reveled in the pleasure of her company. In the softness of her smile, the beauty of her long dark hair, her angel eyes, her sinfully delectable body. She'd worn a maddening little skirt that barely reached midthigh, leaving her long tanned legs stark naked. And her blouse looked as if he could open it with one tug to the knot nestled just below her full breasts. The garment left bare the curvaceous little waist and sleek flat abdomen that he'd kissed a hundred times...or more, if he counted his dreams.

How could he have ever called her a prude? She'd always been too damn sexy to deserve that, even when dressed in her old jeans and T-shirts. In fact, if she hadn't been determined not to "go all the way," she would have been the easiest girl he'd ever known. At least, with him.

All he'd had to do back then was glance at her breasts, send a message with his eyes, touch his tongue to his lips, and her color would rise, her nipples would harden, her gaze would invite him, beseech him…turn him hot and hard and ready. He'd simply rested his fingertips beneath the zipper of her tight, soft jeans, and she had undulated against his hand, increasingly needy, until he'd unzipped her, slid his fingers inside….

Memories swamped him with startling heat.

And she had come so easily. So passionately. She gave as good as she got, too, with lusty enjoyment. He couldn't honestly say that she hadn't satisfied his sexual needs.

But that hadn't been enough for him. No, he'd wanted more. He'd wanted it all. Intercourse. Lovemaking. *Her.* The very core and essence of her. And he hadn't been able to tolerate the thought that he couldn't have her, that she was saving herself. For what, he didn't know. Or rather, for *whom.*

The question had rankled and nagged. And the need for her had obsessed him.

That wouldn't happen again. Before he left her and returned to Colorado, he would put a satisfying end to all unfinished business here. That was what he needed from her. Closure. Hell, yes. *Closure.*

And she needed "sexual adventure" from him.

As well as protection from an abductor. Cade had deliberately lost anyone who could have been tailing them, though his professional instincts told him no one had been. And scanning the crowd for potential threats had become second nature to him. No one would hurt her while she was with him. And he would keep her with him—away from the inn—for as long as he reasonably could, while John's team investigated all the leads they'd gathered.

Meanwhile, he intended to make the most of his time with Brynn. The very most she would allow. Anticipation sang through his veins and injected every muscle of his body with tense readiness. For her. For them. For anything.

They reached the restaurant in no time. Not much had changed in their favorite hangout. Students still slammed balls across the Ping-Pong table at each other. Onlookers still chugged beer, wolfed down pizza and cheered on the players. Music still shook the floorboards.

Cade led the way to the outside patio deck, to a relatively quiet corner. He ordered the beer. She chose the pizza. He then tugged her hand across the table and squeezed it, kneaded it, molded it to his own.

Brynn smiled and closed her eyes, soaking in the magic of the moment. The aroma of pizza and beer on a sultry breeze. The hard-driving beat of the music and the rumble of cars passing by. The inexplicable charge coursing through her from Cade's masterful grip of her hand. This magical mix could easily whisk her back to the time when they'd been college kids riding high on the first heady wave of romance.

When she opened her eyes, though, she saw not the brooding, passionate boy she used to date, but a rock-solid, self-assured man with a dangerous new glint in his gaze, a readiness to his pose and a determined set to his strong, lean jaw and powerful shoulders. He wanted something from her.

She knew what it was. The knowledge thrilled her. This time, she was game. Wasn't she?

"We have serious business to take care of," he reminded her in a low, intent voice that played havoc with her insides.

"You mean, gathering details for your book?"

"Well, that, too. You help me with my work—" he leaned in closer, as did she "—and I'll help you lick your sleepwalking."

Just the word *lick* coming from his mouth turned her on. Conjured up naughty, sensuous thoughts. Naughty, sensuous memories.

"I take it you've come up with a plan." She nearly breathed the last word, remembering how they'd finished this morning's discussion…and the heated interlude in bed that had led up to it.

A charming series of crescent-shaped grooves deepened along one side of his mouth. "A form of therapy, yes."

"Therapy. Interesting." She wanted to trace those curved, elongated dimples with her fingertip. Or maybe with her tongue, on her way to his mouth…. "Does it have anything to do with satisfying the underlying need?"

His hand tightened on hers, and his thumb swept in slow arcs across the tender inside of her wrist. "Yeah."

The rub of his thumb aroused her, made her skin heat and throb in all her private places. Incredible, that a simple touch from him could do that to her.

Their beer arrived, and she reached for hers without

letting go of his hand or breaking intimate eye contact. She sipped her beer slowly, needing its frosty bite to calm her. Cool her. Help her regain some sense of control.

Cade ignored his beer altogether. "I believe your sleep disorder stems from traumatic deprivation," he whispered, "that occurred during your freshman year of college."

"Deprivation." She knew, of course, what he meant. So she just had to ask, "What exactly was I deprived of?"

"Sex. With me."

Brynn didn't reply. The flare of hunger in his stare left her too breathless.

"The way I see it, we need to go back to the places where we used to make out," he said. "But this time, we finish the job."

"The job?"

"Making love. All the way. No holds barred."

Her pulse accelerated and warmth shimmied through her in waves. "There were quite a few places where we made out," she said. "Some were…risky."

"True."

She swallowed against a suddenly dry throat, unsure if she was quite that adventurous. She was, after all, a respected member of the community. A mature, responsible adult. "To revisit every one of those places…" She paused, seriously considering his proposition and all it entailed. "That would take some time."

"All good therapy does."

"Don't you think we can accomplish the same thing in the privacy of our rooms?"

"Well, I wouldn't *exclude* the privacy of our rooms," he answered, lifting one side of his mouth in the hint of a smile. "But to get to the very root of the problem—the unsatisfied need that's sending you to me every night—I think it'll take some serious digging into our past. We need to relive it as much as we can, but get it right this time. Take every encounter to its fullest, most natural conclusion. Leave no need unmet."

An electrified silence pulsed between them. She found it hard to breathe. He was waiting for her to agree to his plan. The time for silly, flirtatious repartee had passed.

Her heartbeat shook her, and warmth rose to her face, but she refused to let herself back out. "Well." She cleared her throat, and her hand clenched his in something like panic. She knew he could feel the hammering of her pulse. "I suppose I'm willing to give your therapy a try," she said in an uneven whisper, "if you really think it will help."

"Oh, I do." With his eyes on hers, he lifted her hand and brushed a kiss across her knuckles, one that sent hot shivers up her arm and to the furthermost reaches of her body. "I most certainly do."

CADE REFUSED TO TELL HER where they would begin. And since the plan of therapy had been his, Brynn allowed him to decide where and how to administer "treatment." There were quite a few sites he could choose from—places where they had come close to making love.

"Just a hint," she insisted as she slid into the seat next to a window on a bus headed downtown. Unlike their first ride today, the bus wasn't crowded. The football game had begun some time ago; the fans were occupied at whatever site they'd chosen to watch the game, be it the stadium, a bar or a tailgating party. Only a few people rode the bus now, all seated near the doors for easy exit.

"You'll see where we're headed soon enough," Cade said as he settled in beside her, his large, manly form and long legs taking up more than his share of the seat.

Brynn knew he was enjoying the suspense he was generating. With the stadium throw she now held in her lap—a blanket he'd bought from a vendor—they could be headed to any of their old make-out sites. "The pasture of the vet school," she guessed, "where we put on a show for those voyeuristic cows."

"Nope."

"Our secret place near the hill behind the stadium."

"Uh-uh."

"The balcony overlooking the quadrangle."

"Don't waste your time guessing. As your therapist, I advise you to keep your mind on more important things."

"Such as…?"

"Visualizing the steps we'll take to reach our goal."

She had no problem picturing what those steps might be. A tingle of excitement raced up her spine. "Ah. The visualization technique. Brilliant of you, Doc."

A smile deepened the crescents bracketing his mouth, and his voice lowered to a husky pitch. "I believe that half the battle is won in the…preparation.''

And he laid his hand on her knee. A tendril of heat unfurled between her thighs.

''Yes, preparation is…good.''

The bus turned a corner, and as he swayed closer to her, his large, pleasantly callused hand slid from her knee upward, tunneling beneath the blanket on her lap…and also beneath her skirt. ''In order to cure you of your sleep disorder, we'll have to explore beneath the surface of your…consciousness.'' His fingertips reached the very top of her thigh. The *inside* of her thigh.

Her breath stalled, and she couldn't help casting a startled, furtive glance at the other passengers on the bus. Though most of the riders were seated with their backs to them, a portly older woman on the sideways seat behind the driver was peering in their general direction.

''I…I'm not sure this, um, preparation shouldn't wait.''

''Visualize.'' Cade's voice was a velvet caress. ''See in your mind how we'll start out just *skimming the surface.*'' Bending his head to hers, he slid the tip of his tongue across her lips. And his fingertips brushed along the sensitive valley between her legs. The sensation jolted her.

''We'll delve deeper,'' he whispered against her mouth, then engaged her in a longer, more voluptuous kiss. And his fingers slipped beneath the satin of her panties, dipping into intimate folds.

Serious heat coursed from the point of contact, and she gripped the blanket in her lap, sliding lower into the seat and tilting her hips. She wanted him *in*. A shocking thing to want, here and now....

He slanted his mouth on hers and his tongue went deep. As did his fingers, radiating a startling pleasure.

He broke off the kiss and, breathing hard, met her gaze. "Preparation," he whispered, "is the key." And his fingers moved again, inciting liquid heat.

Her throat muscles worked to hold back a groan. The woman at the front of the bus was covertly watching now, or so Brynn believed with what little part of her brain was still functioning.

The bus slowed and whined, approaching a stop.

Cade slowly withdrew his fingers, causing a quivering reaction and leaving a needy throb in its wake. "Our stop." He pulled her skirt into place.

Then he rose from the seat, took the blanket from her and helped her to stand. With her knees wobbly and her blood rushing, she allowed Cade's strong arms to steady her.

They exited the bus on Broad Street, the main thoroughfare between the campus and historic downtown Athens. With a hungry glance at her—one that caused a surge of heat from deep inside—he hurried her along. She no longer cared where they were headed, only that they'd get there soon. He'd stirred up an awesome need in her, the kind she'd almost forgotten about over the past nine years.

He guided her not toward the downtown area, but up the concrete steps to the legendary University of Georgia arch. He swept her at a brisk pace through the wrought-iron gateway and down a tree-canopied walk onto North Campus.

Although most of the football fans were now corralled in Sanford Stadium, some clustered around tents where radios and televisions broadcast the game. Cade steered her away from the biggest, most active gatherings. Clearly he didn't want to be waylaid.

He barely spared a glance for the architecturally stunning historic buildings they passed or the majestic oaks and poplars shading the walkways of the grassy quadrangle. He didn't even pause to listen to broadcasts of plays being made in the stadium "between the hedges," as it was called.

His single-mindedness aroused Brynn, kept her inner heat on a low simmer.

On some rational level, she knew she should be balking at having sex somewhere here. Too many people were milling about. But caught up in a Cade-induced spell, she ignored her customary caution. She wanted adventure. She wanted *him*.

When they reached the end of the quadrangle, Cade led her down a maze of walkways bordered by exotic trees and fragrant hedges. Twilight had descended around them, and tiny white track lights flicked on to illuminate the walkways.

Deep within the heart of the mazelike garden, a familiar sight met her eyes: a gargantuan magnolia tree with broad leaves glimmering in a solid mass from the ground to its towering top.

"Our tree!" she exclaimed with hushed reverence. This sweet-smelling evergreen had been the site of their very first make-out session, when the compulsion to kiss and feel and taste had overcome them. "How did you remember where to find it?"

"You'd be surprised what I remember." Hoarseness roughened his voice, and her pulse quickened in reaction. Catching her hand in his, he led her around to the back of the magnolia and pushed aside a heavy branch.

She ducked and entered. Once inside, she was able to stand erect within the roomy space beneath a leafy, umbrellalike canopy. The dark green outer wall had grown thicker and more concealing over the years. The branches were sturdier now, the interior more spacious. From outside, the glow of the white bulbs bordering the walkway provided just enough illumination to see by, like moonlight.

Cade allowed the limb he'd been holding to spring back into place, enclosing them in a cozy space fragrant with magnolia and peat. "Be quiet now," he whispered as he came up behind her, infusing her with a hot, prickly awareness of him. "You never know when someone will walk by."

He then ran his hands beneath her skirt, caught the sides of her panties and tugged until they whispered down her legs and pooled around her spiky black high heels.

Her adrenaline surged, and she stepped free of the black lace. The risk of what they were doing heightened all her senses, making her vibrantly aware of her intimate scent mingling with the redolence of the woods, the lingering taste of beer and this morning's luscious kisses, the stirring of the evening breeze like phantom fingers beneath her skirt. Feeling drugged with sensuality, she lowered herself onto a smooth, broad limb and leaned against the massive trunk. Her breasts ached for his touch, and the wet heat he'd aroused between her legs pulsed to a greater intensity.

Cade tossed the blanket onto the ground and

dropped to his knees. "This time, we're going all the way, Brynn," he stated. *"All the way."* As if to assert the fact, he unzipped his jeans, freed his erection and sheathed it with a condom.

Dizzy with desire, Brynn unbuttoned her blouse, untied its sash and unhooked her bra. And then he was there, taking her breasts in his hands, in his mouth, drawing her into a wet, hot heaven. Awash in sensation, she dug her fingers into his brawny shoulders and leaned her head against the tree.

But after he'd suckled her nipples into hard, sensitized points—a brusque, purposeful undertaking—he broke free, his gaze golden fire, his face intense. Leaving her nipples glistening and tingling in the open air, he pushed her skirt to the tops of her legs, wrapped a hand around each naked thigh and parted them.

With a breathy cry, she gripped the branches above her head to brace herself as he kissed, licked and nipped along her inner thighs, his silky hair brushing against her, his beard-shadowed face rasping here and there. She struggled to hold back a moan. *Be quiet now.*

The first hot glide of his tongue across the intimate center of her nearly brought her off the limb. He tightened his grip on her, though, and continued the sensual assault, every lick, swirl and probe increasing the pleasure, escalating her tension.

She couldn't hold back the groans and cries any longer. Couldn't resist the overpowering tide. Like a woman possessed, she writhed, moaned and rocked her pelvis while he continued his ministrations, her hands locking fiercely around the tree limbs as if to keep her earthbound.

His tongue went deep, forcing her body to arch. Sensation speared her, spiked her into a long, hard, shuddering climax. The tree itself seemed to convulse around her, the leafy limbs jerking and quivering until she managed to release her grip and reach for Cade.

He rose from his knees to catch her, and stifled her cries with a kiss. As she answered every thrust and parry of his tongue, she ran her hands down his body—one beneath the open waistband of his jeans to the taut muscles of his buttocks, the other to the thinly sheathed erection that pulsed with awesome heat and hardness.

She longed to feel it pulse within her. But she also longed to push Cade beyond all control, into the sweet madness that now possessed her.

Breaking their kiss, she slid from the tree limb to her knees and swept her fingers down his backside within the most sensitive of valleys. She wrapped her other hand around the base of his erection and took the plum-shaped tip into her mouth. He jerked and tensed and hissed in a breath. And as she licked and laved in ever-deepening revolutions, he groaned, undulated and tangled his fingers in her hair.

But when she tightened her lips around him and pulled with a steady suction, a hoarse cry broke from his throat and he caught her face in his hands. ''Brynn. Brynn!''

Urgently he gripped her shoulders and pulled her up, until his gaze burned into hers. They surged together then in a voracious kiss. And in one fluid motion, he hefted her off the ground, wrapped her legs around his hips and pushed into her.

The penetration jolted her, stunned her. And as she

hovered on the upswing of the most incredible thrill, he said in a gruff whisper, "This is where I want to be, Brynn. This is where I've always wanted to be. Right here, inside you."

She flexed her inner muscles to embrace him there.

And Cade lunged with deep, possessive thrusts. Ablaze with need, he was ruled by compulsion: to fill her, body and soul. To brand her from the inside out. To make this moment go on and on. He'd wanted her for so damn long, needed her so damn badly.

But too soon, the fiercest, keenest pleasure gripped him, blinded him, and he couldn't hold out. Neither, it seemed, could she. Her orgasmic contractions milked him relentlessly as he bucked in the throes of a soul-shaking climax.

He kept her locked against him as they panted, gasped and trembled, her legs around his hips, his shoulder wedged against the tree, until the aftershocks mellowed to a point that he could think and see and possibly even move. Slowly, then, he slid down the tree trunk onto the blanket, where he held her tightly on his lap.

For a long moment, neither of them attempted to speak.

"Brynn," he finally said, mystified more than ever by something she'd said the first time she'd spoken in her sleep to him. "How could you ever have thought you were frigid?"

She didn't answer at first, just hugged him harder and pressed her face against his chest. "No one else does this to me," she finally whispered. Drawing back to look at him in tender awe, she repeated, "No one else."

Emotion reared like a wild stallion in his chest, and he took her mouth in another kiss, this one charged with a passion that bordered on devout. It seemed impossible that he could want her again so soon, but he did. God, he did. And she returned the kiss as if she felt the same.

In a distant corner of his brain, he noted the ringing of a bell. The victory bell. For a moment, he connected it with his own personal victory. The most exhilarating victory of his life.

But Brynn ended their kiss. "Cade. The bell. *The bell!* It means—"

"Victory."

"—the game is over."

"Over? No." Their game was far from over. It was just beginning.

"The stadium is letting out. The crowd's coming our way."

No sooner had the words left her mouth than footsteps and voices sounded nearby. A few yards away, at the most.

"I know what I heard, Walt," a woman said in a hushed, frightened tone. "It sounded like groaning, or growling. Didn't you see the tree shaking?"

Brynn's eyes grew round with horror.

"It was probably just the wind, Louise."

"It was not. And don't go any closer to that tree! There's a big wild animal in it. Maybe a bear."

"A bear? There ain't any bears on campus."

Footsteps plodded closer, and Brynn jolted into action. Pulling back from Cade's embrace, she jerked her blouse together and tugged at her skirt, which was bunched up around her waist.

"There! Did you see something move in the tree?" Louise cried, while Walt cursed in amazed fascination.

With a soft curse of his own, Cade spoke up. "The only animals in this tree," he said, tugging Brynn's skirt into place, "are a couple of Georgia dawgs."

Stunned silence greeted that announcement. Then a burst of masculine laughter.

"Oh, for heaven's sakes," Louise muttered.

"Go, dawgs!" Walt said.

"I told you something was shaking that tree."

And as they walked away, Cade heard Walt say, "Gives new meaning to the term 'between the hedges,' don't it?"

9

THE THERAPY HE'D prescribed for Brynn's sleepwalking had been too effective, Cade decided later that night as he lay in bed alone, watching the digital clock turn to 1:00 a.m.

She should be with him now. She should be lying in his arms, sweaty and exhausted from wild, mind-altering sex. He'd been ready for another go shortly after they'd left that magnolia tree.

But he'd known as they'd strolled across campus toward the inn that something was going wrong. He had no idea what or why, but a chasm had opened between them as surely as if she'd pushed him away. It happened when he whispered into her ear, "I want you in a *bed* now. Naked. Both of us."

Her face flushed with arousal, but she'd said, "I can't sleep with you at the inn, Cade. It would get awkward if Trish realized we were together."

"Why?"

"Antoine is her cousin. I've been dating him. I need to break things off with him, and let Trish know, before I'd feel right about sleeping with another man at our inn."

Not a very good reason, in his estimation. She was making excuses not to sleep with him. Why?

"Call Antoine." He handed her his cell phone. He

wanted the guy out of her life as soon as possible. And if he *was* the abductor, he'd come running back to reestablish his connection with her, and Cade would be waiting for him. "Break it off with him."

"I tried to do that earlier, but our cell phones weren't connecting very well. And he hasn't called me back yet."

Cade suspected he was busy courting another victim. Wanting to learn more about his main suspect— and the man who had too intimate a relationship with Brynn—Cade asked in a casual tone, "What does he do for a living?"

"Sells art supplies wholesale." No surprise there. Trish had told him that much. "But his real passion is art. He paints. Oils, mostly. Some watercolor."

"Have you seen his work?"

"No. He hasn't had it shipped over from France yet. He studied at the Sorbonne in Paris, you know."

"I have a friend in the art supply business. Wonder if he knows Antoine. What's his company called?"

She told him, and Cade added that information along with the rest to his mental file. Even if Antoine wasn't the abductor, Cade didn't trust him. Of course, that might be because he was a personal rival. The very idea that he *had* a rival in regards to Brynn stuck in Cade's craw.

"*Are* you going to break up with him?" he asked her.

"Of course."

"Why?" He found himself holding his breath as he waited for her answer.

"After what I just did with you, do you really have to ask?"

"Yes." He really, really did.

"Because I feel I'm wasting my time with him."

That was good. But not quite good enough. "Wasting your time...sexwise, you mean?"

She'd then given him an enigmatic look and replied in a gentle yet firm tone, "That's none of your business, Cade."

Just remembering the conversation shook him up again. And now he lay in bed alone, tensing at every creak and footfall, hoping the alarm on his watch would beep, indicating she was coming to him. Whether she was sleepwalking or not. He didn't have to make love to her again tonight, he supposed, but he *did* have to hold her. With a frustrated sigh, he shut his eyes.

And the alarm on his watch went off, a quiet but rousing *beep.* She'd opened her door! Light footsteps headed his way. His blood rushed and his spirits rose.

But then he heard heavier footsteps and another door opening. A loud thud, as if someone had hit into a wall. A feminine gasp. A masculine mumble.

Cade raced to his door and threw it open. Between his room and Brynn's stood one of the Kappa Alpha guys, helping Brynn up from the floor. She looked stunned and bewildered, as if she'd been rudely awakened from a deep sleep.

"Sorry, Brynn," the pajama-clad Kappa Alpha was saying. "Didn't see you coming. Jeez, you bounced right into that wall. You okay?"

"Y-yes." She nodded, blinking repeatedly. "I'm fine."

"Brynn." Cade strode down the hall to make sure she was okay. And to lead her to his room....

But before he reached her, she glanced at him, backed up a step and murmured, "I'm okay." She then whirled around, fled to her room and shut the door behind her.

Not the reaction he'd been looking for.

"She came out of nowhere," the Kappa Alpha said to him, looking shaken and defensive. "Darted out at a full run."

Cade didn't bother to answer. He knew she'd been dreaming, and assumed she'd been on her way to his room—until she'd woken up and run in the opposite direction. Swallowing his disappointment, he returned to bed.

He didn't understand Brynn's refusal to sleep with him. They'd finally made love, and it had surpassed his wildest dreams. She'd told him she hadn't felt that way with anyone else. But her barriers were still in place against him, or she wouldn't have made flimsy excuses to sleep alone. She'd be with him right now.

He'd just have to do something about those barriers.

"THE NAMES AND PHOTOS you sent of the guests all checked out," John Sutherland informed Cade over the phone on Sunday morning. "Nothing suspicious there."

"Yeah, I figured as much. Most are repeat customers, and all but one old lady left this morning. As far as I've been able to tell, there are only two newcomers to Brynn's circle of acquaintances. One is Lexi's boyfriend, a guy she's been dating for four months. Lived in the area his entire life. No police record. The other is Antoine Moreau, who showed up five weeks ago, claiming to be Trish's cousin. She told me he was born

in the United States, but lived in France from age
three, when his mother died. His French father wanted
nothing to do with his wife's American family, so the
ties were broken. Seems like the perfect setup for an
imposter to step in. Have you found anything on him
yet?''

"Only that Trish does have a cousin by that name
with dual citizenship. His U.S. driver's license has him
at 5'11, 180 pounds, brown hair, blue eyes.''

"Lexi told me Antoine is over six feet tall. Of
course, she might have overestimated, but…'' With
mounting certainty that something was off with Moreau, Cade gave John the name of the company Antoine allegedly ran and the information that he'd supposedly attended the Sorbonne in France. "Brynn
talked to Moreau from her cell phone yesterday. We
can get his number from her phone records, and information about him from his account. Trish told me
he's living in a hotel nearby until he finds a permanent
place. I've got a man checking into that, too.''

After hanging up, Cade signed on to his laptop and
tested the surveillance equipment he'd planted in various locations around the inn. Moreau was bound to
show up soon. No way would he be able to spend a
single moment alone with Brynn without every word
and action being transmitted to Cade while he stood
nearby. He'd already placed movement sensors on the
door and windows of her private suite, and he'd
bugged her telephone. Now he would install video
cameras in her suite and a locator chip on whatever
vehicle Moreau arrived in.

Cade didn't give a damn about the legality of the
surveillance or its usefulness in court. He simply

wasn't going to give a possible abductor—maybe even a killer—access to Brynn. He'd stick like glue to her until the Piper was caught.

The "sticking like glue" part of the plan appealed to him immensely. He only hoped that her aloofness after their lovemaking didn't mean that she no longer wanted to be with him. That would present a problem.

But it wouldn't stop him. Regardless of how she felt about him, she *would* be with him until the Piper was apprehended.

"BRYNNIE, ARE YOU OKAY?"

"Me? Sure," Brynn answered absentmindedly as she filed credit card forms after the Sunday morning checkout. When it occurred to her to be curious over the question, she glanced at Trish, who stood beside her behind the registration counter. "Why do you ask?"

"Because you're putting those credit card forms in Lexi's recipe file."

"Oh." She blinked at the file cabinet drawer that was clearly marked Lexi's Recipes, and mentally scolded herself. "Must be more tired than I thought. I didn't sleep well last night." She'd been too preoccupied with thoughts of Cade, as well as with her anxiety over the sleepwalking debacle that could have injured a guest. And…well, with more thoughts of Cade.

The sex had been *too good.* Better than she'd ever imagined. And the way he'd held her afterward had moved her *too much….*

"You looked distracted when you came in last night, too." Curiosity lurked in Trish's keen blue eyes. "Around nine-thirty, I believe it was. Guess you and

Cade spent a lot of time gathering info for his book, huh?''

Not wanting to talk about her intimacy with Cade, Brynn nodded, then felt bad about lying, and shook her head. But when she couldn't think of an explanation for why they hadn't worked on his book, she ended with a shrug. The movement caused an ache in her shoulder that reminded her of the collision she'd had in her sleep. Which in turn brought her thoughts back to Cade. She'd run from him last night. She'd actually turned tail and run!

If she hadn't, she probably would have ended up spending the rest of the night cuddled with him in his bed. And that was something she couldn't allow herself to do.

She'd made an important realization after their lovemaking yesterday. She finally understood why she'd been sexually dissatisfied with other men. It wasn't because of what they did or didn't do, but because they didn't look, sound, feel, smell or taste like Cade. And for some crazy reason, she needed that particular mix of sensory input to fully stimulate her.

How sick was that? She had to get over it! But how? Maybe he'd been right about the therapy. Maybe she really did need to exorcise him from her subconscious by satisfying the sexual need she'd neglected during their past relationship. But even if that was true, she couldn't let herself get too attached to him in the process.

And that meant no more cuddling in his bed all night. It could get to be habit-forming. After just one morning of waking up there, she already felt lonely in her own bed—and it had only a little to do with sex.

This constant craving for his company, for strengthening their new bond, wouldn't do. They would have sex between them—hot, wild, mind-blowing sex—but nothing else. Nothing else!

"Brynn, honey, you're scaring me."

Startled out of the thoughts that had been dominating her mind all morning, Brynn realized Trish now loomed nearer, frowning suspiciously. "What happened between you and Cade?"

"Happened?" She would *not* tell Trish to mind her own business. Conflict between business partners could only lead to trouble. "What do you mean?"

Trish's eyes widened and her mouth grew slack. "You had sex with him, didn't you?"

"Sex!" Not exactly a denial, but not a confirmation, either. Instinctively she knew Trish was upset that she, Brynn "Boring Brunette on a Budget" Sutherland, had attracted a man that she, "Dazzling Blond Queen of the Cosmopolitan Elite," had wanted.

It was then that Brynn realized with mild shock that, despite all the years they'd been friends, they'd never outgrown the roles they'd assumed in the sorority house. She still felt anxiety claw at her because she had displeased the most influential girl in the sorority. None of their crowd purposely displeased Trish. Ever.

"I never thought you were such a hypocrite, Brynn. You warned me away from Cade, then went after him yourself."

Brynn bit her tongue to keep from reminding her that the warning hadn't stopped Trish from trying her damnedest to get him into bed. The fact that he hadn't taken the bait was what irritated Trish the most, Brynn guessed. "Everything I told you about him was true, Trish…and for your own good."

"Did you work on Cade's book yesterday *at all?*"

Guilt flushed through Brynn, but before she could reply, Cade sauntered in from the dining room, looking impossibly handsome in a black, chest-hugging Henley T-shirt, tight jeans and a disarmingly attractive smile. "Morning, ladies." His deep, masculine voice sang through Brynn like a favorite song. "My compliments to the chef for the, er, muffins this morning. Nothing like homemade blueberry muffins."

"They were blackberry," Trish snapped. She stalked out from behind the registration counter and aimed a cool glare over her shoulder. "By the way, Brynn, Antoine called last night. Seems he couldn't get through on your cell phone." After a chastising lift of one golden brow, she strode away with the arrogant grace of a royal princess.

"Trish." Brynn came around the counter to follow her. On her way past, though, Cade caught her arm, braced a hand at the small of her back and diverted her into the small office that had once been the sorority house's supply room. Shutting the door behind him, he blocked her only path of escape.

"So, what do you think?" he muttered in a conspiratorial tone. "Does she suspect something's going on between us?" The gravity of his question was belied by the amusement in his brown-gold eyes.

"This isn't funny, Cade. I've really upset her."

"Annoyed her," he corrected. His gaze then wandered over Brynn's face with a warmth that recharged the energy she'd been trying to contain since their interlude in the magnolia tree. Brushing his finger down the curve of her cheek, he murmured, "You've been avoiding me."

His nearness, his touch, scattered her thoughts and activated every one of the nerve endings in the path his finger had taken. "I've just been busy," she replied breathlessly. "Sunday morning checkout is always hectic."

"What about last night, in the hallway?"

"If you'll remember, one of my Kappa Alphas was standing there in his pj's, embarrassed because he thought he'd knocked me down. I felt it best to put a quick end to the awkwardness by retiring to my room."

"You could have retired to *my* room."

Helplessly aroused by the huskiness in his voice and the heat in his gaze, she evaded the comment by sliding her arms around his neck and resting her pelvis against his taut thighs—a vivid reminder of yesterday's powerful thrusts. "Since my sleepwalking does seem to be getting more dangerous," she murmured, "we'd better schedule our next therapy session soon."

"Mmm," he agreed, tilting his face toward hers to nip at her mouth playfully, adding a soft, sensuous tug. "Real soon." He nipped again—at her bottom lip this time, drawing it into the moist heat of his mouth.

She pressed closer, craving more of his hardness and heat. She was allowed to do this—a strictly sexual thing, kissing him in a darkened office and lusting after his touch. And this would be a fine place for their next therapy session, she realized. They had kissed against this very wall during her sorority days. She'd nearly lost her virginity here. Where had she ever found the strength to resist him back then?

But in a far corner of her mind, she knew. Fear had stopped her. Not fear of Cade or of sex, but of making another huge mistake. One that could send her on ruinous detours from her goal.

But she was older and stronger now. She had her degree. Her career was on the right track. And as long as she kept things in perspective, sex with Cade wouldn't hurt.

And that's what she wanted now. Sex with Cade. Before she had time to think too much about why he and he alone held such a strong sexual appeal for her.

Luring him into a deeper kiss, she ran her fingers up his muscled thighs and relished the ripples of reaction she felt and the low moan that rumbled within him. Heat gunned through her, and she brushed her fingers across the hardness within his jeans.

He gasped, slid his hands around her buttocks and backed her against the wall, lifting her just high enough to press against his erection. Reaction leaped in her like a flame, and she wrapped her legs around his hips, wanting him inside her.

Breaking from their kiss with a harsh exhalation, he said in a hot whisper against her jaw, ''Not here.''

''Why not? It would fit with our therapy.''

''I want to lie with you. Naked. And take it slow.''

Anticipation stirred her blood, and heat throbbed between her legs, in her womb, in her breasts. ''Where, then?''

''A bed. Any bed.''

A bed. Yes. But then alarm bells rang through her head at the thought of taking him to her bed or going to his. It was a step in the wrong direction. If they went to bed now, she might not have the fortitude to stop from going to bed with him tonight, too. And the night after that. She could end up spending every night in bed with him for as long as his stay lasted. And when he left, she'd have a terrible time trying to adjust to lying in bed without him. A terrible, terrible time...

No, the "therapy" they'd discussed was as far as she could go with him. She'd agreed to make love in the places where they'd made out during their college romance. To add any more intimacy to that plan was a danger to her state of mind. She had to stay within the boundaries of their agreement, or she would be lost.

"A bed?" she repeated, undulating against him with provocative friction that made his color rise, his breathing deepen. "But that's not on our therapy agenda. We never made out in a bed back in college."

He angled his face to capture her mouth in another kiss, but then stopped. "You avoided beds back then because you were afraid we'd go all the way. We've already done that. And we're going to do it again. So what's wrong with a bed?"

"You're the one who prescribed my therapy. Don't you think we should stick to it?"

"Yeah, but that doesn't mean we can't supplement the program." As he said it, he rocked his hardness against her again, sending hot sensation shooting through her core.

"No bed," she said with a groan. A bed was simply too real. Making love to him in a bed would leave an indelible imprint on her everyday life. Fooling around outdoors was an adventure that would always remain outside her normal life. Like a fantasy. And that's what she would have when he left. Fantasies. "So what's your second choice?"

He frowned and narrowed his gaze. She distracted him with another kiss—and the press of her breasts against his chest, and the gyration of her hips, coaxing his erection to strain harder against his jeans...and against her.

But as he gave in to the deliciously carnal kiss, a loud, intrusive voice crackled from the radio she wore on her belt.

"Brynn." It was Trish, and her voice had a smug tone. "You have a visitor waiting for you on the porch."

STRUGGLING TO REGAIN control of his body after the abrupt end to a kiss that had been only one hammering heartbeat away from full-fledged sex against the wall, Cade plowed his fingers through his hair and followed Brynn at a distance.

She finger-combed her tousled mane, too, and drew in a deep, audible breath before stepping through the front door of the inn and onto the front porch. Cade remained inside, assuming a casual stance by a partially open window where he had a clear view of her caller.

He knew who the guy was the instant he set eyes on him. He stood about six-feet tall—slightly over the five-eleven on his supposed driver's license. His light brown hair was streaked with blond, and shoulder length. His blazer, matching gray shirt and pleated khakis were tailored with European elegance, and probably cost more than a weekend getaway for your average family of four. He could be no other than

Antoine Moreau. Or the man posing as Antoine Moreau.

Cade disliked him on sight, even before Brynn greeted him. "Antoine. I didn't expect you until tonight."

"*Bonjour,* Brynn," he murmured in response, then kissed both her cheeks and gifted her with a smile meant to dazzle.

Cade wondered if it had.

"I missed you too much to stay away for even one hour longer." His French accent was subtle—nothing more than a melodious cadence that distinguished him as continental.

Oh, yeah. This guy could lure women away from their homes as easily as the fictional Pied Piper had lured the children. Cade held on to one important fact as Moreau opened his arms to the woman he himself had just been holding: Moreau hadn't satisfied her in bed.

She hesitated before stepping into his embrace, or so it seemed to Cade. But maybe that was just wishful thinking.

"Spying on the competition?" Trish's tart question sprang from directly beside him.

Annoyed that she'd startled him, he slanted a mildly admonishing glance at her, then returned his attention to the porch. "He looks familiar," Cade lied. "I think I've met him somewhere before. He's your, er, cousin, I take it?"

"I hope you're not counting on Brynn choosing you over Antoine for the rest of your stay. She might have gotten carried away with you yesterday, but she's strictly a one-man woman. And for now, she's Antoine's. Her relationships last a long time, too. Years, usually. That is, unless a guy really screws things up with her. You know, like *you* did?''

He felt the jab go deep. ''Retract the claws, Trish.''

''She hasn't really forgiven you, you know.''

He wondered if that was true. His head still rang from the metaphorical slap she'd dealt him only moments ago—refusing to go to a bed. He craved time and privacy with her. She hadn't wanted that. She'd been more than willing, though, for him to take her against a wall. God knows he wasn't opposed to sex with her any way or anywhere, but her refusal to come with him to a bed bothered him.

Maybe it was that sexual adventure thing she'd mentioned in her sleep. Was that what she wanted from him—and *all* she wanted? A few bouts of sex in risky, unusual places?

Feeling vaguely used, he forced the thought aside and focused on the couple on the porch. Which one had ended the hug—Moreau or Brynn? Either way, Cade was glad it had ended.

Trish let out an annoyed sigh and walked away.

When she'd stalked out of sight, Cade took out his cell phone and typed in a coded text message to the undercover team, alerting them to Moreau's presence. He'd be under constant surveillance from now on. Cade also activated the camera on his phone, snapped a few digital photos and, with the press of a button, e-mailed them to John.

He then remained at the window, tense with readiness. He hadn't a shred of hard evidence yet, but his gut told him that the man claiming to be Antoine Moreau was also the one who had sent photographs of his victims to the police with a note signed "The Pied Piper."

ANTOINE, as he thought of himself now, had come fully prepared to smooth Brynn's ruffled feathers. From their phone conversation, he knew that his recent absences had upset her, and that he would have to exert more effort to mollify her.

But from the moment she stepped out onto the porch to greet him, he knew the problem went much deeper than he had supposed. Her smile wasn't genuine. Was that guilt in her eyes, or regret? What had she done, or what was she planning to do?

He felt the reserve in her hug, too, so he didn't attempt to kiss her. She'd never been a very physical woman, and he'd given up trying to woo her with seduction. Yet for some reason, she looked incredibly available right now. The tumble of her hair, the color in her cheeks, the sparkle in her eyes… She looked ready for sex. Yet he'd felt her coolness toward him.

Maybe he'd made a mistake in accepting the sexual limitations she'd set. Maybe he'd missed some tiny cue that she wanted him to come on stronger. Overcome her inhibitions. Use a little force. It was worth considering.

One thing was clear: he had to reestablish his connection with her. "Antoine," she was saying, "I need to talk to you."

"Of course." He half smiled, half frowned. "But first…" He withdrew from the inner pocket of his jacket an oval canvas, the size of a wallet, and felt his heart lope into a heavier beat.

Sharing his work was never a casual thing. Reaction

was too important. His very soul fed off of admiration, appreciation, awe…and shrank from anything less. This was the first of his paintings he would allow her to see.

"What is it, Antoine?" She waited with open curiosity.

He had to concentrate before speaking, or the magnitude of the occasion might compromise the French rhythm he'd perfected in his speech. "This is something I have worked on every night I've spent away from you, *mon coeur*." With solemn ceremony, he murmured, "I give you roses."

She peered in surprise at the miniature painting he handed to her. "Oh, Antoine!" She studied it silently. Every second of her silence increased the force of his heartbeats. When he didn't think he could stand another moment of waiting, she raised her hazel-eyed gaze and smiled. "It's beautiful." Her face was radiant with admiration, her tone reverent. "You truly are a gifted artist."

In that moment, he loved her. No matter what had gone wrong between them, he would make it right. She was too perfect to let slip away. She was the model he had chosen first, before the others. He had taken the longest time with her, the most detailed care. She would sit for him willingly—more or less—and her portrait would be his masterpiece.

"Let me put this in my room," she said, holding the painting of roses carefully. "I'm so honored you've given it to me, Antoine." She smiled her soft, sweet smile and hurried inside.

And he knew he had chosen well. She had everything he needed: physical beauty along with an inner glow that would enhance the portrait he would paint of her. She also had a strong bond with an Atlanta cop—the lead detective on his case, at that. And, of equal importance, she harbored a guilty secret she wanted to keep hidden. He'd searched long and hard for women like her, and she was the best he'd found. He wouldn't lose her at this late stage of the game.

Which meant he had to discover the nature of the problem that had arisen between them.

"Antoine." Trish strolled out onto the porch, looking as chic and gorgeous as ever. Too bad she didn't have the other qualities he needed in his models, or his so-called cousin would have been among his top choices. "Has Brynn told you about the surprise visitor we have staying with us?"

"What visitor?"

Brynn, who had returned to the porch in time to hear Trish's question, said, "He's not really visiting us. He's in town on business, and happens to be staying at our inn."

"He's an old friend of Brynn's," Trish insisted, "from college." With an odd twist to her smile, she called through the screen door, "Cade? Come meet my cousin Antoine."

The man who pushed through the door a few moments later was about his own height, but wider through the shoulders, with arms and chest clearly more muscular, as if his work involved heavy manual labor. Or deliberate physical toning. Antoine wondered what this Cade did for a living.

The grip of his handshake confirmed the impression of strength, and his direct gaze, though not openly hostile, nearly backed Antoine up a step. He felt as if this cool-eyed stranger were somehow peering into the furthest reaches of his mind. Not a pleasant sensation.

They shook hands. "Cade, meet Antoine Moreau," said Trish. "Antoine, Cade Hunter. You two have a lot in common."

Brynn's gaze flew to Trish. Cade Hunter, on the other hand, looked only at him, his expression unreadable, his stance as solid as a mountain. "Do we, now." He hadn't phrased it as a question, but as a comment. And not a complimentary one.

"You both work in creative fields," Trish said. "Antoine is an artist. Cade a writer."

"A writer?" The occupation didn't fit him.

"Why, just yesterday, our very own Brynnie helped him put some local color into the travel book he's writing."

"Really?" Now this was interesting, especially since Brynn was looking annoyed with Trish for mentioning it. "And how, exactly, did you help him, *chérie?*"

"Oh, I didn't do much at all."

"She showed me around campus on game day," Cade said. "Refreshed my memory about certain things. Pointed out a few colorful details."

"Which of those colorful details will you use in the book?" Trish's question sounded suspiciously tongue in cheek.

"Really, Trish." Brynn was scowling at her now. "An author doesn't give away his material before it's in print. But I suspect he'll include the historical and architectural importance of the buildings on North Campus."

"Along with the characters of old-time Athens," Cade said.

"And the merchants of Five Points."

"Oh, and the various meanings of the term so often applied to Sanford Stadium—'between the hedges.'

For some reason, Brynn flushed at that, glanced away from Cade and hurriedly added, "And the many generations of Uga, our bulldog mascot."

"And, of course, I can't leave out the story of my own personal *first time* with Brynn."

Her gaze jerked to Cade, her eyes wide, her mouth open. With a resurgence of her blush, she stammered, "I—I—I'm not sure what you could possibly mean—"

"Walking under the arch together." Cade's look of innocence was flawless. "You never walked beneath it with me before. You were afraid the legend might be true and that you'd never graduate. Now that you have your degree, you finally, uh, did the deed." Humor warmed the eyes that had been cool and hard as agates, Antoine noticed, now that Cade was focusing on Brynn. "A personal first."

She bit her lush bottom lip, stifling a smile, or maybe a retort. When the compulsion had presumably passed, she said, "I didn't think you'd noticed that momentous occasion." She sounded pleased that he had, and her glow of sexual allure heightened. "The legend of the arch would be an excellent detail to add."

"But my personal all-time favorite," Cade added, his husky voice as sexually charged as Brynn's heightened color, "is the giant old magnolia tree."

Something flashed between them then—something

so brief and subtle that the average person wouldn't have picked up on it. But Antoine was not the average person. He'd made an art, a science, out of reading people, studying every expression, until he understood their emotions and motives better than they themselves did.

She'd been intimate with Cade.

When Cade again aimed a gaze his way, a subtle insolence in the man's otherwise veiled expression let Antoine know that he didn't give a damn who knew it. In fact, he was deliberately flaunting their intimacy. Brynn would be mortified to realize it, Antoine knew. She'd been drawn despite herself into making those innuendos, and clearly hoped Antoine hadn't understood the double meanings. She wanted to spare his feelings, allow him his pride.

To his way of thinking, she hadn't tried hard enough.

"Sounds like Brynn's tour was everything you'd hoped it would be," Antoine remarked, hating Cade.

"Oh, it was."

The tension between them prevented Antoine from attempting a smile.

"Um, excuse us, Cade and Trish, but Antoine and I have a lot to…catch up on." She glanced at him meaningfully. "Let's go up to my suite where we can talk."

He nodded and smiled, but it wasn't easy. She was going to throw him over for Cade Hunter.

Or so she thought. A nobody like Hunter would never win out over Doyle Fontaine—or, as he was called at the moment, Antoine Moreau. He'd do everything in his power to make sure of it.

For now, he merely hooked an arm around Brynn.

It would grate on Cade's nerves, seeing them go to her private suite. Antoine intended to keep her there for as long as possible.

Not surprisingly, Cade shifted into their path. "I hate to mess up your plans, Brynn, but you've already promised the rest of the day to me."

She lifted a brow in clear surprise.

"To take me on another tour of the area," he said.

"Oh, that's right." She nodded, and Antoine suspected their plans had been of a very different nature. "But…can it wait until later?" Cade started to object, but she overrode him. "Let's say thirty minutes from now."

Antoine struggled to maintain his temper. She assumed she could be done with him in thirty minutes, then get off for her little tryst with Cade Hunter?

"If we're upsetting your work schedule, Cade," Antoine suggested, "why don't you ask Trish to help you?"

Trish brightened. He'd known she would. Her sexual availability to Hunter was almost as apparent as Brynn's. An interesting situation, that. "I'd be happy to show you whatever you'd like to see, Cade."

"No offense, Trish," Hunter replied, "but I'm really after Brynn's outlook as a native of Athens."

"Native?" Antoine couldn't resist throwing a wrench into Hunter's plans, as well as showing him how little he knew about Brynn. "For some reason, Brynn, I thought you'd been raised elsewhere."

Cade and Trish looked to Brynn to straighten him out. She clearly didn't relish the chore. "Well, I've lived in Athens for almost half my life." She tossed her thick, gleaming hair over her shoulder in a nervous gesture. "So I do consider myself a native."

"*Half* your life?" Trish said. "That means you were about thirteen or fourteen when you moved here."

"About that age, I'd say."

Antoine knew she'd been fifteen when she moved here…to escape scandal. But of course, she didn't want anyone to know about *that*. Or worse, about the complications that had followed. Antoine would keep her secrets safe…as long as she cooperated with him when the time came.

"But I always thought you were from Athens, Brynn," Trish insisted. "Where *are* you from?"

"What does it matter? I was born in a small town south of Atlanta that you probably haven't heard of, okay?"

"Oh. Okay." Trish didn't seem interested in the details. Turning to Hunter, she said, "I moved here when I was eighteen, so I'm only four years behind Brynn."

"That might be true," Hunter said, "but I find her outlook on things uniquely valuable to my work." He locked gazes with Brynn, and in a silent way that infuriated Antoine, they resolved the issue between them. "I'll meet you here, on the porch," he said, "in fifteen minutes. That's…" he glanced at his watch "…one-fifteen."

Fifteen minutes! She'd said thirty, which had been insulting enough. But before Antoine could find a reason to object, Brynn nodded and ushered him toward the door.

Hunter thought he'd outwitted him, but his satisfaction wouldn't last long, Antoine swore. Because very soon, Brynn would be leaving him.

10

THEY'D BEEN THE LONGEST fifteen minutes of his life.
And by the time he was driving down a highway in
his open-topped SUV with Brynn beside him, Cade's
insides were tied up in knots.

He'd sat in his room with his laptop and surveillance earphones, watching every move Brynn and Antoine made, listening to every word, waiting for the
first hint of trouble. And though he stood not more
than fifteen feet from her door, with motion sensors
on all her windows, and the inn surrounded by plainclothes cops, nightmare images of worst-case scenar-
ios had flashed through Cade's brain like lightning.

He couldn't help thinking that the abducted women
hadn't been found. *They may have been murdered.*
The thought of Brynn alone in a locked suite with a
killer made Cade break out in a cold sweat. The likelihood was low—the guy couldn't think he'd get away
with it. Then again, from the tone of the Piper's note,
Cade believed he wanted notoriety. Maybe he didn't
care whether he was caught. Which meant he might
try anything in there with Brynn. It took only a moment to break a neck, or slit a throat, or…

Those fifteen minutes had been hell.

But Cade had to admit her physical safety hadn't
been his only worry. What if Monsieur Smooth Moves

found a way to sweet-talk her into bed? Cade had thought up all kinds of last-resort options—like setting off the fire alarm, or banging on her door until she opened it. Shooting off the lock. Kicking in the door.

That was when he realized how bad he had it. He'd completely lost his mind over her.

He should have realized that when he'd crossed swords with her boyfriend. If he'd been thinking straight, he would have played it cool. Kept a low profile. Come across as just another guest at the inn.

But no. He'd let Antoine know in subtle but unmistakable ways that Brynn was no longer his. That Cade would be breathing down his neck at every turn if he persisted in thinking he could ever, ever have her.

Cade had let his emotions rule him. His professional judgment was so skewed that he had no business working this case at all. Yet there was no way in hell he'd walk away and leave Brynn's safety to someone else.

"Cade?"

"Hmm?"

"What's wrong?"

He shook his head and steered the car around another curve in the road. Brynn probably thought he was upset with *her*. He wasn't. Not really. He could have done without her rendezvous in the bedroom with the French Don Juan, but at least she *had* broken up with him.

More or less. She'd explained to Antoine that, although she'd had a wonderful time with him, she wanted to be friends, nothing more. Antoine had said he would value their friendship and wished the very best for her.

But before their fifteen minutes were up, he had wrangled a promise for more time alone with her. He'd asked if she'd come by his place—the house he'd just leased today—to give him ideas for decorating. She was, of course, delighted to help. "I'll call you," he said, "and we can set a time for some day this week."

Cade had no doubt that would be it. If Moreau was the Piper—and he firmly believed he was—he'd make his move on Brynn "some day this week."

Cade and his men would be ready. Unless, of course, his crazy, knee-jerk reactions regarding Brynn interfered with his judgment. He couldn't afford to be distracted by anything, let alone irrational feelings he barely understood.

Frustrated by his lack of self-control, he made a sharp left onto a road leading to the Oconee River, aware that he was gritting his teeth, but unable to stop.

"You're obviously angry," Brynn said, her lustrous hair blowing wildly about in the wind despite the red bandanna she'd worn to contain it. "I'd like to know why."

He forced his jaw to loosen enough for him to reply. "I'm not angry."

"Does it have anything to do with Antoine?"

I don't want him to touch you again. Ever. And I don't want you taking another man to your bedroom. Ever. "You broke up with him, right?"

"Right."

"Then why would I be angry about him?"

She studied him doubtfully, her eyes intensely green

in the afternoon sun. "Are you upset because I...let you think...you know—that I was born and raised in Athens?"

That was so far from the truth he almost snorted. But now that she'd mentioned it, she *had* led him to believe she was from Athens. Not that it mattered where she was from. Why should it?

With a bemused glance at her, he noticed she looked as guilty as if she'd been caught red-handed in a crime. Which, of course, piqued his curiosity. "Care to explain?"

"Why should it make any difference where I'm from?"

"You tell me."

She compressed her lips and fidgeted with the strands of vividly colored beads she wore around her neck to complement her gypsy-style blouse. "If you'll remember, I didn't actually say I was born in Athens. I said I grew up here. Which is true. I didn't 'grow up' until I was living in Athens. I mean, you wouldn't call a girl in her early teens a grown-up, would you?"

"You're trying to get off on a technicality."

"I never meant to lie."

The angst she obviously felt over this seemingly inconsequential subject raised his interest level from mild curiosity to a definite need to know. "You're hiding something."

She pressed her lush lips into a thin line again—a crime in its own right.

Unwilling to tolerate her evasion, Cade swerved the car to the side of the road, parked under a cluster of pines and turned to her. "Are you going to tell me why you're making such a big deal out of where you're from?''

''*I'm* not making a big deal out of it. You're the one who's angry.''

Hell yes, he was angry. She was keeping something from him. Something that bothered her. Which meant she was still holding him at a distance. And that distance, more than anything else, ticked him off. ''Where are you from, Brynn?''

Lifting a dark, satiny brow in a stubborn refusal to answer, she presented him with her pert profile. Ironic that John thought she couldn't keep a secret because of her sleepwalking and talking. Cade then remembered her refusal to sleep with him last night, and wondered if she'd refused for fear of telling her secret.

He then wondered how Antoine had known about it.

Under the pressure of his glowering stare, Brynn finally replied in cool, clipped tones, ''I'm from a small, ordinary, unremarkable town south of Atlanta called Summerton.''

''So, why didn't you say that from the start?''

''It seemed irrelevant.''

It *had* been irrelevant, until she'd hidden it. And she was still hiding something. He wondered if John would know what it might be. But Cade didn't want to learn about her from John, or from any of his other readily available resources. He wanted her to open herself to him. *All the way.* He wanted that so much it hurt.

''How did Antoine know you weren't from Athens?''

''I don't know.''

"You didn't tell him?"

"No."

But he'd definitely known. He'd flaunted his knowledge of her in a silent but malicious taunt. Maybe he had researched her background—the Piper's probable method of choosing his victims. How else would he know about the women in a cop's life without researching the cop's history? If he knew John was from Summerton, he'd know his sister was, too.

"Oh, Cade, let's not waste time on arguments." Brynn turned a beseeching gaze to him. "What's past is past. Why don't we get on with today and the, uh, important stuff?" Her smile emerged only enough to activate a dimple near her chin, and her voice softened with sensuality. "Like that second session of therapy."

Desire sliced through him, low and sharp. God, he wanted her. Wanted to carry her off into the woods, lay her down on blankets and thrust deeply into her. Make her cry out his name, and quake in his arms, and take him places he'd been only while inside her.

He could do all those things—the very things he'd been obsessing over since college. Ironically, though, he couldn't make her talk to him. Couldn't make her trust him enough to share whatever secret she kept.

"I'm not sure I'm ready for another therapy session," he said, even as his body hardened and throbbed for her. "Unlike you, Brynn, I prefer to know a person I'm having sex with."

Her mouth opened in protest. "You know me!"

"What are you afraid of revealing about yourself?"

"I'm not afraid of revealing anything about myself." But he saw the startled look in her eyes.

She was flat-out refusing to trust him. Frustration filled him to near bursting. A familiar sensation. Before he could rein in his tongue, he heard himself saying, "Do you know, Brynn, that during the entire time I stayed at my father's home—six months a year until I turned eighteen—he never gave me a key to the house, or trusted me to be alone there?"

She blinked in clear surprise, probably because of the sudden change in topic. "Why not?"

"I used to think it was because my mother was a stripper, and he didn't believe any son of hers could be worth a damn. But, looking back, I see that I wasn't blameless. I spent half the year in my mother's inner-city neighborhood, and it always took me time to readjust to the suburbs. I smoked. Cussed. Drank beer with the guys. Cut class now and then. Dressed like a Hell's Angel. So every time a crime was committed nearby, my father suspected me. And my mother wasn't much better. She didn't trust anyone of the male gender. She constantly suspected me of plotting with my father to deprive her of alimony."

"Oh, Cade, that's terrible."

"I'm not after your sympathy, Brynn. Things turned out okay for me. What I want to know is—" he sharpened his gaze on her "—what reasons have I given *you* not to trust me?"

"I never said I didn't trust you."

"Not in words, but in actions. You never opened up to me, Brynn. Never talked about your life, or took me to meet your parents." He shut his mouth in self-disgust, embarrassed that he'd mentioned those things. He hadn't admitted even to himself that they'd bothered him.

"I didn't realize you wanted to meet my parents."

"I suggested it more than once." It made no sense, really, how much he'd wanted to. Whenever she and John had mentioned family matters, they'd spoken with affection. Affection had been a rare commodity in his family. Maybe he'd just wanted to see it in action.

"Well, it's too late to introduce you. My mother passed away, and my father retired to Florida. But I don't see why my parents or my past should mean anything to you."

Of course she didn't. Because he didn't mean anything to *her*. Other than a sexual adventure. A "carnival ride."

Seething with emotions too complex to sort out, he yanked the SUV into gear, lurched out of their parking place and sped down the graveled road until it ended. He then turned the vehicle down a narrow, rutted path through the forest, allowing a hazy memory to guide him. When at last he found his destination, he parked the car, reached into the rear seat, grabbed the backpack from the floorboards, hoisted it onto his shoulder and stepped down from the SUV.

If all she wanted from him was sex, that was what she'd get. But not right away. He couldn't touch her anytime soon without losing his cool altogether.

She climbed from the SUV and walked beside him, half running to keep up. Even with his emotions in turmoil, she couldn't fail to stir his blood. Her dark hair tumbled every which way from beneath her red bandanna, and above tight, slim jeans, a semisheer peasant blouse rode low across her creamy shoulders.

A blouse that could be *off* those shoulders with one good pull.

The roiling in his chest grew more chaotic. If protecting her wasn't so damn important, he would have left her here, on the path to the river, and hiked deep into the woods to lose himself.

BRYNN COULDN'T UNDERSTAND why he was so angry. She'd always thought that if she gave in and had sex with him, he'd want little else from her. But it seemed he did.

He wanted to know her better.

The realization warmed her, but also stirred vague feelings of alarm. Why could he never settle for what she was willing to give?

In surly silence, he led her to a grassy overlook above the Oconee River. If their therapy plan was on his mind, he'd chosen a perfect place. The memories of the things they'd done here—and thoughts of what they hadn't done—breathed like a living thing from the deep woods around them.

Cade didn't pause to appreciate the serene beauty of their surroundings. With brisk moves he opened the backpack, tossed out a sleeping bag and applied his efforts to erecting a camouflage-green pup tent on a reasonably level plateau. He positioned the tent with one end toward a thick grove of hardwoods and the other to the steep drop-off above the river, ensuring a good deal of privacy even if someone were to wander upon their campsite. The setup also allowed for a cooling, river-scented breeze to tunnel through.

He'd always been good at finding pleasant places to be alone with her. They'd spent considerable time making out in tents—the closest they'd come to a bed. The sensual pleasure of those memories came back to her with surprising clarity, strengthening the longing he'd ignited in her this morning with his slow, hungry kisses.

Unfortunately, the heat she'd stirred in *him* seemed long gone. Yet she swore she sensed volcanic activity brewing just beneath his cool reserve.

He crouched to spread out the sleeping bag on the floor of the tent, and she knelt at the other end to help him, stealing glances at him as they worked. If he was so blasted angry, why had he brought her here?

When they finished, she crawled into the cozy enclosure and propped herself up on an elbow, expecting him to join her. He remained outside the tent, though, sitting against a boulder and throwing pebbles into the river, his jaw taut, his expression dark.

She wished she hadn't upset him, but didn't see how she could have avoided it. The secret she kept could impact people she loved. There was more than just the minor issue of where she was from. She'd withheld that bit of information simply to stop anyone who might know folks from her hometown from connecting her with the scandal she'd caused. The important secret had to do with her father's and brother's attempts at damage control. The less anyone knew, the better off her family would be.

Besides, if she confided too much to Cade, his respect for her might die a terrible death. He had that good-guys-versus-bad-guys thing going on. Just look at how angry he'd become over one tiny falsehood about her hometown. What would he do if he knew that she, her brother and her father were, technically speaking, criminals who hadn't been punished?

But no good could come from thinking about that. She had only a limited time with Cade before he left her. She wanted to make the most of their time together. *Needed* to make the most of it. Their lovemaking had the potential to solve more than her sleepwalking problem. Regular doses of uninhibited sex might help her resolve whatever hang-ups she'd had with other lovers.

Bleakness settled over her. She didn't like to think about moving on to other lovers. Another symptom of her unhealthy preoccupation with Cade, she told herself. She really did need closure.

"Come lie with me," she called out to him. When he acknowledged her with a grudging glance, she smoothed her hand in invitation over the empty place beside her.

His mouth tight, his jaw hard, he ducked into the tent, settled onto his back and crossed his arms behind his head. He didn't reach for her or even look at her, but stared unseeingly at the tent's central beam.

"I can't believe you're this angry," she said, peering down at his sullen face from her half-reclining position, "just because I'd rather have sex with you than talk."

That got him. He abruptly shifted his gaze to her.

"I'd have thought you'd be thrilled," she added.

And she knew she'd angered him more. But at least he was looking at her now. "You thought I'd be thrilled," he said in a low yet penetrating voice. "At what, Brynn? You seem to think I'm good enough for sex in the bushes or a quick bang against your office wall, but not to spend the night with. Or to take to your bed. Or to confide in."

Dismay washed through her. She couldn't confide her secret to him because it involved her father and brother. And she didn't dare spend the night with Cade, or take him to her bed, because she was having a hard enough time keeping their relationship in perspective. Sex was okay. Intimacy was not. Otherwise, she just might fall in love with him. And then she'd surely fall apart when he left.

"What if our positions were reversed," he said, "and after our sex games, I refused to let you spend the night, or come to my bed, or know anything about me? How would you feel, Brynn?"

Used. She didn't admit that out loud, though. The realization disturbed her too much.

"If you're trying to turn the tables on me," he said, "to show me how you felt when I gave you that ultimatum, you're doing a damn good job."

Her throat tightened. That idea had never entered her mind. If he thought she'd had sex with him as part of a scheme for revenge, he'd been right that he didn't know her.

She raised herself a little higher on her elbow to look squarely down at him. "So, you think I set out from the beginning to get revenge, teach you a lesson?"

"Maybe it just turned out that way."

She stared at him, appalled that he'd seen their lovemaking as anything other than what it had been. But then, what *had* it been? If she was honest, she'd have to admit that she *had* used him. And planned to continue using him. He had, after all, agreed to administer therapy. Agreed to lend himself to her cause. Hadn't he, in effect, been asking her to use him?

She wasn't about to let him out of that agreement now, though. It seemed more important than ever to get closure—true closure—from their sexual relationship.

"If I'm using you, Cade," she said, trying for a light tone but not quite succeeding, "and you're not *enjoying* it…" she drew her fingers down the curve of his face, from his temple, along his thick, shining hair to his strong, hard jaw "…I guess I'll have to change my tactics."

He frowned and opened his mouth in what she knew would be a rebuke. He didn't want her to trivialize his feelings.

She laid her finger across his lips to shush him. He'd said quite enough already. "I'm thinking I should concentrate on *using* just one body part at a time."

At last, she'd succeeded in rendering him speechless.

11

"I THINK I'LL START with your tongue."

Cade's brows scrunched together above wary eyes and a deepening frown.

Brynn pressed closer, looming above him now, her hair pooling onto his chest as she swept her finger lightly, teasingly, across his mouth, then tapped his lower lip. "Stick out your tongue."

She thought he might refuse, but after an indecisive silence, he obeyed.

Heartened by the victory, she leaned in and caressed his tongue with her own. A silky, swirling lick. A bold, sensuous foray. He rose to meet her, to draw her into an actual kiss.

She pulled back, evading him. "Uh-uh," she scolded, her face ablaze with erotic warmth. "I'm using your tongue now, not your mouth. I'll let you know when I'm ready for that."

Surprise sparked where the wariness had been, deep within the brown-gold gaze that so mesmerized her.

Holding that gaze, she shifted onto her knees and unbuttoned her peasant blouse. She let it fall from her shoulders, catch on her forearms and drape across her back, while she unhooked the strapless lace bra from between her breasts.

The dusky color of arousal deepened the natural

bronze of Cade's skin as he watched her. He pushed himself up onto his forearm so his face was level with her breasts as she bared them.

With a slight arch of her back, she projected one nipple toward his mouth, and was rewarded with the instant darkening of his eyes. "Open," she murmured. "I'm not done using your tongue yet."

Sexy little crescents creased alongside his mouth in the hint of a sardonic smile. And with a slow, deliberate reach of his tongue, he licked that nipple—only the nipple—with the very tip. Shards of pleasure radiated through her from the light, brief contact, and her nipple puckered. He then blew a soft, cool current of air against it, causing it to draw into a tight bead.

A rush of breath escaped her.

He raised his eyes to hers with a heated gleam—an unspoken dare to continue.

Her voice shook only slightly as she whispered, "Again."

He extended his tongue once more and circled the pebbled tip of her breast, moving his head in tiny rotations, his eyes closed in concentration. The sight alone turned her on. The sensation nearly undid her. Quicksilver stabs of pleasure flashed into her very core.

But she didn't intend to lose control. At least, not until he did.

He closed his lips around the highly sensitized crest and drew it in deeper with hot, wet suction. Feeling the tug resonate between her legs, she breathed, "No," and forced herself to pull back when she wanted to press forward. "We're still using the tongue," she croaked, "and only the tongue. Not the whole mouth yet."

Blinking as if disoriented by the sudden withdrawal of her breast, he frowned at her.

Light-headed with voluptuous heat, she brought the other breast to his mouth. "Tongue."

He obeyed without hesitation, setting instantly to work, gliding over the already marbled tip with the flat of his tongue in long, slow licks, as if savoring a particularly luscious lollipop.

She wallowed in erotic bliss. She couldn't allow this to go on for very long, though. Her womb was now contracting in hot waves of reaction. Her breath skidded and surged in her throat. Light flashed beneath her eyelids, like flames leaping and dancing to a compelling beat.

So involved was she that she barely noticed when he tugged her forgotten blouse from her arms, splayed his hands across her back and pulled her to him, taking her down, until she lay writhing in pleasure beneath his questing mouth.

But when sensation shot through her other breast, too, she grabbed at the hand that fondled her there.

"Did I say 'hand'?" she cried, trapping the marauder against her breast, even as he drew her other nipple into the hot, swirling vortex of his mouth. "No, I didn't." She wrapped her fingers in the silky thickness of his hair and lightly tugged. "Who's using whom here?"

With a moan of protest, he raised his head and regarded her with hot-eyed impatience.

"*I'm* using *you*," she said in emphatic reply to her own question, her dominatrix tone spoiled by the tremor in her voice. "And I believe we'll have fewer complications if I use you *one body part at a time.*"

He received that mandate with unblinking composure, then hoisted himself forward with athletic ease, pinning her beneath him and positioning his mouth in general alignment with hers. He maintained just enough elevation to scour her face with a hungry gaze. In a low, throaty rumble, he asked, "Which part do you want next?"

Heat curled through her. Decisions, decisions. Not that this one had to be rushed. His very nearness titillated her. The warmth of his breath against her mouth, the evocative scent of his hair and skin, the tension emanating from every muscle in his large, strong body...

"Illegal contact," she admonished. And she shoved at his powerful shoulder in an ineffectual attempt to dislodge him from his advantageous position above her.

With a wry slant of his mouth, he rolled onto his side, still high enough to peer down at her, but allowing her the freedom of movement she would need to drive him utterly out of his mind. Which was, after all, the goal of her siege. He would soon be begging her to "use" him, and he'd forget all about the questions she couldn't answer, the intimacies she couldn't risk.

"Let's get one thing straight." She propped herself up on her own forearm to face him eye to eye. "Whichever part of you I choose," she murmured, sweeping her hand with teasing slowness down her body to the zipper of her jeans, "will be used as a *tool.*" In no particular hurry, she unfastened the button and unzipped her jeans as she spoke. "I will be the only one to manipulate that tool. You'll have nothing to do with it."

She wasn't sure he'd heard a word she'd said, let alone understood her. His gaze, which had been lingering on her breasts, now traveled to the slowly parting zipper of her jeans.

"I'd say it's time to open the toolbox," she whispered.

That reclaimed his attention, though he looked too distracted to know exactly what she meant. Pursing her lips to hold back a pleased smile, she gestured toward his body-hugging Henley shirt. He immediately sat up, tugged the shirt from the waistband of his jeans, yanked it over his head and tossed it over one broad shoulder, leaving his magnificent, lightly furred chest bare.

Fighting the urge to run her hands and mouth across his powerful pecs and abs, she waggled her fingers in the direction of his jeans. He knelt to unbuckle his belt, then cautiously guided his zipper down—an undertaking complicated by the massive swelling behind his fly. When he'd finally succeeded, leaving the column of his erection straining beneath the white cotton of his briefs, he turned his efforts to pushing the jeans down his trim, virile hips and muscular thighs.

Brynn watched with a steadily increasing pulse rate, and a blossoming sense of awe. Despite a few mysterious scars marring his dark, smooth flesh—proof of violent confrontations, which jabbed at her heart—he was stunningly, shockingly beautiful.

And if she'd had any doubt about his willingness to play this game of hers to the very end, he laid those doubts to rest. Without a break in the fluidity of his movement, he drew a packet from his discarded jeans and smoothly applied a condom. His most prominent tool now stood tall and proud and entirely at her service.

He then turned his attention to her—a large, sleekly muscled warrior stretching out with single-minded intent. Fully aroused. Undeniably ready. His eyes, a burnished gold, were lit by a fire within. "Have you made up your mind yet," he said in a low, gruff purr, "as to which tool you'll, uh, *manipulate?*"

So he *had* been listening. She should have known. He always listened to her. Even when she didn't realize she was talking.

To her dismay, a dreadful, paralyzing shyness struck her. Throughout their previous sex games, she'd insisted they remain at least partially clothed, and so had never seen him entirely naked before. Never fully appreciated the majesty of his body at the peak of desire. He wanted her, as he always had, without the slightest hint of reserve. She felt honored, and humbled, and somehow out of her league.

But much worse than that, while he waited at her side, allowing her to take the lead, allowing her to make light of concerns that had bothered him to a surprising degree, she felt an inexplicable swell of emotion that nearly brought tears to her eyes.

Determined to overcome this foolishness, which hit her out of nowhere, she said through an alarmingly constricted throat, "Your hand. I've decided to go with your hand." Briskly she held out hers. "Give it to me."

With a small frown—he'd clearly been hoping

she'd choose a different tool—he did as he was told. His strong, callused palm nestled against her own with sensual perfection. The simple yet somehow intimate contact threatened her with another wave of fiercely tender emotion, so she shut her eyes to block out his face, lay down beside him and brought his hand to her mouth.

She hadn't planned this move. It wasn't particularly seductive. Swallowing the ridiculous lump in her throat, she turned his hand around with both of hers and pressed her lips to the center of his palm in a compulsive kiss.

She heard him expel a breath, felt a quickening of his pulse. And eroticism heated her blood again. In mimicry of what he'd done to her breasts, she extended her tongue and licked with light, teasing strokes across the spot she'd just kissed. She then brought his hand to her breast and rubbed the exquisitely hardened peak of her nipple with the moistened center of his palm.

Cade watched in helpless arousal. He'd been ready to love her during the worst of his anger. This sex play had pushed him into desperate territory. And the indescribably tender kiss she'd pressed into his palm had added a dangerous depth to his need.

Unable to stop himself, he reached forward to catch the extended peak of her breast between his fingers.

With a cry of surprise and an arch of her back, she opened her eyes and met his gaze—something he'd been wanting her to do since she'd first closed them. She looked dazed and aroused and sexier than sin.

"You're bad." The breathy chastisement rolled from deep in her throat like a moan. "Very bad."

Tightening her grip on his hand, she pressed his fingers together, her nipple still caught between them. Arching again in involuntary response, she said, "When I want your help, I'll tell you."

"Yes, *ma'am*," he murmured, though he couldn't help kneading her breast slightly and squeezing the rigid crest between his fingers, which caused a reflexive parting of her lips and dilating of her pupils. The heaviness in his loins pulsed with greater urgency.

She then pushed his hand downward in a slow, sensuous movement, from the velvety swell of her breast, past the beguiling dip of her navel, to the shadowed expanse of flat, sleek abdomen revealed by the open zipper of her jeans. His thumb lodged beneath the confining denim. His fingertips brushed the body-warmed satin of her panties.

The heat within him leaped and burned.

And with her eyes tightly shut, her bottom lip caught between her teeth, she slid her fingers over his and pushed them beneath the layer of red satin, into the hot, moist cluster of feminine curls.

The compulsion burned in him to move, to push, to take over from here. But he also wanted her to go on. Wanted to see and feel and experience everything she'd allow.

She stopped short of the expected target, though— barely within the silken nest, at the very top of the sloping valley. She mashed his fingertips there, her hand curving over his, and initiated tiny, circular movements...a gentle press and stroke...a sensual rhythm that further enflamed him.

Her hips took up the rhythm with slight undulations,

and he felt sure that if he couldn't bury himself deep within her very soon, he'd die.

And in some far corner of her mind, beyond the compelling blaze of sensuality that drove her, Brynn knew she'd crossed some border of intimacy she'd never planned to cross. But now that she had, she lost herself in the sheer carnal pleasure. Gave in to the wickedly sexual demands of her body, knowing Cade was there with her, in every sense.

She expanded the movement of their fingers, pressing his downward along the fleshy folds. But the tightness of her jeans and panties soon compromised the rhythmic slide. She reached with her free hand to push them down. He reached with his, and together they tugged her jeans and panties down to her thighs, her knees, then off.

He leaned above her, his breathing labored, his face intense, his gaze traveling between her face and her manipulations as she worked his hand, rolled her hips and broke out in a fine sweat. Only after she'd wrapped her hand around two of his fingers and pushed them inside her—a shallow, angled penetration at first, then deeper with each fluctuation of her hips— did his resolve break.

With a soft curse, he took over the thrusting, earning a surprised gasp and long groan. Though he'd always known how to get her hot, how to make her come, he now had inside knowledge of the quickest path to take, the optimum rhythm and pressure, to drive her beyond conscious thought.

He used it shamelessly, up to a point. A very fine, tentative, hair-trigger point. As she teetered at the edge of orgasm, he stopped. "Ready for more?"

"More?" she repeated with a gasp, comprehension beyond her.

He took that as a yes. And brought into service his ultimate tool—the one that had been straining and pulsing against her naked thigh for far too long now.

She arched with a cry as he entered her slick, hot tightness, and he had to stop and grit his teeth to keep from exploding then and there. While he struggled to regain control, he grabbed hold of her hips to keep them still.

And in a tremulous, panting whisper, she told him again, *"I'm* using *you."* She then caught him off guard with a sudden lurch, and before he knew what had hit him, he'd lost his balance, taking her with him in a tumble…and jarring him into deeper, hotter penetration.

While he lay stunned by the onslaught of pleasure, she twisted around to straddle him, maintaining their intimate union the entire time. Her dark hair streamed in shimmering abundance from her gypsylike bandanna, the ropes of beads swaying across her breasts adding to the exotic effect, and her curvaceous body glistened in the golden light of late afternoon. He feasted on the sight of her. He'd never had her entirely naked before.

"Do you want me to keep *using* you, Cade?" Her hoarsely uttered question ended with a slight tilt of her pelvis, bringing his shoulders up from the ground.

"Yeah," he mouthed on his way back down, unsure if his voice had emerged at all.

She clearly understood what he meant. With a sensuous arch to her sinfully beautiful body, she rode him. Every revolution of her hips, every throaty groan that escaped her, every subtle change in her rhythm and speed, propelled him further into mindless bliss.

But he wanted more than that. Wanted more from her. He would not be distracted. With a superhuman effort, he gritted his teeth, held his breath and resisted the tide as it took her. With a guttural cry, she went into a spasm, her inner muscles pumping, her body shuddering.

He caught her in his arms and held on tightly. She breathed his name and pressed her face to his neck. He fought with every ounce of his might to keep from ejaculating into her.

When he'd quelled the voracious need enough to risk movement, he rolled her onto her back and peered down into her flushed, glimmering face, aware with every jolting beat of his heart that he was still buried within her, hard and thick, clamoring for release.

"Brynn." He barely recognized his rasping voice.

Her responding gaze, warm and vibrantly tender, heightened a profound need in him that surpassed even the physical. "Hmm?"

"It's my turn to use you."

Her angel eyes smiled into his with sweet consent.

"Mouth," he said. Her brows raised, and he added for clarity, "Open."

With a slight, provocative smile, she parted her lips. He kissed her. Slid his tongue inside. And she gave in to a full-bodied kiss. Though he hadn't intended to move within her, he couldn't quite help it.

But he broke the kiss and suspended his gyrations yet again, his body taut from the effort, his face beading with sweat. "Mouth open," he whispered again.

She obeyed.

"Now say 'I love you.'"

The request pulsed like a heartbeat between them. Time itself seemed suspended.

Brynn heard his instruction, but thought she'd misunderstood. With her blood drumming through her head and heat blurring her vision, she felt sure she must have heard wrong. Must have pulled the words from somewhere deep in her subconscious—dangerous, forbidden words. And so she merely stared at the wildly sexy, ruggedly beautiful man whose erection pulsed within her.

"I played your sex game, Brynn," he uttered. "Now play mine. I want to hear you say it."

She swallowed against a suddenly dry throat. "Say…?"

His arms tightened around her, and she felt the tension coiled in every muscle. He was holding back a ferocious physical need. Holding back, just to hear her tell him…

"Say 'I love you.'"

How could she refuse when he'd obeyed all of her commands? How could she refuse, even though this game was much more dangerous than the one she'd played? But this *was* just a game. For sexual dominance. Did he think he'd hit upon her secret weakness? *Had he?*

With her heart throbbing in her throat, in her head, in her feminine core, she obediently said, "I love you."

Releasing a torrential breath, he drew back his hips and thrust fully, solidly, into her. Reaction spiraled through her loins to every region of her being. "Again," he urged.

"I love you."

He thrust again, and she arched at the keen, un-earthly pleasure of it.

"Keep on," he growled.

So she did, repeating the words at first by rote, care-ful to keep a proper emotional detachment. He greeted each refrain with a forceful push of his hips, a gasp, a groan, flooding her with hot sensation and ever-growing need, until somewhere along the way, she lost all objectivity.

"I love you. *I love you.*" She wrapped her legs around his waist and angled her body to take him in as deeply as she could, and when he'd filled her to capacity with a jarring thrust, she fought for breath and swore again, "I love you."

Cade savored the words, savored her intensity, which fed and fueled his passion. Grasping her arms and then locking them beside her head, he peered into her eyes and drank in her reaction while he thor-oughly, utterly possessed her.

"I love you!"

He believed her. He heard the sincerity in her voice, saw it in her gaze, felt it in her body's welcome. At the first rippling squeeze of her inner contractions, he gave a mighty lunge. A shout tore from his throat, and he let go of his control, giving in to the most blind-ingly explosive climax of his life.

And when, a good while later, the pieces of his soul loosely reunited, he drew her closer, pulled a blanket over their naked, glistening bodies and held her with stronger purpose than ever before.

He believed with his whole heart and soul that she'd spoken the truth, even if she didn't know it. But he also sensed that her feelings for him scared her. He could think of only one reason—the same reason she refused to confide her secret to him. She didn't entirely trust him.

At one time, the pain of that knowledge would have had him drawing back from her. Would have sent him on his way, licking his wounds, shoring up his defenses, swearing to never open himself again. It was how he'd handled their breakup in college, once he'd failed to move her with jealousy.

He wouldn't be put off that easily now.

Sometime during her evolution from shy temptress to brazen seductress, his course had become crystal clear: he had to make her his, entirely his, for as long as they both would live. Though he hadn't consciously faced it before, he knew now that he'd wanted that from the very first moment he'd met her.

The silence between them spun out much longer than it should have, but he wasn't sure what to say or do to advance his cause. Had he made another crucial error by insisting she say, ''I love you''? Should he laugh it off as part of the game, or force a serious discussion? He'd messed up his chance with her so badly before....

''Cade?'' She lifted her head from his chest to level a searching gaze at him. ''Why did you want me to say that?''

''Say what?''

A subtle flush tinted her cheekbones. ''You know what.''

So. She couldn't bring herself to even repeat the words outside of their game. ''You mean, 'I love you'?''

She nodded.

He brushed a thick, silky lock of hair from her face, savoring the softness, hoping he could trust what his gut was urging him to do. "I guess because I love you."

Her breath surged out as if she'd been squeezed too hard. She remained perfectly still, her expression unchanging, though he saw shadows gathering in her eyes. Her voice, when she finally spoke, was hushed and tentative. "It might just be the sex. It *was* pretty good sex."

A colossal understatement. "The best."

Color warmed her entire face then, and an enticing softness came into her gaze, though he sensed she wouldn't be pleased to know it. "We've always had a special…chemistry between us. People sometimes mistake sexual chemistry for love. You think, maybe… you have?"

She sounded ready to be convinced otherwise. Which gave him hope. But he had to tread carefully. If he made the wrong move, she might bolt from him like a deer through woods.

"That's a question worth exploring," he murmured. Sliding his fingers into the heavy, shining mass of her hair, he held her profoundly beautiful face between his hands and wished upon his soul that she'd believe in him. "Don't be afraid to explore it with me, Brynn. I'll never hurt you again, I swear. You can have your secrets, whatever they are. I have a few, too. When the time is right, I'll share them with you. You can keep yours forever, if you want. All I ask is that you give me the benefit of any doubt you might have about me. Give me a chance to prove myself. Will you do that? Will you trust me not to hurt you?''

A sheen of tears welled in her eyes, and she nodded.

Intensely pleased by that response, he kissed her. The kiss turned immediately hot, deep and searching, charged with a need that transcended the physical.

He loved her, and he would do whatever it took to allay her fears. He would change anything in his life that needed changing to make her happy. He would open himself completely to her in order to win her trust.

But, of course, that complete openness would have to wait. Her safety had to come first. Cade had to put the Piper behind bars before he could be completely honest with her.

Caught up now in the passion he believed came straight from her heart, he closed his mind to that one little caveat.

And Brynn closed her mind to the doubts and fears that had ruled her for so long. She'd made mistakes in judgment, but she was wiser now. She'd been hurt before, but she was stronger now. He'd broken her heart, but he was also mending it. He'd said he loved her. And she wanted his love. Why should she let old insecurities interfere?

"Spend the night with me, Brynn," he said. "The whole night. I brought everything we need to camp here."

She met him in another blood-stirring kiss, then surfaced from the depths of passion with a deeper need than before. "We could stay here," she whispered, "or go home. To my bed. Or yours. Anywhere you want."

He answered with a slow smile that engaged his dimples and beamed from his eyes with special warmth. "I've wanted you in bed for a long, long time...but I like you where I have you now, too. Let's give it more thought." And he bent to take her mouth in a meltingly tender kiss that made her heart sing.

And she needed plenty of heart-song. She hadn't forgotten the risk. Just because he said he loved her didn't mean he meant forever. His definition of love might not match hers. By letting down her defenses, she might grow too accustomed to having him in her life, only to be crushed when he left. But she had to face another truth, too. If he left her right now, she'd be lost and lonely, anyway.

So why not open her heart and let him in all the way—or, rather, acknowledge that he'd always been there?

She'd taken risks before, and they'd ended catastrophically. This one would not, she swore. She needed to prove that to herself, if she was ever to fully live.

She would trust him.

12

"UP TO NO GOOD?" Lexi tilted her head in thought, then shook it. "You have to consider the source, Trish. Antoine is raising questions about Cade out of jealousy." Lexi stirred the apple bits gently into the batter, then poured the fragrant mixture into a muffin tin. The muffins would be ready just in time for the Monday morning buffet. Although only two guests remained at the inn, Lexi prided herself on always setting out a great breakfast.

"I don't believe Antoine is jealous of Cade," Trish countered, leaning against the work island with her morning cup of coffee in hand. "He's just suspicious of his motives."

"Antoine said that Brynn broke up with him, right?"

"Well, yes, but—"

"And then she left with Cade."

"Right. But still—"

"Antoine must have noticed the sizzle between Cade and Brynn. Any guy would feel resentful."

"But the questions Antoine raised are valid."

If Trish hadn't risen this early to talk about these concerns, Lexi would assume she was just peeved that a handsome, virile guy like Cade had chosen Brynn over her. Her worry over Brynn seemed genuine. "What questions did Antoine raise?" Lexi asked.

"To start with, he said he didn't believe Cade was a writer. So after he left, I did some research on the Internet. The web address on Cade's business card brought up a list of his titles and a phone number to order them. But his books aren't available through any of the online bookstores."

Lexi shrugged. "It's probably one of those small, regional publishers that market their own books."

"But I signed on to the public library catalog, and didn't find his books there, either."

"Not all books are in the library."

"Then I called a friend in the publishing business. You remember Mimsey Sullivan, our sorority sister, two years ahead of me? With a sort of caved-in face, bless her heart, but her daddy owns half of Manhattan? She said she never heard of that publisher. And when she checked her sources, she found that his books aren't listed as being in print."

Lexi slid the muffin tin into the oven, then glanced at Trish in puzzlement. "That *is* strange." She would suspect Cade of lying about his writing career to impress Brynn, but she doubted he'd have gone through the trouble of building a Web site that listed his books if he wasn't a real author. "Maybe he's self-published." A disappointing possibility. It wouldn't do them much good to have their inn mentioned in his book if it wasn't distributed properly.

"But that's not the only question Antoine raised." Trish's fingers tightened around her coffee cup in an uncharacteristic show of anxiety. "Have you heard about that creep who sent the cops a note signed 'The Pied Piper'?''

Lexi nodded, hoping Trish wasn't about to make some bizarre accusation against a guy they'd both known since college—a guy whom Trish herself had invited to the inn.

"The police believe the man gets to know his victims and wins their trust before he abducts them."

"So?"

"Antoine believes the Piper's victims go with him unsuspectingly because he's *from their past.*"

"Don't tell me you're thinking that Cade is the abductor!" That was too melodramatic even for Trish.

"I thought it was ridiculous, too, until I went online to CNN. According to the latest report, every woman abducted by the Piper has been related to an Atlanta cop."

Lexi stared at Trish in surprise. Brynn's brother was an Atlanta cop. No wonder he'd been warning Brynn about the abductor. "But if that's true," she said, airing her thoughts aloud, "why didn't John tell Brynn the details, so she'd know she was one of a select few he might go after?"

"Maybe the cops were trying to keep the details under wraps, and John wasn't allowed to tell Brynn. Or maybe he *did* tell her, but made her promise to keep quiet about it."

Lexi waved that last suggestion aside. "She'd have told us something like that. Besides, she's not very good at keeping big secrets from me."

"The point is, what if Antoine is right? Maybe Cade had been planning to come to the inn, even before I invited him."

"I understand why you're concerned, Trish, but…" A sudden thought hit Lexi. "Oh, my gosh. Cade majored in criminal justice." When Trish frowned, Lexi explained, "I read that some highly intelligent criminals study police procedure and forensic science so they can pull off the perfect crimes."

Trish spread her French-manicured fingers across her mouth in horrified dismay. "She's alone with him right now. She called last night to say they were camping out. But she hadn't *planned* on camping out. What if he's snatched her? The camping thing might have been a ruse to buy him time before we alert the authorities."

"Oh, Trish, we can't jump to conclusions like that."

"Personally, I don't think it's too far of a jump." At the sound of the age-sharpened female voice behind them, Lexi and Trish swung around, to find Mrs. Hornsby in the kitchen doorway. After a cautious glance behind her—as if she didn't want to be seen meeting with them—she bustled into the kitchen, closed the door and dropped her voice to a harsh whisper. "He's been watching every move Brynn makes. And he asks a lot of questions about her. He even took pictures of her with his cell phone."

Trish blinked. Lexi frowned.

"It's true. I saw him. Yesterday. While she was standing on the porch with her beau. Cade aimed his cell phone at them and took pictures."

"There *are* cell phones with built-in cameras," Trish said, sounding doubtful nonetheless.

"I think he hypnotized her, too," Mrs. Hornsby added.

Trish stared blankly at the older woman. Lexi drew in a breath to hold back a giggle. This was what she got for letting her imagination run wild.

"Go ahead and laugh," said Mrs. Hornsby, although no one was actually laughing. "But you won't be amused when he abducts Brynn and sends her photo to the cops. Remember how upset she was when he first got here?"

"She wasn't too happy to see him," Trish agreed, eyeing the old lady with doubt, but clearly hoping to be persuaded by whatever theory she held.

"That same night, real late, Brynn glided right past me in the hallway without seeing me. And guess where she went?" Leaning closer to them, she said with dramatic flair, "Cade Hunter's bedroom."

Trish's jaw dropped. "Why, that deceitful little witch. And she had the nerve to tell me the next day that she wanted nothing to do with him."

"She was hypnotized, I'm telling you," Mrs. Hornsby insisted. "I know a trance when I see one."

"Sleepwalking," Lexi said, more to herself than anyone else. "She had to be sleepwalking."

"Oh, I'll just bet she was," Trish muttered, her face flushed with vexation. "Probably snored all the way to climax, too."

"Trish!" Lexi admonished, on behalf of their older guest.

"Don't believe me if you don't want to," Mrs. Hornsby said, ignoring the climax comment, "but just last night, they showed those abducted women on television, and I recognized them right away."

Lexi felt her eyebrows raise of their own volition.

She couldn't wait to hear how the old lady connected the abducted women to Cade.

"You recognized them from where?" Trish prodded.

Mrs. Hornsby hesitated then, looking oddly sheepish. After a moment, though, her chin came up in a defensively aggressive manner. "You might not like this, seeing as how you own this inn, but when I realized that that young man was up to no good, I felt it was my duty to investigate."

"Investigate how, Mrs. Hornsby?" Lexi asked, almost afraid to hear.

"I waited until he went out of the inn on game day, then used an old bobby-pin trick of mine to pick the lock and get into his room. You really do need to get computerized locks, you know."

Lexi swallowed a groan, and Trish set down her coffee to pay the fullest attention possible. "What did you find?"

Mrs. Hornsby spoke now with unbridled enthusiasm. "I couldn't get into his luggage, his briefcase or his laptop. They were all locked tighter than a bank vault—which, to my way of thinking, only proves he's up to something. But I did find a portfolio in the side pocket of his briefcase."

She had their undivided attention now.

"He's got photos of those women. The gals who were abducted. And to make matters worse, he's got a gun."

IT HAD BEEN THE BEST night of her life, Brynn decided. Cade had surprised her with a picnic dinner of roasted chicken, gourmet salads and other goodies that Lexi had prepared for him. They'd then spent long, languid hours making love, holding each other and talking.

He'd told her about his house in the Colorado Rockies, just west of Denver, and they'd laughed about the quirky friends he'd made in his small mountain community. She'd talked about the ordeal of buying the sorority house and opening the inn, the antics and peccadilloes of her guests, and the complexities of her relationship with her partners.

They'd then gone back to lovemaking. During a tender exploration of his body, Brynn had asked about his scars. He'd explained each one, most of which stemmed from the mean streets of his mother's neighborhood. A couple of them, though, were from skiing accidents at his father's vacation home in Utah. The worst scar—on his upper thigh—he hadn't explained at all. It had looked to Brynn like a gunshot wound.

He'd distracted her with insights he'd gained from growing up "on both sides of the tracks." *There are good guys and bad guys on both sides,* he said. *The difference is, the ones with money get away with more.* At that, her age-old worry had surfaced again. How could she ever tell him her darkest secrets without destroying his respect for her? The death of that respect would hurt all the more now....

But she'd soon forgotten her worry in another round of loving that left them sleeping exhaustedly in each other's arms.

The morning dawned bright, warm, fragrant with honeysuckle and pine, and humming with thrilling possibilities. She couldn't remember being happier to have a day off to use however she pleased. She intended to spend every possible moment with Cade.

On their drive back to the inn, she felt incredibly euphoric, as if she were soaring through the heavens, far above the ordinary world she had once occupied.

A call from Trish on her cell phone tugged her a little closer to that ordinary world. The first words out of her partner's mouth were "Brynn! Are you okay, hon?"

Lexi then took the phone and instructed Brynn to "act normal," but to casually mention her location— exactly where she was and what direction the car was headed.

Thoroughly mystified, Brynn said, "We're pulling into the driveway of the inn."

"Thank God," Lexi exclaimed.

That bit of oddity did not prepare her for what was to come. The moment Cade veered off toward his room to shower and change—with the understanding that she'd handle whatever problem had cropped up, and join him for the rest of the day—Lexi and Trish herded her into her private suite. Once there, they not only jerked her down from the heavens, but shoved her facedown into the dirt.

THE MOMENT CADE REACHED the privacy of his room, he called John for an update on the investigation.

"He's not Antoine Moreau," John reported, an undercurrent of excitement in his otherwise stoic voice. "We ran the photo you sent us of Brynn's boyfriend through the database. He's an ex-con by the name of Doyle Fontaine."

Satisfaction rushed through Cade.

"Seems he did a few years in Atlanta for fraud and grand theft," John added. "Was taken down by the

Atlanta PD. Explains his animosity toward us Atlanta cops—*if* he's the Piper.''

"Oh, he is."

"Problem is, we don't have anything linking him with the abductions yet. We don't even have much to issue an arrest. Charging him for using false identification to get a hotel room and a rental car won't hold him for long—and he'd know we were on to him."

"We'll get the bastard," Cade assured him. "At least now we know who we're after. We'll monitor his movements until he slips up or leads us to his victims. That means we can keep Brynn out of it. We'll tell her what's going on and get her the hell away from here until we have him." He'd never been more relieved in his life.

"But we can't risk tipping him off," John said. "He's expecting her to meet with him sometime this week, remember? He's probably planning to make his move then. I'd like him to prepare as much as possible for that move, so we can nail him in the process."

"Yeah...as long as Brynn is out of here. We'll send her away today. She can leave a message for him, saying it's a family emergency."

"But what if we're wrong and he isn't the Piper? What if he's just a grifter out to scam a couple of innkeepers?"

"You and I both know he's the Piper."

"We're assuming that."

"Brynn is out of this, John," Cade insisted, fully prepared to take that matter into his own hands. "And Trish needs to know that this dirtbag isn't her cousin."

"Just give me another hour. We'll keep him under maximum surveillance. We're contacting the hotel maid who saw the suspect at the hotel in Florida. Maybe she can identify him from the photo. I've also got a team ready to search his hotel room when he leaves it. And last night we lifted fingerprints from his car. Just one more hour. Then we'll fill my little sister in on the facts and send her away.''

Cade didn't want to wait, but John's reasoning made sense. One thing Cade would do from now until the case was closed: keep Brynn safely at his side.

He brought the cell phone with him into the bathroom while he showered, not only in anticipation of John's call, but in case his men were alerting him that there'd been contact from the suspect. The bastard wouldn't speak a single word to Brynn without Cade listening in.

And certainly wouldn't meet with her.

''THE PIED PIPER? Cade? Just because his books aren't listed where you think they should be?'' Brynn gaped at Lexi and Trish in astonishment. ''What have you two been smoking?''

''Look at these.'' Trish handed her photos. ''Victims of the Pied Piper. We found these photos in Cade's room.''

''I can't believe you invaded his privacy like that.'' Brynn tossed the photos aside, feeling as if she'd wandered into some alternate reality. ''You actually stole something from a guest's room!''

''All we're asking you to do, Brynn,'' Lexi said, ''is to call your brother. Tell him what we found. He told you to be cautious of strangers, and since this is the first time we've seen Cade in nine years, he's practically a stranger.''

"No, he's not." She didn't want to listen to another word of this nonsense. She wanted to be with Cade. And she would be, very soon.

"Oh, Brynnie, you've got to listen!" Trish cried. "Didn't you hear on the news that this Pied Piper has been abducting loved ones of Atlanta cops? Your brother is an Atlanta cop, sugar. You're walking around with a big ol' target on your back...and Cade Hunter is taking aim."

The very idea was ludicrous. But Brynn hadn't known that all the victims were loved ones of Atlanta cops. No wonder John had been warning her.

"Call John," Lexi insisted. "Better safe than sorry."

"If I call him and he tells us not to worry about Cade, will that satisfy you?"

They replied with a resounding "yes."

With a stiff spine and churning stomach, Brynn dialed John's number at the Atlanta Police Department. When he came on the line, she switched to speakerphone and told him of her partners' concerns, with both of them adding details to build their case against Cade.

When they'd finished, John let out a hearty laugh. "I wish you'd faxed me about this so I could put it on my bulletin board. I need a good chuckle now and then. Cade Hunter—the Pied Piper?" He laughed again. "Don't you worry about Cade. He was a good guy back in college, and I'm sure that hasn't changed."

Brynn nodded triumphantly.

"I hate to imply you're wrong, John," Lexi said,

"but what would a travel journalist be doing with photographs of the abducted women?"

"Maybe he's working on a novel," John theorized. "Yeah, I think I heard one of our old classmates say something about that one time—that Cade was interested in writing true crime books. He's probably too embarrassed to mention it."

"I knew there had to be an explanation," Brynn said, ready to breathe fire on Cade's behalf. If his travel books hadn't done well, of course he'd be embarrassed about writing a novel. He had every right to keep it a secret. Though it did irk her a little that he hadn't confided in her.

She'd wondered last night why he hadn't talked about his writing. He'd deliberately steered the conversation away from the subject whenever she'd brought it up. But she supposed she had little room to complain about his keeping secrets from her....

"To tell you the truth, I'm glad Cade's there," John continued, lightening Brynn's heart all the more. "Doesn't hurt to have some reliable muscle around in case things go wrong. The abductor really is a threat, and it's good that you're keeping a careful lookout. I'd have told you about the Piper targeting family members of Atlanta cops, but we were keeping that detail quiet, until someone leaked it to the media. So, is Cade there right now? I haven't talked to him in years. I'd like to say hello."

"He's in the shower," Brynn replied hastily. She didn't want John talking to him now. Didn't want to take the chance that he'd tell Cade why she'd called. Cade's boyhood had left him vulnerable when it came to doubts about his trustworthiness. She didn't want to hurt him with the knowledge that Trish and Lexi believed the worst about him.

"Uh, John...if and when you do speak to Cade," Brynn said, "please don't mention that we asked about him. I'm sure it would make the remainder of his stay here uncomfortable."

"We wouldn't want that," he agreed, still sounding amused. "Tell him I said hello. And keep your guard up, Brynn-Brynn."

Brynn-Brynn. She rolled her eyes as she disconnected the call. He so enjoyed coming up with oddball nicknames. A surge of sisterly affection helped take the edge off the tension she felt regarding Trish and Lexi.

"I don't want to hear another word against Cade from either one of you," she told them. "Is that understood?"

They nodded, although she didn't believe they were entirely convinced of his innocence.

Before she could confront them, though, Trish's cell phone rang. "Antoine," Trish exclaimed, turning away from Brynn as if for privacy. "What did you find? Uh-huh. Yeah. I see. No, she won't listen to a word we've been telling her. And her brother the cop won't listen, either. No, Cade's taking a shower or something. Don't worry about that—he couldn't have overheard us."

Anger rose in Brynn at the realization that Trish had shared her outlandish suspicions with Antoine, and that she'd summarily dismissed John's assurance of Cade's innocence.

"Brynn, Antoine would like a word with you." Trish held out the phone to her.

With a glare at Trish, Brynn briskly took the phone, intending to break her tentative plan to meet Antoine sometime this week. He'd have to decorate his house without her.

"Brynn, we have to talk." Antoine's smooth, accented voice was surprisingly grim. "I've done research with the help of a detective friend. It's important for you to see what we've found."

Foreboding weighted her down. "Research about what?"

"This man who has turned your head, *chérie*. This Cade Hunter."

"I don't need to see anything about him. And I don't appreciate you or Trish sullying Cade's good name over groundless theories."

"I haven't told Trish what I've found. I thought I should show you first, since you seem to be, uh, particularly fond of Hunter. After you've seen the facts for yourself, you can decide what, if anything, should be done."

Brynn held the phone tightly, torn between her desire to hang up on him and her need to know what he was talking about, if only for the sake of debunking untruths about Cade. "Just tell me what you've found, Antoine."

"No, no…you must see this yourself. You can interpret my findings in whatever way you will. Meet me at Country Cousins Diner on Atlanta Highway. Come *now*, Brynn. Alone. Don't let Hunter see you leave. It's urgent."

Don't let Hunter see you leave. As if he'd try to stop her from learning whatever Antoine knew. Anger gushed through her in currents so strong that some inner dam burst its restraints. *She'd had it!* She'd had enough of Antoine's accusations, enough of her partners' refusal to listen to her, enough of her own doubts about the validity of her judgment. Cade was a good man. She knew that for a fact. And she wouldn't tolerate slander against him. She would meet with Antoine, but only to end their relationship in no uncertain terms. He would not be calling her again. Ever. She would also take whatever "proof" he offered against Cade and show it up as false—not only to Antoine, but to Lexi and Trish, too.

When she finished with the three of them, they wouldn't dare utter a word against Cade in her presence—or out of it, for that matter.

Strength born of resolution buoyed her high above the anger. She would not fail Cade, or herself.

"I'll be there, Antoine. Count on it."

HE HUNG UP THE PHONE with a satisfied smirk, pleased that he'd managed to use Brynn's feelings for Hunter against her. It was a crime, really, how easy he found it to manipulate women's emotions.

Wouldn't she be surprised when he talked to her, not about Hunter's past, but her own? He'd played the part of tabloid reporter and "interviewed" people from her hometown. Amazing what folks would tell you when they expected big bucks in return. He'd then researched every lead until he hit pay dirt. The time had come to use that dirt to the best advantage. He wouldn't broach the subject of her brush with the law until he had her on the expressway, a good ways out of town.

She'd be putty in his hands. She'd come with him

to his hideaway at the beach, and she'd sit for him to paint her.

And the headlines would scream that the Pied Piper had snatched the sister of the detective heading up his case, and Detective John Sutherland and Marshal Cade Hunter would know they were dealing with a genius.

Never did Doyle feel as alive as when the heat was on and he was pitting his wits against the so-called experts.

Not that the law wouldn't get him eventually. They knew too much about him now. He'd realized that last night, when he'd learned of Hunter's true occupation. But once his rage and panic had died down, he'd realized that his plan for Brynn could still work. It would be risky, but he considered her well worth the risk.

Brynn, Trish and Lexi clearly didn't know that Hunter was a marshal, or they wouldn't have discussed their suspicions about him—or, in Brynn's case, her lack thereof. Trish had even agreed to keep Hunter distracted for as long as possible when Brynn left the inn. Once he had Brynn alone, Doyle felt sure it would take weeks for the law to track them down.

Now that he knew he was being watched by the cops, he could plan around their surveillance. Calling Trish's cell phone instead of Brynn's or any phone at the inn had been his way of avoiding tapped phone lines. It had been pure genius to draw Trish into his game, Doyle decided, almost gloating, and pure luck that she'd been so receptive to his suggestions about Hunter's guilt. He congratulated himself at being such a master at manipulating emotions.

He'd have to lose whatever tail the cops had on him before he met with Brynn, of course. He would dress as a woman to leave the hotel—a disguise that had come in handy more than once since he'd begun this Pied Piper gig. He'd wear his own clothing underneath the oversize dress, his pants rolled up to the knees and his shirt bunched up within the bodice, both to fatten up his form and to facilitate a quick change when needed.

He'd then hop on a bus, leaving his rental car here. That should keep the cops off his track for a good long while. He'd then hot-wire a car from a parking lot. Shouldn't take but a minute. By the time the police realized he wasn't in his hotel room, he'd be long gone.

He expected Brynn would be followed from the inn, but the cops wouldn't realize whom she was meeting, since they'd assume Antoine was at his hotel. Her tail would surely be in communication with the team staked out at his hotel, so wouldn't be expecting trouble. And her tail wouldn't recognize him at the diner. By that time, he'd be wearing a shady hat, concealing sunglasses and a Hawaiian shirt.

Brynn would recognize him, though. He'd worn the same outfit the first day he'd met her.

All he needed was a few minutes to get her out the back door of the restaurant—one he'd chosen for its layout and proximity to multiple freeways. He had no doubt he could lose any tail once Brynn was with him. In his experience, cops weren't particularly hard to fool.

The law would eventually catch him, of course. Yet his arrest would be just another step on the road to notoriety. That was, after all, the ultimate goal of his game.

He intended to have a good start on his portrait of Brynn before his arrest, though. He'd already captured the essence of his other models on canvas. His paintings of them would command huge prices, once his legend had been firmly established.

He hoped to add one more portrait to that collection—a decision he'd reached that morning. If time permitted, he would take a final model. One a good deal younger than the women he'd used so far. One that would add an extra degree of sensationalism to his case. One whose "secret shame" would get splashed across the headlines upon his arrest…thereby punishing a certain deputy U.S. marshal.

13

THE CALL CAME JUST AFTER Cade's shower, as he was dressing.

"Our lady left the premises," said Vinny Venducci, one of the plainclothes cops on the surveillance team. "Wasn't sure you knew, Marshal."

Cade paused in the act of buttoning his shirt. "Brynn left the inn?"

"Affirmative."

He frowned. He'd been expecting her to come to his room any moment now. Where the hell was she going? Anxiety twinged in his stomach. "Is she alone?"

"Yes, sir."

"On foot?"

"Driving her Chevy coupe."

So she wasn't just visiting a neighbor or checking up on the motherless sorority girl next door. His anxiety deepened, and he jolted into high gear, his fingers flying over the buttons of his shirt. "Follow her. Stay close. Keep her in your sight at all times. What's her location? What direction is she headed?"

While he listened, Cade strapped a holster over his shoulders, shoved his gun into place, then shrugged into a lightweight, charcoal-gray blazer. "I'm on my way, Vin."

As he approached the bedroom door, he saw a note lodged beneath it. He scooped it up and read "Have an errand to run. Be back within the hour. B."

Muttering a curse, he crumpled the note and tossed it away. What the hell kind of errand was she running? He hoped to God it didn't involve meeting with Antoine. "Where's the suspect?" he asked into the cell phone.

"Hasn't left his hotel. Don't worry, Marshal. We've got men watching every exit, another in the lobby and another assigned to his car. He ain't going nowhere without us."

Cade had too much experience under his belt to take that as gospel. With his heart hammering in his temples, he hurried downstairs.

In the foyer, he nearly collided with Trish as she rounded the corner from the parlor. "Cade!" He caught her arms to steady her. "I was on my way to see you. I—"

"Where did Brynn go?"

"Brynn? Oh, she's around here somewhere, I'm sure."

He moved to step around her, but Trish shifted into his path, deliberately blocking him. "I wanted to talk to you about Brynn," she said. "She's a very complex woman, and I thought you might like a little feminine insight to understand more about—"

"Later." Gripping her shoulders, he shifted her out of his way and strode past her. His gut told him to hurry, to catch up with Brynn, to watch every move.

Though he knew his personal feelings were probably skewing his professional instincts, he didn't intend to take any chances by ignoring that sense of urgency.

"HE'S GOING AFTER BRYNN," Trish cried the moment the door closed behind him. "And I think Mrs. Hornsby was right—he has a gun. I felt it under his jacket when I ran into him."

"A gun!" Lexi emerged from the parlor where she'd been watching with phone in hand, her finger poised to dial if Cade tried anything with Trish. "It's so hard to believe."

"Did you see his face? He looked ready to kill someone. He *must* be the Piper."

"John's probably blinded by his friendship with him."

"We've got to do something, Lex. He's going after Brynn *now*. I just know it."

"He won't catch up with her. She had a head start."

"But she might have told him where she was going. You saw her slip that note under his door."

Lexi felt herself blanch. "My God, you're right. He might know she's headed for the Country Cousins Diner. Maybe he'll try to stop her from meeting with Antoine. But then, why did he ask you where she went?"

"Maybe to see if she told him the truth. Or to throw us off his track…and give him time to snatch her."

"I'm going to call the police."

"And tell them what? John's in charge of the Piper case, and he already thinks we're nuts."

Resolutely, Lexi pressed the button to dial 911, and when a voice answered, she cried, "Send the cops to the Country Cousins Diner. Cade Hunter is the Pied Piper! And he's on his way to abduct Brynn Sutherland. He—"

"Excuse me, ma'am, but you'll have to slow

down,'' the emergency technician answered. ''I'm having trouble understanding you. What exactly is your emergency?''

''An abduction.''

''In progress?''

''No, but any minute now.''

''At your house?''

''At the Country Cousins Diner.''

''Are you at the Country Cousins Diner, ma'am?''

''No, I'm at home, but—''

''How do you know an abduction is taking place?''

''It's complicated, but my business partner and I have just figured out that a man by the name of Cade Hunter is the Pied Piper.''

''You say you figured this out, ma'am?''

''Yes. And he's going to the diner with a gun.''

''Did you see the gun?''

''Well, no, but—''

''Did he threaten to use a gun?''

''No. Of course he didn't *admit* he was going to use it.''

''Are you or anyone with you in immediate danger, ma'am?''

''No, not me, but—''

''If you're not in immediate danger, please call your local police station to report your concerns. That number is—''

With a frustrated curse, Lexi disconnected the call, and Trish wailed, ''We've got to get to Brynn before Cade does!''

''I know a shortcut to the diner. Let's go.''

White faced and tight lipped, they hurried to Trish's Porsche. Before they reached it, though, a crotchety feminine voice called out from behind them, "Don't you need me to come, too? You know, as backup?" Mrs. Hornsby stood at the door of the inn with a hopeful expression.

"No, but could you stay here and watch the inn for us?" Lexi suggested.

Before she replied, Trish said from behind the driver's wheel, "Get in, Lex. We can't waste any more time!"

Only after they'd peeled out of the inn's parking lot and down Milledge Avenue did Lexi realize they had no weapons to use in case things got ugly. "Weapons," she cried. "We might need weapons."

"I don't have any weapons."

"Then I guess we'll have to improvise."

"SHE PARKED AND WENT INTO the Country Cousins Diner. I'm turning in there now."

"Keep a clear view of the door, Vinny," Cade ordered, swerving through the lunchtime traffic on one of Athens's busiest thoroughfares, only a block behind him. Cade had closed the top on his SUV to maintain a lower profile, inserted an earphone into his ear to stay apprised of Brynn's movements, and had attached a microphone to his shirt to keep in constant contact with John and the surveillance team. "If she comes out with someone else—anyone else—stop her from leaving," Cade instructed. "The perp might be in disguise."

The cop trailing Brynn grunted in vague agreement, but Cade knew he wasn't entirely convinced they had cause for the heightened vigilance. The team at the suspect's hotel swore that Fontaine hadn't left there, and they'd intercepted no calls from him on the wire-tapped phones.

Cade had his doubts, though. Why had Brynn suddenly dashed across town to go to a restaurant alone? And why in her note had she called this impromptu trip to the Country Cousins Diner "an errand"? If she'd intended to meet someone for lunch, she would have told him.

Wouldn't she?

Foreboding rode heavy in his gut as he cruised by the diner, turned down a side street and circled back to the rear entrance. Only one car was parked in the small lot behind the brick building.

Parking his SUV behind the older-model sedan, Cade called in a check on its license plate. If he were the perp, he'd have a car waiting at the rear entrance to spirit her away without witnesses.

It didn't take long for the info to come back on the sedan. It was a stolen vehicle.

Cade called for discreet backup. Keeping a cautious lookout, he then slipped from his car to the other, opened its hood and removed the distributor cap. This sucker wasn't going anywhere. He then returned to his own vehicle and crouched behind it, his hand hovering near his gun as he maintained a clear view of the restaurant's back door.

A call from John came through on his earphones. "I hope like hell he's there, Cade-man. The hotel maid in Florida identified Fontaine from his photo. We went in for the arrest, and guess what? No one there." John cursed explicitly. "The bastard slipped out from under our noses. If he's at that diner, we've got to take him down."

Cade murmured in agreement, his gaze trained on the restaurant door.

"Stay back and let my guys apprehend him, Cade. If Brynn sees you, she might cause enough disturbance to give Fontaine an advantage."

"If he comes out," Cade replied, his voice barely above a whisper, "I'm taking him down."

"Backup is almost there. Keep out of sight. Brynn already suspects something's up with you."

Cade frowned. "What do you mean?"

"She called me this morning, right after I talked with you." Amusement lightened John's tone. "She asked if I thought you could be the Piper."

Cade's breath congealed in his lungs. He couldn't have heard right. No damn way had he heard right.

"Trish found out your travel books don't exist," John said. "Lexi remembered you majored in criminal justice, and figured you'd been studying to pull off the perfect crime. They found photos of the kidnap victims in your briefcase—"

"Brynn believed I was the Pied Piper?" Cade managed to ask, despite the sudden paralysis of every muscle in his body, including those in his face, mouth and throat.

"Yeah. Talk about irony."

Cade couldn't talk at all. He felt as if he'd been kicked in the chest by a mule. *Brynn believed he could be the abductor.*

It seemed then that everything happened at once. The restaurant door opened, and Brynn stepped out, accompanied by a man in a blue Hawaiian shirt, panama hat and sunglasses.

Cade's professional training cut through the mind-numbing shock brought on by John's disclosure, and he drew his gun. But as he rose to yell "Freeze!" the bushes behind him rustled.

A form loomed up on his left side and sprayed a mist into his eyes, while a woman on his other side cried, "Drop the gun!" and clubbed the wrist of his gun hand with a slim, blunt object.

The stinging, sticky mist blinded him. It smelled like hair spray. Someone jumped onto his back and choked him with two slim forearms, screaming in his ear, "Run, Brynn—he has a gun!"

His other assailant took to batting him with her weapon—the handle of a tennis racket, he decided— shouting, "Someone call the police!"

The only thing that stopped him from seriously disabling his attackers was the fact that he recognized them from their voices. Trish and Lexi.

His forbearance cost him. As he flipped Lexi from his back, disarmed Trish and wrestled them into arm locks against his car, a third form bustled out from the bushes and shouted in a harsh, age-warbled voice, "I knew you girls would need me!"

And she zapped him with a paralyzing jolt of electricity.

BRYNN TOOK A DEEP BREATH in the middle of her tirade against Antoine as he led her to the back door of the diner. The scene she'd caused at the table had embarrassed him, it seemed, since he'd begged her to step outside to finish their conversation.

He'd also claimed to have proof against Cade in his car, which caused her to clench her teeth and ball her fists as she followed him. She'd look at whatever he had to show her, repeat her warnings to leave her and Cade alone, then get back to Cade as soon as possible.

But no sooner had she and Antoine stepped out of the restaurant's back door than a ruckus broke out in the parking lot—screaming, yelling, grunting. A scuffle of some kind.

"Run, Brynn—he has a gun."

Lexi! That was Lexi, hanging on some guy's back and screaming at her to run. And Trish, wielding a tennis racket. And Mrs. Hornsby...!

Before Brynn could begin to make sense of it all, Antoine grabbed her arm and shoved her toward a nearby car in the rudest possible way. "Get in the car, Brynn."

Another vehicle roared around the corner of the building and squealed to a halt behind the car, very near to the SUV where the scuffle was taking place— an SUV that looked a lot like Cade's. A police siren wailed nearby on the main highway. *And that was Cade,* falling to his knees, surrounded by the three angry, shouting women.

"What are you *doing?*" Brynn cried at them, jerking free of Antoine's fierce grip on her arm to run pell-mell toward the fracas. "Stop that! Quit hitting him. Can't you see he's hurt? What have you done?"

"Zapped him with my stun gun," boasted Mrs. Hornsby. At the same time Lexi cried, "We caught him red-handed, taking aim at you with a gun, Brynn."

"He's the Piper," Trish swore simultaneously.

"Freeze!" came a deep, hostile bellow from behind Brynn. "Police. Hands in the air, all of you. Hands in the air, goddammit!"

Sirens shrieked all around them. Blue lights flashed. Cops swarmed the parking lot with guns pointed at Antoine, Lexi, Trish, Mrs. Hornsby and Cade.

Things only grew more bizarre from there.

A DEPUTY UNITED STATES marshal. She should have known. How could she have believed that Cade Hunter had given up his law enforcement aspirations?

Now that she saw him in his true element, Brynn felt especially foolish for having accepted the falsehood about his career. He'd set up a command unit in the back offices of the local police station, where he directed a crew of men and women, some in uniform and some not, in the task of collecting, handling and analyzing evidence against the suspect. Clustered around desks and tables, his staff went through boxes of the items found, flipped through files, worked on computers and talked earnestly among themselves, while Brynn watched them through an open doorway from the bench to which she'd been relegated.

When he wasn't issuing curt orders or speaking intently on the telephone—to her low-down, secret-keeping brother, Brynn assumed—Cade himself disappeared for extended periods of time into the interrogation room with the suspect.

Brynn wished Cade would take a moment to speak with her. He didn't, though. He acknowledged her presence only once, when he told a patrolman to drive her home.

She refused to go. "I'm not leaving until my friends are released and I've had the chance to talk to Cade Hunter."

"Sorry, ma'am," the patrolman said, "but Marshal

Hunter will be too busy to see anyone for quite some time."

"Especially when it comes to women," said another cop standing at the nearby water cooler. "Can't say I blame him. A U.S. marshal taken down by two former sorority sisters and an old lady. That's got to hurt."

Brynn glared at him until the amusement left his eyes. She'd had enough with the quips and jokes about the attack. She could only imagine the ribbing Cade was taking.

How she wished he would talk to her! His refusal filled her with a terrible sense of loss. She wanted to apologize for her friends' behavior and make it clear that they'd acted without her knowledge or approval. She also wanted to know if their attack had hurt him more than he was letting on. Though his eyes were slightly red from the hair spray assault, and the front of his hair stood up in stiff tufts, he looked stronger and steadier than ever.

Brynn wanted to ask him, too, why he hadn't told her about his work with the U.S. Marshal Service. Hadn't he trusted her to keep quiet about his undercover mission?

But, most of all, she wanted to hold him, and be held by him. The shocking developments of the last few hours had left her shaky and disoriented.

She could barely believe that Antoine was the Pied Piper. Or, rather, Doyle Fontaine. An ex-con. A fraud. An abductor! She shuddered to think what else he might be. Until they found the women he'd abducted, no one would know the true extent of his crimes. She'd been so fooled by him.

Trish was taking the news especially hard. She'd been thrilled at having her long-lost cousin in her life. She was now anguished and infuriated to discover that he was a criminal who had used her. Lexi had also expressed her deepest regrets for her part in the entire affair.

As they were being marched from the police car in handcuffs, both her friends, along with Mrs. Hornsby, had profusely apologized to Cade for jumping to the wrong conclusion about him. He had said, with only the slightest inflection of the driest humor, "I'll bet you are."

He'd then gone off to the interrogation room, while the local police went about the preliminary motions of charging them for assaulting an officer and obstructing justice.

So Brynn paced beside the bench outside Cade's main workroom. By six o'clock that evening, she'd almost given up hope of ever talking with him. Frustrated beyond bearing, she called John on her cell phone.

"Can't talk long, Brynn."

No nickname. His situation must be serious indeed. "Just tell Cade that I need to talk to him," she said. "You owe me that much, you secretive jerk."

"Cade's got his hands full. He's one awesome interrogator, though. He already got the perp to confess. Fontaine's trying to make a deal with the info of where he's keeping the women. Claims they're alive and well. The Atlanta PD is on pins and needles, waiting to see if they are. These women are wives and daughters of our own."

"I know, John. I hope you find them safe."

"Fontaine says he didn't take them by force, but 'lured them with his charm.' Somehow we doubt that. Gotta go now. Another call's coming through."

"John, about my friends and the charges against them—"

"Cade's getting the charges dropped. They'll be released soon." After a pause, his voice gentled, as if he'd just remembered her part in the ordeal. "Hey, how are *you* holding up?"

Oddly enough, her throat tightened at his concern. "Fine. I'm fine."

"Good. I'll call you as soon as I get a break, okay, Brynnola?"

Brynnola. That was the brother she knew and sometimes hated. "Okay, John-boy."

Minutes later, a dour-faced desk sergeant approached her. "Marshal Hunter would like to see you, Ms. Sutherland."

She followed him to the office where Cade sat behind a massive desk, dividing his attention between a phone call and two cops at his elbow arguing about overlapping jurisdiction. He did indeed have his hands full.

When he noticed Brynn, though, Cade ended his phone discussion and sent the arguing cops out of the office. After shutting and locking the door, he paced back to the desk, sat on its edge and slid his hands into the pockets of his charcoal-gray jacket. That jacket now bore a Deputy United States Marshal badge.

The warmth that had once been in his gaze for her was markedly absent. Not that he looked at her coldly, just impersonally. Which, to her, was just as bad. "Are you okay?" he asked.

"Oh, Cade." She crossed the distance between them, her chest both hollow and heavy. "I'm so sorry—"

He stopped her with an upraised palm. "Don't touch me, Brynn."

She froze in the act of reaching for him. Nothing could have communicated his change of heart more succinctly. Nothing could have pierced her more deeply. She'd never dreamed he'd say those words to her, much less mean them. And he clearly meant them.

Only when she drew back into her own space did he continue. "There's no need for you to apologize for anything." His tone remained quiet and even. "I take full responsibility for the conclusions you and your friends reached. And, under the circumstances, I don't blame them for trying to stop me."

"I didn't reach any conclusions, and I didn't know they were going to attack you, and I certainly didn't—"

The upraised hand stopped her again, along with a darkening of his expression. After acknowledging her outburst with a quelling stare, he continued, "The local police aren't too happy about dropping the charges. They believed the three of them were working with the suspect to facilitate his escape." At Brynn's gasp, he assured her, "I think I've convinced them otherwise. The charges will be dropped."

"Thank you." Her throat grew tight and dry. Despite his lack of overt animosity, he was astoundingly unreachable. "But you could have trusted me enough to tell me what you were doing. You didn't have to lie about being a writer.''

"As I said, I take full responsibility.''

That wasn't nearly good enough. ''Was everything you told me part of your cover?'' She couldn't keep the sharpness from her tone. His treatment of her was starting to rankle. ''Was everything you did with me part of the grand plan?''

''Of course not.'' A glimmer of emotion surfaced, then faded. ''But my personal involvement with you was a mistake.''

Incredible pain rendered her silent. Had he reached that conclusion because of her friends' attack, or because the case was drawing to a close and he'd soon be leaving?

''I never thought you were the Piper,'' she stated flatly.

''You didn't call John and ask if I might be?''

That caught her off guard. So John had told him about her call—after she'd asked him not to. She supposed he'd had little choice, though, considering Cade's cover as a writer had been blown. ''I only wanted to prove to Lexi and Trish that they didn't have to worry about you.''

''Is that why you came to me with their suspicions? Is that why you let me know you were meeting 'Antoine'?''

His sarcasm cut deep. But at least he was responding. ''I didn't want to hurt you.''

''Good job.''

Amazing, how she felt so overcome by guilt, yet so wanted to lash out and blame everything on him. She was sure she could find a way to do it.

"I called you in here to clear up another matter," he said. "Something that has me puzzled, and a little concerned."

"What matter?"

"Among the suspect's possessions, we found a computer printout, dated yesterday, that has to do with Rhiannon Jeffries."

"Rhiannon Jeffries?" The surprises just kept on coming.

"Why would the Piper have any interest in Rhiannon?"

Brynn hadn't a clue. The only time she ever thought about Rhiannon was in connection to her long-ago relationship with Cade. The relationship that had broken Brynn's heart and shattered her trust in love. Of course, she'd since changed her mind about that whole affair. Cade said they hadn't been intimate, and she now believed him.

But she had told Lexi about their alleged affair. She'd also mentioned it to Trish....

A terrible possibility entered Brynn's mind. "What kind of information did he have about her?"

"Just a printout from her personal Web site. Photos of Rhiannon, her home, her daughter."

Brynn's heart dropped. "I...I want to talk to Trish."

"Why?"

"Can you bring her in here, or get her on the phone?"

He pulled out his cell phone, punched in a number, instructed someone to put Trish on the line, then handed the phone to Brynn. A few moments later, Trish picked up.

"Trish," Brynn said, trying unsuccessfully to keep a tremor out of her voice. "You know how I told you that Cade, um, was involved with a sorority sister of ours?" She avoided Cade's eyes, hoping her suspicion was wrong.

"Yeah?"

"I didn't tell you who it was, did I?"

"No." The reply sounded oddly tentative, though.

"Did you...talk to Lexi about it?"

"A little."

Foreboding pulsed through Brynn. "Did you come to any conclusions about who that sorority sister was?"

"Sheesh, Brynnie. It wasn't some classified government secret or anything. Lexi reminded me of how Cade brought Rhiannon Jeffries to that party. What's the big deal?"

"And did you then surmise anything from that?"

A thick silence followed the question. "I did wonder if Cade had fathered Rhiannon's baby."

"Did you mention that possibility to Antoine?"

"I might have," she hedged. "Just in passing."

Brynn shut her eyes and disconnected the call...and wished that the floor would open and swallow her whole. She felt Cade's gaze on her, growing more intent.

"Why would Fontaine have information about Rhiannon?" he asked again, his voice immeasurably harder than before.

"If he'd figured out you were a cop," she said, forcing herself to meet his gaze, "he might have decided to go after another victim."

"Rhiannon?"

"Maybe, but…I'd be willing to bet he was more interested in her daughter."

"Why?"

"Well, I'm just theorizing, but we know the Piper targeted wives, sisters and daughters of cops. So I'm thinking he might have wanted revenge against you for going undercover to catch him."

"What does that have to do with Rhiannon's daughter?"

"Trish might have mentioned the possibility that… um, she was also *your* daughter."

Never had she imagined Cade's gaze could grow so cold. "You thought I fathered Rhiannon's baby."

"Well…" She lifted a hand in a helpless attempt to express a jumble of explanations.

"And that I'd left her to raise the child without me."

She winced. That had, of course, been her belief at one time. "You led me to think you were sexually involved with Rhiannon. When she turned up pregnant a few weeks later, it wasn't too big of a leap."

Cade pushed away from his perch on the desk and strode past her, his face a dark, angry storm cloud ready to burst.

"Cade, I jumped to that conclusion years ago, but lately, I—"

"Go home, Brynn." He unlocked the office door and stiffly held it open, his anger a palpable force. "And cancel the rest of my stay at the inn. I'll have my things out of there today."

"Don't do that, Cade. We've got to talk."

"There's nothing left to say."

14

THROUGH INFORMATION Cade had extracted from Fontaine during interrogations, the victims were found on Thursday morning at an isolated beach house on Florida's west coast, alive and seemingly unharmed.

That evening, at the height of the media frenzy, Cade escaped a scourge of reporters in Athens, drove two hours through traffic to Atlanta and checked into a high-rise hotel near Hartsfield International Airport.

His job here was done. The perp had been apprehended, the victims had been rescued and evidence linked Fontaine to each of them, with crates of his belongings from his residence in Atlanta yet to be examined.

Even so, conviction wasn't a foregone conclusion. The admittedly odd circumstances under which the victims had been held presented another unique challenge. John Sutherland and the district attorney would take on that challenge. Cade would not. His role in the Pied Piper case was over.

He would leave for Colorado on an early flight tomorrow.

Settling into an armchair in the Atlanta hotel suite, he toasted to himself with a double bourbon on the rocks. After three nights at the Top Dawg Motor Lodge near the Athens police station, he felt as if he'd fallen into the lap of luxury—a shower that actually got hot, a television with remote control and bourbon delivered by room service.

Now all he had to do was make it through another night. He wasn't looking forward to lying down and turning out the lights. That was when thoughts of Brynn tormented him most.

But he refused to think about her. To resist the onslaught of unwelcome thoughts, Cade turned on the television. John's rescue of the abduction victims was, of course, the lead story on the eleven o'clock news, not only because of the case's notoriety, but also because of the surprising twist it had taken.

"The three missing women who had been linked to the Pied Piper abductions were found today, alive and well," the anchorwoman announced. "*Surprisingly* well." The rueful note in her voice grated on Cade's nerves. "Police tracked them to an isolated Florida beach house, where they were found sunning on lounge chairs and sipping margaritas."

News footage showed the police escorting the three pretty young women, clad in short shorts and summer tops, to a patrol car. "None of them was bound or physically restrained, which has left the district attorney asking were they, in fact, abducted or, as the man who calls himself the Pied Piper claims, were they lured by his promise to paint their portraits?"

Doyle Fontaine's face then appeared in the upper corner of the television screen while a reporter interviewed the three women. "Did he use force to bring you here, or keep you here?"

Two began talking at once. A stern-faced blonde with a ponytail then commandeered the microphone.

"He promised to paint our pictures. Other than that, we have no comment."

A redhead with long, corkscrew curls grabbed the mike. "You might have no comment, Jo, but I do. He promised I'd get twenty-five percent from the sale of my portrait, and that it would go for big bucks. But he hasn't finished it. I'd better get the—'beep'—money he promised, or I'll kick his—'beep, beep, beep.'"

"I just want my parents to know," broke in a soft-spoken woman with dark brown skin and dreadlocks, "that I'm fine, and I'm sorry for how worried they must have been. I'll explain everything, Daddy, when I—"

"There's nothing to explain, Kayla," the ponytailed blonde interrupted. "We wanted our pictures painted, *period.*" To the redhead, she said, "And I'm sure he'll finish your picture, Viv…if you just *keep your mouth shut.*"

Cade leaned forward in his armchair, his attention caught. They were keeping some secret. The blonde was especially nervous about that secret getting out.

"I'm tired of you telling me what do," snapped the redhead, "and I'm tired of Antoine's lies, too." To the reporter, she grumbled, "He said he'd bring us movies, but did he? Nooo. And there's no television reception here. He didn't bring the *Cosmo* magazines, either."

"Or the diet protein bars," Kayla with the dreadlocks added.

"And he insisted I pose in yellow," Viv the redhead complained. "*Buttercup at the Beach,* he's calling my painting. But yellow is not my color. Why couldn't it be *Bluebell at the Beach?*''

The scene then shifted to the reporter, who faced the cameras and mused, ''Were these wives and daughters of Atlanta cops bribed with promises? Or were they brainwashed into cooperating with their captor? Police have yet to determine a motive, since ransom was never demanded....''

Cade turned off the television. The son-of-a-bitch was after notoriety and the sick thrill of controlling others. He'd forced those women to cooperate—with threats against them or their loved ones, probably. Or blackmail.

Cade's gut was telling him blackmail. He'd bet that somewhere in the crates of belongings taken from Fontaine's apartment in Atlanta, John would find dirt of some kind against the victims. Viv, Jo and Kayla were clearly afraid to cross Fontaine, afraid to accuse him of wrongdoing. Fontaine was holding something over their heads.

Cade suddenly remembered how Brynn had withheld a secret from *him,* and his stomach clenched. Was there something in her past that Fontaine had intended to use to coerce her into cooperation? Cade found that hard to believe. He couldn't imagine Brynn having a secret serious enough to use as blackmail material.

But he would call John, first thing tomorrow, and mention the likelihood of blackmail. He hated the thought that Brynn might be vulnerable to exploitation of that kind. He also couldn't accept the possibility that Doyle Fontaine might get off on minor charges. He wouldn't get much time for using false identification, and they hadn't conclusively linked him to the stolen car outside the diner.

It's not your concern, Cade told himself, *and neither is Brynn.*

That didn't stop him from thinking about her, though. Continuously, at every unguarded moment.

The memories were the worst—of holding her while she slept, and waking with her pressed against him. Making the sweetest, hottest love. Playing their sex games. Kissing, laughing, talking.

Promise you'll trust me not to hurt you, he'd said. And she'd promised. *I love you,* she'd said, and though it had only been part of their game and he'd insisted she say it, he'd believed her.

Obviously, he'd been wrong. The very next morning, she'd been ready to believe he was a deranged abductor taunting her brother with notes signed "The Pied Piper," scheming to do God knows what to her.

After learning of her suspicions, he shouldn't have blinked an eye to discover she'd assumed all these years that he'd impregnated Rhiannon, then abandoned her and the baby.

Other people in his life had held low opinions of him, but never that low. And nobody's lack of faith had ever hurt as much. He felt as if a hole had been blown through his chest, and the essence of his life was seeping steadily out.

He needed another bourbon.

As Cade rose from the armchair to ring for room service, a knock sounded at his door. Pulling a robe on over his briefs, he looked through the peephole into the hotel corridor.

Trish and Lexi stood there.

Annoyed by their presence, but too curious to ignore them, he swung open the door. "How did you know I was here?"

"John told us." Lexi walked past him uninvited into the room, her step not as perky as usual, her platinum hair not as spiky and her ears surprisingly devoid of studs and hoops.

"We've got to talk, Cade," Trish insisted, looking elegant as always in a classic skirt and sweater, though her eyes were noticeably puffy and red. "About Brynn."

The mention of her name sent little daggers through his heart. "She's no longer my concern." He turned his back on them and retreated to the armchair.

As he sank down into it with deliberate nonchalance, Lexi said, "She quit as manager of the inn."

"What?" He gaped at her, too astounded to remain unaffected. He couldn't imagine Brynn quitting the business she'd worked so hard to build. Her future as an entrepreneur had always been her top priority.

"And she's leaving for Barbados," Trish said.

"Barbados?" She'd never said a word about Barbados. Why the hell was she going there?

"Oh, Cade, it's terrible," Lexi cried, sinking heavily onto the bed. "She's selling us her stock in the business. Says she's going to find work at some resort."

"Why?"

"She said she can't run a business with...with—" Lexi's voice broke. Trish finished for her. "With partners who don't trust her judgment."

"What brought this on?"

"You," Trish said.

Lexi quickly amended. "Us. When we figured out you weren't a writer, and Mrs. Hornsby found those photos in your room, we tried to tell Brynn you were the Piper. She refused to even consider the possibility. She called John to ease our minds, but when he laughed at us, we thought he was blinded by his friendship with you."

Cade stared at them as the significance slowly sank in. Brynn had left her business—the one she had worked so long and hard to build. For as long as he had known her, the focus of her life had been to build a flourishing, successful business that would ensure her economic independence and stature in the community. Nothing had been more important to her.

Yet Brynn had abandoned that business, that hard-won security, because of him. Because her partners had refused to trust him.

Which left him with only one logical conclusion. She had trusted him. She had disregarded their evidence and blindly trusted him.

He hadn't believed her when she'd told him so. He'd regarded her declarations of faith as nothing but empty words. But he couldn't dismiss her actions.

"So now she thinks we don't value her judgment," Trish lamented. "But the only reason we didn't was because we knew she was too crazy in love with you to think straight."

Too crazy in love with him.

"I've never seen her so unhappy." Lexi blinked back the tears in her wide dark eyes.

"If I'd known how she felt about you," said Trish, her blue eyes growing shiny, too, "I never would have interfered. And I'm so sorry I jumped to conclusions about Rhiannon. Please don't blame Brynn for that.''

"Brynn jumped to the same conclusions."

"When she was eighteen," Lexi said. "Do you really think she would have gotten involved with you if she still believed you'd fathered Rhiannon's baby and left her without support?''

Like light flooding a dark room, the truth hit him. Brynn would never ignore a sin of that magnitude.

His throat muscles contracted and his heart surged into a heavier beat. "Where is she?''

"Room 371," Lexi said.

Cade frowned and blinked. "In this hotel?''

"The room next to yours, actually.''

"She's *here? Now?*" He could barely comprehend it. He'd been feeling a million miles away from her, in every sense. "But how—?''

"John," Lexi said by way of explanation. "When she told him she was leaving for Barbados in the morning, and asked to spend the night at his apartment, he gave her some excuse why she couldn't and made a reservation for her here. So she'd be close to the airport, he said.''

"*John* did that?" Another shock. Although John had asked for his help in keeping Brynn safe, it had been only because of his expertise as a U.S. marshal and the fact that he knew Brynn—a vital advantage in the undercover work needed. But John had never been especially in favor of an intimate relationship between Cade and Brynn. Yet he'd known Cade was staying here. In fact, John's assistant had booked the reservation.

"John wants Brynn to be happy, too," Lexi said.

She then stood and offered him a tentative, apologetic smile. "We're sorry, Cade. For everything."

Trish nodded in white-faced agreement.

Cade stood and pulled Lexi into a hug. "All you were trying to do was protect Brynn," he murmured against her stiff platinum hair. He released Lexi and hugged Trish. "I'd never hold that against anyone."

Both women shed a few tears, patted his back and encouraged him to go talk to Brynn.

Cade remained where he stood, though, long after they'd left. He felt caught in an emotional crosscurrent. Hope flowed like a warm, wild river through the frozen regions of his heart. It seemed possible that Brynn just might love him, after all.

But cold fear flowed with equal force. He had believed the same many times before—whenever he'd kissed her, held her, loved her. And he'd been grievously hurt by that belief.

For the first time ever, he understood why she hadn't given him a second chance during their college days.

TALK ABOUT IRONY. For years she'd doubted her own judgment, living in fear of making another catastrophic mistake like the one she'd made in Daytona Beach with the Firebird. Then finally, she'd taken a stand and refused to be swayed from her convictions…only to realize that no one else trusted her, either. Not her business partners, obviously. And not the man who'd claimed to love her.

He'd immediately believed the worst, and turned off his warmth as if from a spigot. *Trust me not to hurt you,* he'd said. She'd trusted him. And he'd crushed her like a bug. *Don't touch me, Brynn.*

The cop who drove Trish and Lexi home after their release from jail had picked up Cade's luggage from the inn. Cade hadn't bothered to contact her, then or later.

But, miracle of miracles, she'd survived. The worst had happened, and though she *had* been crushed, she knew that when the heart-piercing pain of Cade's abandonment eventually wore itself out, she would be okay.

She also realized that mistakes would always be made, by her and others. The important thing was to believe in herself, and in her own wisdom. Which, at long last, she did. By God, she did.

From now on, she would live life on her own terms. No more kowtowing to Trish, or struggling to guard her deepest secret from Lexi, or striving to be an urban adventuress with multiple notches on her bedpost. She'd had her sexual adventures with a red-hot lover, thank you very much, and if the day ever came when she was able to think of those adventures without crying, she'd probably treasure them.

Until then, she'd expend all her time and energy in starting over someplace new, far away from Athens, which would always remind her too much of Cade. She would save her money, build her credit and open her very own inn.

With that solemn vow, she wiped her eyes, blew her nose and tossed the crumpled tissue into the over-flowing wastebasket beside the desk in her hotel room. She then whipped back the bedcovers, settled beneath them and reached to set the alarm clock for tomorrow's early flight to Barbados—a trip that she should, by all rights, be looking forward to.

The message light on the telephone caught her eye. She must have missed a call while she was bathing. With a hit of a button, she lay back against the pillows and put the receiver to her ear.

"Hey there, Sis-boom-bah." John, of course. "Just thought you should know that Cade has a room at the same hotel." Brynn shot up from the pillows. "So if you see him in the hall or on an elevator, don't think he's stalking you." She bit her lip, mortified. John wasn't letting her forget her call to him about Cade. "He's got a flight home to Colorado tomorrow, so my assistant booked a room for him. If you happen to run into him, go easy on the guy, okay?"

Go easy on him. As if she might leap onto his back and blast him in the face with hair spray.

Those despicable tears blurred her vision again, and longing gripped her—to see him, talk to him. But what good would that do? He hadn't cared enough to listen to her explanations, and he would never believe she *had* trusted him.

But had you really? asked a doubting inner voice.

Yes! Entirely. With a sinking sensation in her chest, though, she realized it wasn't quite true. She had known he wasn't the Piper, but she hadn't been able to bring herself to tell him her darkest secret.

Which was just as well. Now that she'd experienced his icy disdain, she could easily imagine how he might have reacted.

Assaulted by fresh pain, she switched off the light and lay down. It took awhile, but she drifted into a restless, uneasy slumber.

And the seriousness of the situation struck her. Cade couldn't leave! They had to finish their therapy! He needed it badly. So did she. She couldn't remember exactly why—her thoughts were too tumultuous—but urgency pumped through her veins, pounded through her head.

"Cade!" she cried. "Cade, Cade, don't leave!" Tossing the covers aside, she leaped from the bed and dashed to the door. Unlocked it. Threw back the safety latch.

And stopped with her hand on the knob. With a violent start, she realized she couldn't walk out that door. She was in a hotel—a huge, unfamiliar, luxury hotel—in only her nightshirt. The door would have locked behind her...with her key, money, credit card and identification inside.

Leaning her forehead against the door, she gave fervent thanks for her self-preservation instincts.

A loud, hard knock startled her into a backward step.

"Brynn? Brynn, open up."

She recognized the voice, and with a rush of jumbled emotions, she opened the door. Cade.

It really *was* him. She could barely fathom it. One moment she'd been chasing him in a dream, and the next he stood before her, not a phantom, but a solid, well-muscled man, his thick ebony hair mussed and falling across his forehead, his powerful chest exposed in a loosely sashed plaid robe, his legs and feet bare. He looked as if he, too, had just leaped out of bed. He also looked tense, and serious, and so breathtakingly gorgeous that her heart ached.

She stared at him in astonishment.

He was the first to break the silence. "I thought I heard you calling me."

Her hand rose to her heart. He'd heard her. He'd materialized out of the night in response to her cry. It seemed impossible, yet so like him. And what could she say about calling out his name? That thoughts of him had tormented her since he'd been gone?

"Let me in, Brynn."

Without a thought of refusing, she moved aside for him to enter. As the door shut behind him, he cupped her face with one gentle hand and scrutinized her intently. "Are you dreaming?"

Maybe she was. If so, she didn't want to wake up— not while he was touching her as if he cared and gazing at her with the old, blood-stirring warmth. "I think so," she whispered. "Or you wouldn't be here."

Contrition darkened his eyes. "No, no," he uttered in an imploring way. "This is real." He held her face with both hands then, his thumbs stroking, his gaze skimming her face, her hair, her mouth. "More real than anything else in my life."

A warm welling of hope rose in her, and with a groan that could have come from him or her, they met in a kiss. And, oh, the sweet, sultry flavor of that kiss! It filled yet intensified a voracious craving. Her fingers slid into his hair; his hands coursed down her back, pressing her body to his.

But even as passion flared between them, she knew passion wasn't enough. Not anymore. The craving went much deeper now—as deep and profound as the pain he'd caused her.

As the kiss drew to a close, the frown in his eyes spoke of an anguish that mirrored her own. "I'm sorry, Brynn," he said, his forehead nearly touching hers, "for not letting you explain. It was just so damn easy to believe you hadn't trusted me. You had every reason not to—the lies I told you about my writing, the photos in my room of the victims…"

"I should have come to you, right away, when Trish and Lexi told me about all that. And I should have told you about my meeting with Antoine. But when he said he had proof against you, I wanted to prove him wrong. I didn't want you to be hurt by their ridiculous accusations—"

He cut off her words with another kiss—hard, urgent, driven by emotion. But then the pace slowed, and the kiss broke into short, sweet quests, each one ending with a needful search of each other's eyes.

"I love you, Brynn," he swore. "I have always loved you. All I need to know is whether you love me."

Her feelings for him rose from a thousand different corners of her being in one tremendous groundswell. She loved him more than she could ever say. But…

Fear knotted the muscles in her throat and, in a strangled whisper, she choked out, "You're wrong." The look on his face and the subtle stiffening of his body—as if bracing for a blow—nearly broke her heart all over again. "There's something else you need to know, Cade."

The stiffness didn't leave him, and wariness veiled all other emotions. "The secret you didn't want to tell me?"

Swallowing an ache, she nodded, then gestured toward the bed. "You'd better sit down."

He looked as if he wanted to refuse, but slowly he

walked to the bed and sank down onto it, his posture erect, his gaze locked with hers. "Tell me."

She took only a moment to fortify herself for whatever reaction he might have. "When I was fifteen, I was...um...arrested."

His brows lifted, but in interest more than condemnation. "For...?"

She drew in a deep breath, squeezed her hands together and twisted them. "Armed robbery."

He stared at her, clearly stunned.

"I drove the getaway car."

He sat perfectly still for a long, long moment, and the silence built up around her until it pulsed through her ears like a death knell.

And then he laughed. A short, disbelieving bark at first, followed by a longer barrage, and capped off with a rich, rolling boom of mirth that astounded her. Bewildered her. Her perplexed stare only made him laugh harder. "Armed robbery?" he repeated between gasps. "You drove the getaway car?"

"You think it's *funny?*"

He let out another laugh, managed to quell it, then shook his head, wiping his eyes. "No, no, it's not really. It just took me by surprise, that's all."

One hell of a surprise.

Cade didn't believe he'd ever been more stunned— not even when Trish, Lexi and the old lady jumped him. Here sat the sweet, demure, eminently moral woman he loved more than life itself, looking soft and cuddly in her kitten-print nightie with her schoolgirl braid curling over one shoulder, confessing that she'd been collared for *armed robbery*.

She apparently didn't see the humor in it. In fact,

she looked a little miffed that he did. He understood why, of course. Armed robbery was a serious crime. Serious enough for Doyle Fontaine to have used in some way against her if he'd had the chance.

Cade leaned forward, resting his wrists on his knees, intent on knowing every detail. "Tell me what happened."

She paced as she explained. The explanation itself wasn't all that surprising. She'd gone to Daytona Beach to visit her grandmother for the summer and gotten involved with a group of bored rich kids.

"I knew they talked kind of crazy, but I thought they were *kidding* about robbing that convenience store!" she cried. "And when they told me I could drive, I was flattered that they trusted me with that brand-new Firebird. I had no idea they were carrying guns."

He pictured her as a trusting, naive fifteen-year-old, fresh from Smalltown, Georgia, impressed and intrigued by the older teens with expensive toys and too much time on their hands. "Were you convicted?"

"No." A flush reddened her cheekbones and a shadow filled her eyes. "The judge dismissed the charges."

Cade narrowed his gaze at her pained expression. "That's a *good* thing, right?"

"There was nothing good about any of it! My brother, seventeen at the time, slugged the guy who owned the Firebird and threatened that if he didn't tell the judge I was duped into driving it, he'd kill him."

Cade shrugged and nodded. Made good sense to him.

"So John was arrested for assault, and my father

was so afraid of what might happen to us..." she paused and bit her lip "...he bribed the judge."

Bribed the judge.

To Brynn's ears, the words echoed with the terrible finality of a bomb dropped. She stood frozen in agony beside the bed, waiting for the enormity of all she'd told Cade to sink in. Cade, a United States marshal, sworn to uphold the integrity of the justice system. He hadn't known all these years that she was one of the very people he held in highest contempt—a criminal who walked away unscathed because of money and dirty dealing.

Not that she'd ever felt unscathed. After making such a horrendous mistake by trusting the wrong people, she'd spent all the subsequent years second-guessing her own judgment, afraid to trust too much in others, and determined to make no further missteps. She'd also focused obsessively on succeeding in business so she could pay back her father.

Another tragic irony was, when she finally *had* succeeded, he'd refused to take a penny from her. She considered that to be part of her punishment. Cade's final condemnation of her would be more punishment. And she deserved it.

But, oh, how it would hurt!

His brows converged, and she braced herself. But then she realized his frown was one of careful thought rather than disapproval. "John told me about this," he murmured.

"What?" She drew a step closer without realizing she'd moved. "Did you say...John *told* you?"

"Yeah. Back in college. Not about your part in it. Just his. The assault charge and how your father mortgaged the house to pay off a judge. But...don't you know the rest?''

"The rest?"

"According to John, your father gave the money to a defense attorney—the guy who'd convinced him the bribe was necessary. But then the attorney took off with the money. Didn't even show up in court.''

"That can't be true." He had to be mistaken! After the charges were dismissed, she'd overheard her mother telling her aunt about the bribe. Soon the whole community had buzzed with news of the armed robbery and whispers of dirty dealings that let Brynn off the hook. Disgraced and ashamed, her mother had insisted they move away.

"Call John," Cade urged. "Ask him."

Without hesitation, Brynn did just that.

"Yeah, the shyster ran with the cash," John confirmed. "Dad made me promise not to tell Mom. Or you, since you'd tell her. Mom never would have let him live it down.''

Brynn felt as if her head was spinning. She could barely comprehend what her brother was telling her. "You mean to tell me that Dad preferred having Mom and I think he'd committed a felony by bribing a judge?''

"Dad didn't realize you knew anything about the so-called bribe. But, yeah. He preferred having Mom think he'd slipped the cash under the table to the judge to save his children rather than admitting he'd lost their life savings to a con man. No one likes being known as a chump. It's embarrassing, being made out for a fool." Brynn could almost picture John's shrug. "I guess it's a guy thing."

She shook her head, astounded. "But if Dad hadn't bribed the judge, why were the charges against us dismissed?"

"Those other kids had a long rap sheet. We were squeaky clean. And Dad argued a good case."

She shut her eyes, overwhelmed by the implications. The bribe had never happened. The charges had been legitimately dismissed. No one could arrest her father or brother for the mistake she'd made. She was free—utterly free—for the first time in eighteen years!

She hung up the phone in a daze, and strong, virile arms encircled her. Gratefully, she turned into Cade's embrace. "Do you have any idea how relieved I am? I've spent half my life worrying that my father and brother would be arrested, or disgraced...and that people like you would despise us."

He lifted a brow. "People like me?"

"Yeah. You know, salt-of-the-earth types. The ones who always want to see justice done. The good guys."

Cade felt a smile growing in his heart, one he was sure would permanently remain there—if, and only if, she answered his original question in the way he believed she would. And though that same belief had kicked him in the teeth many times, he wasn't afraid to embrace it. To have faith in it. In *her*. In *them*.

He pulled her down onto the bed, against the pillows and into a lingering kiss. He then prodded in a hoarse, hopeful whisper, "Anything else you want to tell me?"

She pressed tender kisses along his neck and jaw. "Only that I love you."

The sun rose with an awesome heat from somewhere deep in his heart. He felt it cast a powerful beam into every nook and cranny of his past, his present and his future.

"Oh..." she added with a brush of her mouth across the corner of his smile, "and that I love you. And, of course, the fact that—" she nipped at his lips "—I love you."

He didn't deepen the kiss, as she'd expected. "Enough to come home with me to Colorado?"

Home, with Cade. To his Colorado mountains. Excitement stirred within her. "Plenty enough for that."

"To stay?"

Her love for him leaped and blazed. "Yes, to stay."

"To...marry me?"

Her breath caught at the magnitude of his question. *Marry Cade.* She'd always been afraid to hope for such profound, permanent bonding. But that had been the old Brynn. She wasn't afraid anymore. Happiness dazzled her in a wondrous rush, and she met his gaze with joyous certainty. "Yes...to marry you." She was already imagining a future of passion and devotion and maybe even a mountain-side inn.

They joined in a poignant kiss, Cade firmly resolving to satisfy her every desire.

Intending to start immediately, he slid his hands beneath her nightie. "If my guess is correct," he said in a husky murmur as he captured her breasts, "you were sleepwalking when you called my name."

She moaned in pleasure at his caress and slipped her hands beneath his robe. "You do realize that I walk in my sleep only when you've got me riled up?"

"Since I hope to keep you *riled up* for many years to come—" he lifted the interfering nightie over her head and tossed it aside "—I prescribe intensive therapy every night for the rest of your life."

She sighed at the exquisite press of her naked breasts against his hot, sinewy chest. "Whatever you say, Doc."

Epilogue

THE JUDGE READ the sentence, and Doyle Fontaine barely flinched, but only because he was in shock. Life imprisonment. He couldn't believe it. How had his careful planning gone so wrong?

In a disbelieving daze, he watched two huge, cold-eyed officers of the court descend upon him. How he hated letting Cade Hunter and John Sutherland triumph over him this way!

He'd seriously underestimated them. A week after his arrest, they'd somehow learned his models' secrets—Jo's liaisons during her marriage, Viv's occupation before her marriage, and the illegal gambling activities of Kayla's policeman daddy. Without those secrets to hold over their heads, Doyle had lost all control of them. They'd been more than happy to testify against him in court, and to sue him in civil court, too.

His models' betrayal had been only one of many disappointments, though. He still needed deep-breathing exercises every time he thought about Brynn's recent marriage to Cade Hunter, which had won prominent mention on the local six o'clock news. It made Doyle sick, seeing them in the courtroom holding hands, whispering secrets, smiling into each other's eyes. He'd never seen Brynn so happy, with a dreamy glimmer in her hazel eyes and serious glitter on her left hand. Hunter looked more cocksure of himself than ever, if that was possible.

Trish looked happier, too. She and John Sutherland had been making eyes at each other in court for weeks now. The four of them left together fairly often—Trish, John, Brynn and Cade. Lexi was probably back in Athens running the inn. She'd be pleased as punch to do that on her own.

Sometimes it was a burden, his ability to read people so clearly.

Especially since he, Doyle Fontaine, the most talented artist of the twenty-first century, was being led away in chains to a life behind bars.

But not even *that* was the worst of it. The real tragedy happened earlier this week, right after the press had picked up on the fact that he'd priced his paintings at top dollar. According to the Atlanta PD, a smoldering cigar butt triggered the sprinkler system in the evidence room, and the paintings they had confiscated had been ruined. Every one of his masterpieces—including the one he'd given Brynn!

With a disgruntled sigh, he trudged along between the guards to a holding cell, where they released him from the cuffs, shoved him onto a cot and closed the door with a final clang.

He'd just have to look on the bright side. If he could get the supplies he needed, he'd have plenty of time to paint. And he wouldn't have to put up with whiny, nagging women, either.

Instead of *Buttercup on the Beach*, he'd paint *Bob Behind Bars. Cecil in his Cell. Lawrence in the Laundry. Sergio in Solitary. Yogi in the Yard...*

HARLEQUIN® Blaze™

"(NO STRINGS ATTACHED) battle of the sexes will delight,
tantalize and entertain with Kent's indomitable style. Delicious!
Very highly recommended."
—*Wordweaving.com*

"(ALL TIED UP) is hot, sexy and still manages to involve
the reader emotionally—a winning combination."
—*AllAboutRomance.com*

"With electrifying tension, creative scenes and...seductive
characters, Alison Kent delivers a knockout read."
—*Romantic Times* Book Club

Find out why everybody's talking about Blaze author Alison Kent
and check out the latest books in her gIRL-gEAR miniseries!

#99 STRIPTEASE
August 2003

#107 WICKED GAMES
October 2003

#115 INDISCREET
December 2003

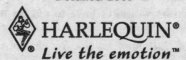

HARLEQUIN®
Live the emotion™

Visit us at www.eHarlequin.com   HBGG

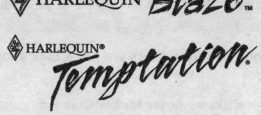

Single in South Beach

Nightlife on the Strip just got a little hotter!

Join author Joanne Rock as she takes you to Miami Beach
and its hottest new singles playground. Club Paradise
has opened for business and the women in charge are
determined to succeed at all costs. So what will they
do with the sexy men who show up at the club?

SEX & THE SINGLE GIRL
Harlequin Blaze #104
September 2003

GIRL'S GUIDE TO HUNTING & KISSING
Harlequin Blaze #108
October 2003

ONE NAUGHTY NIGHT
Harlequin Temptation #951
November 2003

Don't miss these red-hot stories from Joanne Rock!
Watch for the sizzling nightlife to continue in spring 2004.

Look for these books at your favorite retail outlet.

Visit us at www.eHarlequin.com   HBSSB

eHARLEQUIN.com

Your favorite authors are just a click away
at www.eHarlequin.com!

- Take our **Sister Author Quiz** and
  we'll match you up with the author
  most like you!

- Choose from over 500
  author **profiles!**

- Chat with your favorite authors
  on our **message boards.**

- Are you an author in the making?
  Get advice from published authors
  in **The Inside Scoop!**

- Get the latest on **author appearances**
  and tours!

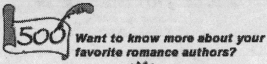

*Want to know more about your
favorite romance authors?*

Choose from over 500 author profiles!

**Learn about your favorite authors
in a fun, interactive setting—
visit www.eHarlequin.com today!**

INTAUTH

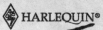
HARLEQUIN®
Temptation.

**What happens when
a girl finds herself
in the *wrong* bed...
with the *right* guy?**

THE WRONG BED

Find out in:

#948 TRICK ME, TREAT ME
by Leslie Kelly
October 2003

#951 ONE NAUGHTY NIGHT
by Joanne Rock
November 2003

#954 A SURE THING?
by Jacquie D'Alessandro
December 2003

Midnight mix-ups have never been so much fun!

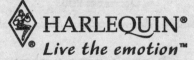
HARLEQUIN®
Live the emotion™

Visit us at www.eHarlequin.com

HTNBN

HARLEQUIN® Blaze™

In L.A., nothing remains confidential for long...

KISS & TELL

Don't miss

Tori Carrington's

exciting new miniseries featuring four
twentysomething friends—
and the secrets they *don't* keep.

Look for:

#105—NIGHT FEVER
October 2003

#109—FLAVOR OF THE MONTH
November 2003

#113—JUST BETWEEN US...
December 2003

Available wherever Harlequin books are sold.

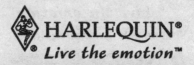

HARLEQUIN®
® *Live the emotion™*

Visit us at www.eHarlequin.com   HBKNT

Is your man too good to be true?

Hot, gorgeous AND romantic?
If so, he could be a Harlequin® Blaze™ series cover model!

Our grand-prize winners will receive a trip for two to New York City to shoot the cover of a Blaze novel, and will stay at the luxurious Plaza Hotel.
Plus, they'll receive $500 U.S. spending money!
The runner-up winners will receive $200 U.S.
to spend on a romantic dinner for two.

It's easy to enter!

In 100 words or less, tell us what makes your boyfriend or spouse a true romantic and the perfect candidate for the cover of a Blaze novel, and include in your submission two photos of this potential cover model.

All entries must include the written submission of the contest entrant, two photographs of the model candidate and the Official Entry Form and Publicity Release forms completed in full and signed by both the model candidate and the contest entrant. Harlequin, along with the experts at Elite Model Management, will select a winner.

For photo and complete Contest details, please refer to the Official Rules on the next page. All entries will become the property of Harlequin Enterprises Ltd. and are not returnable.

Please visit www.blazecovermodel.com to download a copy of the Official Entry Form and Publicity Release Form or send a request to one of the addresses below.

Please mail your entry to: **Harlequin Blaze Cover Model Search**

In U.S.A.	In Canada
P.O. Box 9069	P.O. Box 637
Buffalo, NY	Fort Erie, ON
14269-9069	L2A 5X3

No purchase necessary. Contest open to Canadian and U.S. residents who are 18 and over.
Void where prohibited. Contest closes September 30, 2003.

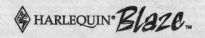

HBCVRMODEL1

HARLEQUIN BLAZE COVER MODEL SEARCH CONTEST 3569 OFFICIAL RULES
NO PURCHASE NECESSARY TO ENTER

1. To enter, submit two (2) 4" x 6" photographs of a boyfriend or spouse (who must be 18 years of age or older) taken no later than three (3) months from the time of entry: a close-up, waist up, shirtless photograph; and a fully clothed, full-length photograph, then, tell us, in 100 words or fewer, why he should be a Harlequin Blaze cover model and how he is romantic. Your complete "entry" must include: (i) your essay, (ii) the Official Entry Form and Publicity Release Form printed below completed and signed by you (as "Entrant"), (iii) the photographs (with your hand-written name, address and phone number, and your model's name, address and phone number on the back of each photograph), and (iv) the Publicity Release Form and Photograph Representation Form printed below completed and signed by your model (as "Model"), and should be sent via first-class mail to either: Harlequin Blaze Cover Model Search Contest 3569, P.O. Box 9069, Buffalo, NY, 14269-9069, or Harlequin Blaze Cover Model Search Contest 3569, P.O. Box 637, Fort Erie, Ontario L2A 5X3. All submissions must be in English and be received no later than September 30, 2003. Limit: one entry per person, household or organization. **Purchase or acceptance of a product offer does not improve your chances of winning.** All entry requirements must be strictly adhered to for eligibility and to ensure fairness among entries.

2. Ten (10) Finalist submissions (photographs and essays) will be selected by a panel of judges consisting of members of the Harlequin editorial, marketing and public relations staff, as well as a representative from Elite Model Management (Toronto) Inc., based on the following criteria:

Aptness/Appropriateness of submitted photographs for a Harlequin Blaze cover—70%
Originality of Essay—20%
Sincerity of Essay—10%

In the event of a tie, duplicate finalists will be selected. The photographs submitted by finalists will be posted on the Harlequin website no later than November 15, 2003 (at www.blazecovermodel.com), and viewers may vote, in rank order, on their favorite(s) to assist in the panel of judges' final determination of the Grand Prize and Runner-up winning entries based on the above judging criteria. All decisions of the judges are final.

3. All entries become the property of Harlequin Enterprises Ltd. and none will be returned. Any entry may be used for future promotional purposes. Elite Model Management (Toronto) Inc. and/or its partners, subsidiaries and affiliates operating as "Elite Model Management" will have access to all entries including all personal information, and may contact any Entrant and/or Model in its sole discretion for their own business purposes. Harlequin and Elite Model Management (Toronto) Inc. are separate entities with no legal association or partnership whatsoever having no power to bind or obligate the other or create any expressed or implied obligation or responsibility on behalf of the other, such that Harlequin shall not be responsible in any way for any acts or omissions of Elite Model Management (Toronto) Inc. or its partners, subsidiaries and affiliates in connection with the Contest or otherwise and Elite Model Management shall not be responsible in any way for any acts or omissions of Harlequin or its partners, subsidiaries and affiliates in connection with the contest or otherwise.

4. All Entrants and Models must be residents of the U.S. and Canada, be 18 years of age or older, and have no prior criminal convictions. The contest is not open to any Model that is a professional model and/or actor in any capacity at the time of the entry. Contest void wherever prohibited by law; all applicable laws and regulations apply. Any litigation within the Province of Quebec regarding the conduct or organization of a publicity contest may be submitted to the Régie des alcools, des courses et des jeux for a ruling, and any litigation regarding the awarding of a prize may be submitted to the Régie only for the purpose of helping the parties reach a settlement. Employees and immediate family members of Harlequin Enterprises Ltd., D.L. Blair, Inc., Elite Model Management (Toronto) Inc. and their parents, affiliates, subsidiaries and all other agencies, entities and persons connected with the use, marketing or conduct of this Contest are not eligible to enter. Acceptance of any prize offered constitutes permission to use Entrants' and Models' names, essay submissions, photographs or other likenesses for the purposes of advertising, trade, publication and promotion on behalf of Harlequin Enterprises Ltd., its parent, affiliates, subsidiaries, assigns and other authorized entities involved in the judging and promotion of the contest without further compensation to any Entrant or Model, unless prohibited by law.

5. Finalists will be determined no later than October 30, 2003. Prize Winners will be determined no later than January 31, 2004. Grand Prize Winners (consisting of winning Entrant and Model) will be required to sign and return Affidavit of Eligibility/Release of Liability and Model Release forms within thirty (30) days of notification. Non-compliance with this requirement and within the specified time period will result in disqualification and an alternate will be selected. Any prize notification returned as undeliverable will result in the awarding of the prize to an alternate set of winners. All travelers (or parent/legal guardian of a minor) must execute the Affidavit of Eligibility/Release of Liability prior to ticketing and must possess required travel documents (e.g. valid photo ID) where applicable. Travel dates specified by Sponsor but no later than May 30, 2004.

6. Prizes: One (1) Grand Prize—the opportunity for the Model to appear on the cover of a paperback book from the Harlequin Blaze series, and a 3 day/2 night trip for two (Entrant and Model) to New York, NY for the photo shoot of Model which includes round-trip coach air transportation from the commercial airport nearest the winning Entrant's home to New York, NY, (or, in lieu of air transportation, $100 cash payable to Entrant and Model, if the winning Entrant's home is within 250 miles of New York, NY), hotel accommodations (double occupancy) at the Plaza Hotel and $500 cash spending money payable to Entrant and Model, (approximate prize value: $8,000), and one (1) Runner-up Prize of $200 cash payable to Entrant and Model for a romantic dinner for two (approximate prize value: $200). Prizes are valued in U.S. currency. Prizes consist of only those items listed as part of the prize. No substitution of prize(s) permitted by winners. All prizes are awarded jointly to the Entrant and Model of the winning entries, and are not severable - prizes and obligations may not be assigned or transferred. Any change to the Entrant and/or Model of the winning entries will result in disqualification and an alternate will be selected. Taxes on prize are the sole responsibility of winners. Any and all expenses and/or items not specifically described as part of the prize are the sole responsibility of winners. Harlequin Enterprises Ltd. and D.L. Blair, Inc., their parents, affiliates, and subsidiaries are not responsible for errors in printing of Contest entries and/or game pieces. No responsibility is assumed for lost, stolen, late, illegible, incomplete, inaccurate, non-delivered, postage due or misdirected mail or entries. In the event of printing or other errors which may result in unintended prize values or duplication of prizes, all affected game pieces or entries shall be null and void.

7. Winners will be notified by mail. For winners' list (available after March 31, 2004), send a self-addressed, stamped envelope to: Harlequin Blaze Cover Model Search Contest 3569 Winners, P.O. Box 4200, Blair, NE 68009-4200, or refer to the Harlequin website (at www.blazecovermodel.com).

Contest sponsored by Harlequin Enterprises Ltd., P.O. Box 9042, Buffalo, NY 14269-9042.

HBCVRMODEL2